Stay Salty

SPRUCE COVE SERIES · BOOK ONE

A SPRUCE COVE NOVEL

Joy Thomas

Beach Road Publishing
South Carolina

Copyright © 2025 by Joy Thomas

This is a work of fiction. Names, characters, places, and incidents are either the product of the author's imagination or used fictitiously. Any resemblance to actual events, locales, or persons, living or dead, is entirely coincidental.

Stay Salty

Spruce Cove Series Book One

ISBN (Paperback-Amazon): 979-8-9930066-0-4

ISBN (Paperback-IngramSpark): 979-8-9930066-4-2

ISBN (eBook): 979-8-9930066-1-1

Instagram: Author Joy Thomas
Facebook: Joy of Fiction
TikTok: Joy of Fiction

Published by Beach Road Publishing

First edition, October 2025

For more information, visit: www.joyoffiction.com

Printed in the United States of America

Chapter 1

Here's the thing about red lipstick: it makes you feel powerful. Until the man who said he loved it, loved *you*, ends up knotted in bedsheets with your roommate.

Ava McCormick leaned into her compact mirror, her hand steady, expression serene. Because ignoring emotional chaos was practically a second major. Her graduation dress hung on the back of the bathroom door, smug in its optimism. Her curls, dyed to match William's fantasy, were lacquered with enough hairspray to survive a wind tunnel or a nervous breakdown. Her lipstick? Fire-Engine Betrayal. Also, William's favorite.

"One week until your parents meet my grandparents," Ava said, aiming for casual and landing somewhere near mildly terrified. It was less a dinner and more a collision of tax brackets. William didn't bother to look up from his phone.

"Uh huh," he muttered, still scrolling.

Classic William. She spoke. He texted. Their conversations had started to feel like background noise in a too-long Netflix series. But this week? It was supposed to be different. Special. Monumental.

She leaned over. A kiss landed on her cheek, absent and cold. "Don't worry. Everyone will get along."

Ava smiled. Polished, pleasant, perfectly practiced. The kind of smile her mother used to wear after a double shift and a stack of overdue bills. It said, "I'm fine." It said, "not now." It said everything Ava didn't have the stomach to unpack before her last college final.

"I'm off to my final," she said, grabbing her bag and flashing a grin that didn't quite reach her eyes. "You can hang here if you want. Sarah won't care. She practically collects stray humans."

William gave a distracted, "good luck," as she walked out the door, still believing, in some small way, that everything was on track.

***

It used to be different. He used to light up when she walked into a room. Used to tuck her hair behind her ear and call her "my girl" in that low, possessive tone that made her feel like the world became just the two of them.

But lately?

Lately, there were signs. Small, easily explained things that piled up until they started to feel like a pattern.

William had changed his phone password a few weeks ago. No big deal, he said, something about security updates. But he didn't offer the new one, and she didn't ask. She didn't want to seem paranoid, or worse, insecure. That's what women did when they were too needy, right?

Then there was the text from "Seth." He jumped off the couch like the message was on fire. Ava had tilted her head, confused.

William didn't know a Seth. In four years together, she'd never heard that name once. When she asked who it was, he said, "Oh, just a guy from class." Too fast. Too light. Like a man reading from a script he'd just been handed.

And then the calls. Quiet ones. Private. He'd leave the room to answer them, his voice barely above a whisper. When she caught his eye as he walked out with his phone pressed to his ear, he'd flash a smile too bright to be real and mouth, "Be right back."

She smiled back.

Because what else do you do when your gut is whispering that something's off, but your heart's still playing house?

***

But that was for another day. Today, she emerged from her final exam an unofficial Yale graduate with a Bachelor's in English and a sensation in her chest she hadn't expected. It wasn't pride, exactly. Or sadness. Or even relief. It was more like standing in a room after everyone else had left. Quiet, echoey, full of things unsaid. An overwhelming sense of *almost*. Almost successful. Almost happy. Almost certain. Like she'd crossed the finish line of a race and realized the person she was running toward had disappeared.

At this very moment, there was only one person she wanted to see: Carla.

Carla worked the front desk of the Office of Student Affairs, where students went to cry behind clipboards and pretend they were just waiting for an appointment. Ava needed Carla's calm gaze and maternal gravitas, the quiet strength that wrapped around her like a hand-knit sweater. The kind that echoed her mother's embrace so precisely, it made her chest ache.

But halfway there, she made a left turn she didn't fully register until she was climbing the worn stone steps of Linsly-Chittenden Hall.

She wasn't even sure why. Habit, maybe. Or the gravitational pull of the English Department, where she'd learned to unpack metaphor and hide behind it at the same time.

She slowed outside Professor Campbell's office, catching sight through the half-open door of his cluttered desk, framed degrees, and that same crooked floor lamp that had lit a hundred office hours.

Taped to the bookshelf behind him was a notecard, yellowed with age, with a quote scribbled in his handwriting: *"Hope is the thing with feathers."* Dickinson, obviously. It looked like it had been there forever. Sun-faded and barely hanging on.

He looked up from a hardcover book, pen still poised between his fingers, a half-dozen sticky notes bristling from the pages like academic porcupine quills. His slim-fit button-down was rolled at the sleeves, and his glasses were smudged from pushing them up mid-sentence, probably more than once. A stack of literary journals teetered beside him, forming a precarious kind of intellectual skyline.

"Ava," he said warmly, the corners of his eyes crinkling. "I half expected you to come say goodbye."

She stepped in, clutching her tote bag like it might anchor her. "I didn't mean to interrupt."

"Nonsense. You may be done with Yale, but Yale's not quite done with you." He gestured to the worn leather chair across from his desk. "Sit."

She did, and for a second, they sat in companionable silence.

"Have you decided what comes next?" he asked gently.

She hesitated. "I had a plan."

"But?"

She gave a small shrug, her smile tight. "The plan made sense on paper. But life doesn't really care about outlines."

He didn't flinch or press. Just nodded. That was his gift. Letting you say what you could, skipping the parts you couldn't.

"I'm not ready to start anything big right now," she said. "But I will."

"I was actually thinking," she trailed off, picking at a thread on her sleeve. "After the wedding, maybe I'd take a break. From writing. Just for a while."

He didn't say anything right away. But the pause stretched, and in it she felt something shift. Something like disappointment, subtle but unmistakable.

"You write with muscle, Ava," he said finally. "There's a pulse to your work. Don't let life talk you out of that."

She looked down, throat tight. "Thank you. That means a lot coming from you."

He gave her a small, knowing smile. "If you ever need a letter of recommendation or just want to vent about the death of print, I'm only an email away."

She left his office lighter than she'd entered.

She stepped out into the spring air, her future brimming with potential as she continued her Yale farewell tour. Next stop: Student Services. Because if anyone deserved to celebrate this victory lap with her, it was the woman who coached her through every meltdown.

***

"Carla," she called as she entered the cluttered room.

The middle-aged woman with wiry curls and a penchant for tacky holiday earrings looked up from her keyboard. Her desk, crowded with student files, a crooked cat calendar, and a steaming cup of coffee that smelled like burnt rubber, felt like home.

"My favorite graduate!" Carla beamed, pulling Ava into one of those hugs that didn't ask permission and didn't let go too quickly. "Look at you! Glowing, exhausted, probably surviving on caffeine and adrenaline. Sit. Breathe."

Ava sank into the chair next to her desk, her shoulders dropping in the way they only did around Carla.

"So, tell me, how are you doing," Carla asked. "Actually doing. Not the curated-for-Instagram version."

Ava gave a half-smile. "Well, I haven't cried in a bathroom stall today, so ... that feels like progress."

Before Carla could respond, a panicked sophomore burst through the doorway, waving a form like it was a crime scene exhibit.

"Carla, I accidentally declared a major in Linguistics because I thought it meant learning cool accents. Is it too late to undeclare?"

Carla blinked. "Did you take any classes?"

"Just one. It was all sentence trees and no British slang. I've made a huge mistake."

She sighed, long-suffering and affectionate. "Sit. We'll rescue your GPA in five."

Then she turned back to Ava and gave her one more hug … briefer this time, but solid, anchoring.

"I'm so proud of you, girl. Four years of late-night studying and instant noodles, and you made it. I'm really gonna miss our morning chats."

"I'll miss you too. I'll even miss your terrible coffee," Ava teased.

"Excuse you, this brew is a work of art. It keeps students humble."

They laughed. It was an easy, familiar sound that settled something in Ava's chest. Carla had been her anchor since freshman year. She didn't just point her to the right office. She handed out perspective, warmth, and the occasional granola bar when it looked like she was one term paper away from falling apart.

Ava tucked a curl behind her ear, more habit than styling. "William's parents are meeting my grandparents next week," she said. "It's … a lot."

Carla gave her that look: calm, clear-eyed, quietly assessing. "And the wedding?"

Ava sighed. "I'm one font away from a full psychological break. The stationery store knows me by name. That's not normal, right?"

Carla paused, her voice soft but sharp around the edges. "Just promise me you won't disappear into someone else's dream while yours is still waiting in the wings."

Ava blinked. "I won't."

"You're not just smart, Ava. You've got that rare kind of voice that is sharp, funny, honest. The kind people don't forget. One day, you're going to write something that breaks hearts in the best way. Don't put that on a shelf because someone else says they've got it covered."

Ava nodded. Her smile faltered, but she didn't try to fix it. "Thanks, Carla. For always being undeniably you."

Before Carla could respond, the same flustered sophomore reappeared at her elbow, this time holding his phone like it had personally betrayed him. "I clicked a link and now I think I enrolled in a philosophy course?"

Carla sighed, long-suffering and amused. "Don't touch anything else. I'll be right there."

"You know where to find me," Carla winked. "And I'll keep the coffee terrible, just in case you ever need a taste of humility."

Exhausted from finals, Ava decided to skip her Pilates class and headed home early.

She grinned as she walked past the smoothie shop where she and her roommate Sarah had spent too many hungover Sundays, sipping green things and pretending they were the kind of women who meal prepped. She could almost hear Sarah's voice: "If I die before graduation, please delete my Tinder." Ava had promised, then added, "But not before screenshotting everything for the group chat."

Before she knew it, she was back at her apartment.

She paused, her fingers resting on the door handle to their shared apartment. The door swung open easily, and her heels clicked softly on the wood floor. She expected silence. What she got was laughter. Familiar. Too familiar.

She paused outside Sarah's door, caught in a moment that didn't feel real. The hallway reeked of jasmine body spray and something ranker, more intimate. Heat and sweat and sex. She heard the unmistakable creak of bedsprings. A gasp. A giggle. Sarah's voice.

Then: "God, baby. You feel so good."

William.

Her knees nearly gave out. Her mind exploded with static, sharp, and unbearable. Like a radio caught between stations. She just stood there. Paralyzed. Her brain knew what was happening, but her body hadn't gotten the memo.

Make a scene. Bang on the door. Scream. Do something. *Anything.*

But she remained frozen, much to her chagrin. What if they stopped? What if they realized she was out there, listening? What if she saw his face? Or worse, what if he saw her and *didn't* care?

Her future fractured silently like a glass dropped in slow motion. The wedding. The white dress. The children they'd named on road trips.

Still, she stood there. Letting it all break.

Maybe she needed to. Maybe she needed to feel every jagged edge. Hear the lies echo through the walls and let them settle in her bones. So, there'd be no room left for excuses. So, she could never, ever go back.

Because knowing it was one thing. Feeling it? That was the truth.

Eventually, her body moved. Not with purpose, but with resignation.

***

She didn't cry. Not yet. Instead, she flung open her suitcase and yanked open drawers with a ferocity that made them rattle. She packed with purpose, or the illusion of it. Grabbing dresses she wouldn't need, shoes she wouldn't wear, socks that didn't match. The zipper shrieked as she yanked it closed, a sound far too loud in a room suddenly pulsing with the echo of voices she couldn't unhear.

What did people pack when their life exploded? She had no idea. But she couldn't stay here. Not another second.

After she slammed a drawer, the silence came, sudden and sharp. The kind that meant they'd finally realized she was home.

A pause. Then chaos. Limbs tangled in panic, a breathless "Oh my God," the creak of a door swinging wide. Sheets snapped back into place; whispers hissed in a rush. Urgent, clumsy attempts to erase the evidence, to rewrite what had just happened.

Ava stood frozen, her suitcase half-zipped and her heart nowhere to be found. The tears came anyway, slow, stubborn things. Like her body couldn't quite believe her life was unraveling this cheaply. Not in some cinematic explosion, not even with the decency of a dramatic fight, but with the pathetic sound of bedsprings and bad judgment seeping through a paper-thin wall.

And then … three soft knocks. William's voice, barely a whisper at first. "Ava?"

He pleaded. Ava didn't answer at first.

Then, she finally opened the door, her eyes were bloodshot and her jaw was tight. "Leave."

"Please, Ava," he said, his voice cracked and ragged, the sound of a man realizing, too late, that he'd just destroyed the best thing in his life. "I made a mistake. I love you."

She pointed to the hallway. "Then go."

He left.

Sarah never showed her face. Not once. No knock, no apology, not even a pathetic excuse murmured through the door. At some point, Ava heard her scurry out, keys jingling, a door creaking open, then slamming shut. Coward.

She continued moving with frantic purpose, like if she packed fast enough, she could outrun the humiliation.

"Do I take the dress?" she asked herself, staring at the white sheath she'd bought for engagement photos. She folded it and stuffed it at the bottom of her suitcase. Then, moments later, she pulled it out and threw it in the trash. Then took it back out again, because it was 40% off and actually made her butt look fantastic.

Toiletries. Chargers. A framed photo of her mom that had lived on her nightstand for four years. She stared at it for a moment. "You'd tell me to key his car, wouldn't you?" she whispered.

She paused at her bookshelf, running her fingers along the spines. Some she'd highlighted to death. Others she hadn't opened since freshman year. She grabbed her favorites: Woolf, Didion, Ephron. And one dog-eared copy of *Tiny Beautiful Things*. The kind of book you didn't read so much as inhale.

By the time she zipped her last suitcase, it bulged like it was holding secrets. Which, in a way, it was.

She gave the apartment one last glance. Couch, table, the wine stain from a New Year's Eve party where Sarah sang karaoke off-key and William watched her like she was a comet.

"You can have each other," she muttered to the empty room, and left.

Before she walked out the door into the abyss, Ava paused in the hallway, hand resting on the photo of her mother that hung crookedly outside her bedroom door. It was a candid shot. Her mom stood in a sundress, holding an ice cream cone and laughing at something off-camera. The photo had a crease down the middle from years spent tucked in Ava's notebooks, dorm cork boards, and eventually, her desk at the apartment.

"You'd hate him," Ava whispered.

Her mother had been a single parent, equal parts steel and softness. She had worked three jobs, taught Ava how to drive in a church parking lot and once punched a guy who tried to snatch Ava's purse at the bus station. "Never be polite when someone's messing with you," she'd said, shaking out her knuckles like a boxer.

Her mother wasn't always the easiest. She thought writing was a lovely hobby but not a job. Ava used to joke that her mother respected her work as much as she respected tofu. It was tolerated, but with suspicion.

Still, her mom would've seen through William. She would've clocked the quiet narcissism. The way he answered questions meant for Ava. The way he made her feel small while calling it love. She would've poured him a glass of iced tea and told him to get the hell out.

Ava ran a thumb along the bottom edge of the frame. "I really screwed this up."

But she could almost hear her mother scoff, flick a cigarette she wasn't supposed to be smoking, and say, *You didn't screw up, honey. He did. You just waited too long to walk out the door. Good news? You're walking now.*

It wasn't enough to fix things. But it was enough to leave.

She wrestled her suitcase down the hall, one arm hooked through her duffel, the other dragging her dignity behind her. The apartment looked like a bomb had gone off. Drawers were yanked open, clothes half-folded and forgotten, the life she'd planned reduced to clutter and carpet fuzz.

Chapter 2

Carla answered the door in plaid pajama pants and a "Book Lovers Do It Between the Covers" T-shirt. Her eyes widened the moment she saw Ava as stood there looking like a human clearance rack: hair frizzy, sweatshirt inside out, mascara smudged just enough to suggest either heartbreak or a really aggressive sneeze. The pile of overstuffed suitcases at her feet didn't help.

"Oh, honey," she said, pulling her in.

Ava hadn't called before showing up at her doorstep. She knew she didn't have to. She didn't speak. Just stood in the entryway like a child who had missed the bus. Carla guided her to the worn couch and wrapped her in a knit throw blanket that smelled like Bounce dryer sheets and mothballs.

That night, Ava didn't cry. She watched at the ceiling as shadows from the streetlamp crawled across it. Carla slept in the recliner next to her, snoring softly.

She stared at her phone.

Her grandparents didn't text. They called. Every time. Which meant she had to say it. Out loud. Not just that the wedding was off, but that William had slept with her roommate who Grandma had knitted a scarf for last year.

The entire next morning, she continued to stare blankly at the screen like it might grant her a script.

Carla finally asked, "You gonna call them, or should I bring you a shot and dial for you?"

Ava groaned. "I don't know how to do this, Carla. I've never called off a wedding before. Is there a protocol? A Google Doc? A sad little meme I can post that says *Never mind* and disappears in twenty-four hours?"

Carla leaned in the doorway, arms crossed, a mug of tea in one hand and that knowing, no-nonsense look only women over fifty could master. "Honey, I've lived through menopause, and three ex-husbands. This is just a speed bump."

"It feels like a head-on collision."

***

Ava finally tapped the screen. Her grandmother answered on the second ring, her voice bright and curious. "Ava, sweetheart! You must be exhausted! Tell me, did the dress fit? I can take it in if …"

"I'm not getting married," Ava blurted out.

Then silence. Heavy and instant. Like she'd dropped a casserole on a church floor.

"Oh," her grandmother said. "Okay."

Ava stared at the ceiling, eyes burning. "He cheated. With Sarah."

Another pause. "Well," she said, "he always did talk too much. I should've known a man with that many words was hiding something."

Ava exhaled. Her cheeks burned, shame blooming hot and fast.

"I feel stupid," she admitted.

"You're not," Grandma Esther replied. "Stupid is staying. You left. That makes you brave."

Her grandfather's voice chimed in faintly from the background. "Tell her to come home," he said. "I'll take her fishing."

Ava's lips lifted. Not quite a smile, but close. Fishing was George's love language. Quiet mornings. Thermos coffee. Room to breathe.

It wasn't a fix. But it was an anchor.

Esther didn't ask questions. She sighed, "just come home."

Ava nodded, even though they couldn't see her. "I'm coming."

Then: "Good. We'll put fresh sheets on the bed. And I'll make that lemon cake you like. Bring a big appetite. Leave the shame in Connecticut."

That's when Ava really cried. This is where she needed to go. It was her home. Because home isn't a place you earned or even spent the most time. It is where you are loved, even at your most broken.

***

At dawn, Carla drove her to Tweed New Haven Airport. They drove past the bookstore where William had surprised her with a first edition of Plath's poems. The corner café where she nearly broke up with him after he spilled espresso on her thesis draft. The fountain where he kissed her in the rain like they were in a movie.

Every landmark felt like a landmine.

Carla reached over and squeezed her hand. "Heartbreak is like stepping on a Lego in the dark. It's sharp, stupid pain that lingers longer than it should. But it won't hurt forever."

Ava nodded, too raw to answer.

"You'll come back from this," Carla said. "And the next man? He better come with receipts, respect, and zero Sarahs.

***

The trip to Alaska was a blur of delays and indignities including an oversold flight and a crying toddler whose screams somehow matched her internal soundtrack. Her only meal? A survival ration of trail mix eaten on the floor of Gate C12 at SeaTac Airport. By the time she boarded the Alaska Airlines flight to Sitka, she was too tired to feel anything but hollow.

Ava sat there, arms crossed, pretending she wasn't watching the clouds like they held the answers to a quiz she hadn't studied for. The world below turned from grids and parking lots into blankets of trees, jagged slices of mountains, and rivers twisting like cursive signatures across land that didn't care who she was or why she was here.

It was beautiful. Stupidly, unfairly beautiful. The kind of beauty that made her feel like an afterthought. Like the world didn't need her to keep spinning.

Ava pressed her forehead against the window as the plane made its way to Sitka. Far below, an eagle soared across the sky like it was performing for a tourism ad. Another followed, flapping slowly and powerfully. She wondered if they were mates or just two loners flying in the same direction. Probably the latter. Probably better that way.

The snow-capped mountains came into view next, like someone had dropped spoonfuls of whipped cream on sharp rocks. Everything looked ancient and untouched. Pure. It made her feel like a speck of lint on an expensive blazer. Like a girl who didn't know how to read a map and was too embarrassed to ask for directions.

She thought about the future she had scripted so carefully. The engagement photos in Central Park, the wedding hashtag she had brainstormed, a future two-bedroom in a gentrified part of Brooklyn with a puppy and a subscription to *The New Yorker*. It all felt laughably distant now. Like someone else's Pinterest board.

She was supposed to have a life plan. A ring. A family of her own. Instead, she had a suitcase packed in rage, a voice that cracked when she tried to order coffee, and a future more uncertain than the plane's exact landing time.

She twisted the thin silver ring on her right hand, a gift from her mother before her death. It used to make her feel grounded. Today, it felt like a paperweight on a pile of unsent emails and failed expectations. Still, she preferred it to the indentation and faint tan line on her left hand that announced to the world, without her permission, that she'd recently separated.

The flight attendant handed her a ginger ale. Ava accepted it, even though she'd hated the stuff since she was nine when her mother forced her to drink it after a long night of throwing up, insisting it would "settle her stomach." It didn't.

But today, it felt weirdly fitting. The kind of drink a person in transition might choose. Not quite soda, not quite juice. Just something to sip when your life no longer fits into a category.

She took a small sip and stared out the window, mentally drafting the bylaws of the "I Hate William" Club. She was founder, president, and the sole voting member.

And yet ...

Her mind betrayed her with flashes. His hands, his voice, the way he used to say her name when no one else was listening. There was the sex. It had been good. Better than good. It was the one part of their relationship that had never asked questions, never let her down.

There was Paris.

There was the way William had stood on the Pont des Arts and kissed her like she was the whole skyline. The way he'd bought her a beret (ironically, of course) and then told her she looked like *Amélie*, even though they both knew she looked more like *Amélie's* sleep-deprived cousin.

There was the bag of goodies he brought her when she had the flu: lemon ginger tea, Vicks VapoRub, a pack of those overpriced tissues with lotion, and a paperback of *Little Women* with a note that just said, "You're Jo."

There was Thanksgiving with his parents, when his mom handed Ava the sacred wooden spoon and let her stir the oyster stuffing. When his dad poured her a glass of Merlot and called her "kiddo." When she let herself believe this, all of it, was forever.

And then there was Sarah. Her *maid of honor*. Had the girl code meant nothing? Was "don't sleep with the groom" somehow optional now?

"I didn't mean for this to happen," Sarah had texted. Message deleted.

Which was funny, because affairs are so accidental, like you tripped and fell naked into someone else's bed. Oops.

Until yesterday, Sarah had felt like family. Their friendship seemed permanent, unbreakable.

Ava remembered how they'd once pulled an all-nighter with chocolate chip cookie dough and bad rom-coms, whispering about their fears of growing old alone. They'd worn matching pajamas and tried on each other's makeup, laughing until their stomachs hurt. When Ava's car broke down during finals week sophomore year, it was Sarah who found a mechanic and fronted the cash, saying, "Pay me back with your first Pulitzer."

They had shared everything: notes, secrets, closet space, tears. Sarah had been there when Ava sobbed over her first internship rejection, and again when she landed the one she'd dreamed about. Screaming so loudly the RA came to check if someone had died.

It wasn't just a friendship. It was a sisterhood.

Now all Ava had was silence, the steady drone of the plane, and a window full of Alaska. A clean slate, blank but not empty.

As the plane dipped lower, Ava pressed her forehead to the window, scanning the horizon for something steady. Across the water, Sitka began to reveal itself. Tucked between the steel-gray Pacific and the steep, green spine of Mount Verstovia. From up here, the town looked like it had been carefully tucked into the wilderness, not built so much as borrowed.

The green onion dome of the Russian Orthodox church still stood like a punctuation mark in the center of town. She could almost hear the hush of the rainforest beyond it, the soft secrets it held.

The runway jutted into the water like a dare, surrounded by the Gulf of Alaska. From up here, it looked like the plane might land in the middle of the ocean. It was beautiful. Wild. Unforgiving. And as the wheels touched down, Ava couldn't help but feel like she was landing on the edge of something. Not just Alaska, but a new version of herself she hadn't met yet.

Her stomach flipped. Not from turbulence, but from the unsettling sensation of trusting a path she couldn't see.

For now, that path led to Sitka, Alaska: population small, weather moody, and apparently, the kind of place where planes aimed for the ocean and hoped for the best.

It felt like a metaphor for her whole life at the moment. Hurling forward, praying there was solid ground somewhere between the waves.

Right before the wheels touched ground, Ava caught her reflection in the airplane window, faint, flickering, barely recognizable. The woman staring back at her looked older somehow. Emptier. But maybe also a little clearer around the edges.

She turned away from the glass. Whatever came next, it wouldn't be William. And it wouldn't be the girl who once built her life around him, either.

Truth was, she wasn't sure who she was without all of that. She hadn't asked herself that question in a long time.

Chapter 3

Here's the thing about heartbreak: it's sneaky. It doesn't crash through the door with a dramatic wail. No, it slides in, settles in your gut, and makes itself at home. It waits until you're boarding your flight to Sitka with a latte in one hand and a one-way boarding pass to nowhere in the other. It clutches at your ribs when you realize your sweater still smells like his apartment. It whispers, *this isn't the life you packed for.*

Ava wasn't supposed to be here. Not really. Not in this liminal space between the ruins of her New Haven apartment and the pine-scented stillness of Spruce Cove. She had a ring. A plan. A man with a golden future and equally golden hair. That last part was busy breaking vows and bed springs with her roommate, leaving Ava alone with a front-row seat to the destruction of her carefully constructed life.

Spruce Cove wasn't unfamiliar, exactly. She'd spent childhood summers here running barefoot through the Tongass, pulling crab pots with Grandpa George and sleeping under a sky that never really got dark. But she hadn't been back since middle school, and now she was just another outsider with too much baggage and nowhere else to go.

Capping off her humiliating exile, Ava had tried to climb aboard the floatplane to Spruce Cove with as much grace as someone in a pencil skirt and emotional freefall could muster. One leg up, a gust of wind. Ava slipped and pitched forward, nearly flashing the pilot and giving an unsolicited view of her control-top Spanx. She mumbled an apology while yanking her skirt down with one hand and hoisting her bag with the other, cheeks burning. The cocky bush pilot smirked. Of course he did.

Now? Now, she was clinging to her seat as the De Havilland Beaver skimmed across icy waters like a skipping stone. The floatplane cabin was packed elbow-to-elbow with fishermen, duffel bags, and a canvas bag of mail. The air reeked of fuel, aftershave and a metallic tang that clung to her nostrils. Most wore bulky headsets to drown out the engine. The propeller buzzed, a mosquito whine that didn't match the grandeur below, snow-dusted peaks and evergreen forests so thick they could swallow your secrets whole.

The wind tossed the floatplane like a ping-pong ball in a hurricane. This wasn't the detached jostle of a commercial jet. It was like the freefall of bungee jumping with no panicked question of whether the cord would hold.

She closed her eyes and tried to breathe. In. Out. In. Out. But each breath only brought another wave of nausea and the sour memory of everything she was running from.

The headset crackled. The pilot made a joke about "a little bump coming up," which translated to: hold on, because this is going to suck.

And it did.

The plane dropped with a violent shudder that made the guy across from her cross himself and mutter something about last rites. Ava gripped the armrest so tightly her knuckles turned bone-white.

She wasn't just flying into Spruce Cove. She was crash-landing into the wreckage of her own life.

She wasn't new to travel disasters. There had been the overnight layover in Phoenix, the suitcase that popped open in JFK, the time she sobbed through a red eye to Seattle after her mother's funeral. But this, this felt different. This wasn't an inconvenience. This was exile.

She peered through the foggy window as Sitka faded into myth, the ocean dark and bottomless beneath her. Somewhere in that vast wild, she imagined her old self slipping under the waves. And maybe that was okay.

Spruce Cove emerged from the wilderness like a memory brought to life: docks painted with peeling stories, small houses on pilings shouldering sea wind, and a general store that hadn't changed its window display since Clinton was in office. Grandpa George and Grandma Esther stood like sentinels, flannel and denim bookends to a life Ava hadn't touched since she was twelve.

"You look like a woman who's done with men and mascara," Grandma Esther said, pulling Ava into a hug that smelled like woodsmoke and lemon balm.

"You look like retirement with a vengeance," Ava replied, managing a shaky smile.

George didn't say much. He just opened the door of the old Ford truck with a nod. That was his way of showing affection, mechanics over monologues.

The drive from the dock wound past everything Ava had remembered and half-invented in childhood. The berry bushes she and her mother used to comb through every July. The carved bear statue outside Annie's Café. The crooked fence where she and the neighbor kid carved "AVA + JARED L" inside a heart. Until Jared moved away and she replaced his name with 'pizza.' Her stomach churned at the familiarity.

"You hungry, honey?" Esther asked. "I made baked halibut with steamed potatoes."

"Living the dream," Ava murmured.

George grunted his approval or perhaps just acknowledged a pothole.

The house hadn't changed. It leaned a little harder into the Southeast wind. The porch swing groaned a little louder. But the wind chimes still clattered the same song and the doormat still said "Wipe Your Paws" even though no one had owned a dog since 2003.

Ava dropped her bag in her mother's childhood bedroom. The same room Ava stayed during her summer visits. Same forget-me-not quilt. Same shelf of Nancy Drew books. Same lump in her throat. Everything was frozen in amber, preserved like a childhood diorama. The curtains still had little sailboats embroidered along the hem.

She stood in the middle of the room, letting the memories push at her like waves. Her knees went soft, and she collapsed backward onto the bed, fully clothed, hands splayed over her stomach. The mattress squeaked in protest.

The ceiling fan blades turned slowly above her, like a hypnotist's pendulum. Back and forth. Round and round. Her eyes followed the rhythm, and just like that, she was twelve again. Gangly limbs. Braces. Wondering if anyone would ever love her enough to stay. She felt regressed, undone, like someone had pressed rewind on her life without asking permission.

Her grown-up life, with its engagements and espresso machines, felt like a dream. A cruel one.

She reached for the edge of the quilt and pulled it up to her chin like she used to after too many ghost stories.

The tears came without asking.

And that's when the memories hit.

William's old apartment. And then came the movie nights. She and William curled up on the couch, her head tucked beneath his chin, his hand tracing circles on her back as he quoted lines from old black-and-white films in terrible accents. The tea that he made when she was writing papers. Or that he'd toast her bagel just right. The bouquet of tulips during finals week with a note that said, "Keep blooming."

She remembered the night he told her he wanted kids.

They were lying on the floor of his tiny New Haven apartment, surrounded by half-unpacked boxes and pizza crusts. The carpet itched, the radiator clanked like it was coughing up hairballs, and still, she had felt safer than she ever had in her life. William had taken her hand like it was a fragile thing, a teacup or a wish.

He'd kissed her forehead, soft, reverent, and whispered, "You'll be the kind of mother they write poetry about."

He talked about little feet padding across hardwood floors, Sunday pancakes shaped like animals, bedtime books read in silly voices. She cried. Hard. The ugly kind tears that didn't belong in rom-coms or engagement shoots. And he pulled her close, holding her like she might vanish if he let go.

She'd believed it. Every word. Every goddamn Hallmark card of it.

She wanted that man back.

The one who looked at her like she was made of starlight and good fortune. The one who never minded when she talked too much or cried during commercials. The one who knew how she took her tea and never forgot to bring her the corner piece of the brownie.

But that man evaporated.

Her throat tightened. The memory soured like milk left too long on the counter. Warm, curdled, impossible to swallow. She blinked fast, trying to fight off the tears that always knew how to find her when she was alone.

What if he'd never been real? What if she'd built him, brick by romantic brick, out of gestures and hope? What if she'd fallen in love with a projection, not a person?

She sat up too fast, her head swimming, heart thudding with that hollow ache that no one warned you about in fairy tales. The part after the ball, after the slipper fits, when the prince says he doesn't want to do this anymore and your world splits like cheap plywood.

None of it was real.

Not the whispered baby names. Not the couch fort dreams. And certainly not the version of him who had once looked at her like she was enough.

She got to her feet and padded to the window, her bare toes curling against the cool floorboards. Outside, the trees swayed under the weight of the wind, steady, rooted, utterly unbothered.

Ava pressed her palm to the glass. At least the trees hadn't lied.

The ache crept in low and sudden, the memory cracking inside her like glass under too much weight. She slammed the curtains shut and told herself not to cry. Not now.

The future she pictured? Turns out, it came with fine print.

***

The next four days unfolded like molasses. Ava cocooned herself in bed, only emerging to pee or drink lukewarm tea. She ignored Esther's bribes, George's silent offerings of peeled apples, and the seagulls waging war outside her window.

Day One: She doom-scrolled wedding inspiration photos she couldn't bring herself to delete. One Pinterest board led to another until she was back on her own saved page titled *"Our Forever Begins,"* a digital scrapbook filled with ivory lace, candlelit barns, and a venue that no longer mattered. She watched a video from a wedding photographer and saw a bride that could have been her. Down to the bun hairstyle she'd bookmarked. When she opened her inbox, she found an email from a florist reminding her to finalize her peony selection. "We can't wait to see you on the Big Day!" the message read, cheery and cruel. She threw her phone under the pillow and screamed into the mattress until her voice cracked.

Day Two: She found a pair of William's socks in her luggage and cried for an hour. They were blue, soft, the ones with tiny boats he used to wear on Sundays while dancing in their apartment kitchen. She clutched them to her chest, and the smell of detergent and a trace of his cologne hit her like a sucker punch. She remembered one night he wore them, balancing a bowl of popcorn on his head while she quizzed him for his final. He kept slipping the wrong answers on purpose, grinning like a kid, just to make her laugh. She missed that grin. She missed the man he'd been or pretended to be. She curled up around the socks on the floor, sobbing so violently she pulled a muscle in her side.

Day Three: She threw the socks in the woodstove. It wasn't dramatic. It wasn't therapeutic. She stood in the living room with the stove door open, holding them like a sacrifice. Her hands trembled. For a moment, she imagined keeping them. Tucking them into her pillowcase like a secret. But then her fingers opened, and they dropped into the flames. The fire hissed as the fabric curled. Ava stared long after they were ash, whispering his name just once. "William." Her voice cracked on the second syllable. The flames didn't answer.

Day Four: She read an old copy of *Little Women* until Jo broke up with Professor Bhaer and sobbed again. She found the book on her childhood shelf, yellowed and softened with time. She read until the afternoon light angled through the curtains, turning the room golden and ghostly. When Jo cried, Ava did too. She imagined Jo begging for love instead, asking someone to choose her, to stay. Ava closed the book, placed it over her heart, and wept. Esther found her like that hours later, curled on the bed, hiccupping silent cries.

"Your heart's bruised, baby girl," Esther whispered, sitting beside her and stroking her hair. 'But that just means it loved big. That's nothing to be ashamed of."

Ava pressed her face into her grandmother's lap and cried harder. They sat like that until the room dimmed and the wind began to whisper through the cedar trees.

On the fifth morning, George tapped on her door, a whisper disguised as a knock.

"Could use a hand on the boat," he said.

It wasn't a request. Not even a suggestion. Just a firm nudge.

Guilt, more effective than any alarm clock, finally dragged her out of bed.

Pulling on her boots felt like slipping into a life she barely remembered. Her reflection was giving off tragic heroine meets coastal breakdown vibes. Mascara smudges, a borrowed Spruce Cove Cannery hoodie that could double as a tent, and the unmistakable aura of someone who'd cried over socks.

Outside, the air kissed her skin with salt and clarity. Seagulls performed aerial stunts overhead, and somewhere in the distance, a buoy bobbed in the surf, its blinking light winking like a signal from another world.

George was already at the dock, elbow-deep in engine grease when she arrived. No words. Just a nod.

She stepped cautiously on the slick dock, her XtraTuf boots squeaking in protest. Her breath misted in the cold morning air as she handed him the wrench he didn't ask for. Lucky guess.

Twenty minutes passed in peaceful clatter. Ava muttered about her underutilized Ivy League degree while George muttered about rusted bolts and fishy gaskets. She wiped grease from her palm with a rag that looked like it had survived the Cold War, definitely older than her brand-new diploma, still unopened in its mailing tube. The cold nipped at her fingers, but the work warmed her bones in a strange, almost ancestral way. Each clang of the wrench was a reminder she was doing something real, tangible. Unlike the ghostwriting gigs and clickbait headlines she'd been grinding through back east.

"Four years of Yale," she muttered, wedging herself deeper into the engine compartment, elbow-deep in grease.

George didn't look up. "Nothing wrong with using your hands. Makes you appreciate what your brain forgets."

She huffed. "My brain forgot to dodge betrayal. Should've paid more attention in Psych 101."

He passed her a socket wrench. "Try this. Better grip."

She adjusted her angle, twisted hard, and the stubborn bolt gave way with a squeal, like it was finally ready to be honest.

"Nice," George said. That was high praise.

Ava glanced at him, surprised to feel the shimmer of pride stir in her chest. She could do this. Maybe not forever, but for now. This was something she could fix, even if it was just a boat engine and not her actual life.

Then, footsteps. Heavy. Confident. Disruptive. She turned. Regretted it instantly.

The man walking toward them was sun-drenched lumberjack meets L.L.Bean catalog fantasy. Plaid shirt. Carhart jacket. Scruff. Eyes the color of smug forests. He was the kind of handsome that should come with a warning label: May cause emotional whiplash.

"Morning, George," he said, voice smooth enough to butter toast.

"Chap," George grunted. "This is Ava. My granddaughter. Fresh outta Yale."

Chap turned to her. His eyes didn't scan like a leer. They observed. They noticed.

"You're the Yale one?"

She raised an eyebrow. "Guilty."

"You don't look clueless."

"Give it time."

He laughed. Short. Surprising. Effective.

Grandpa cleared his throat, the universal signal for "Stop flirting near my torque wrench."

Chap tipped his head. "Catch you around."

He walked away, but not before glancing back once right at her. Caught mid-stare, Ava jolted, spinning so fast she nearly knocked a bait bucket into the water. Her face flamed hotter than a bonfire. She could feel George watching her sideways, that slow smirk tugging at the corners of his mouth.

"Don't hurt your neck watchin' that boy walk away," he muttered without looking up.

"I wasn't!"

"Mmmhmm," George said, which was old-man speak for *you totally were.*

Ava went back to handing him tools, but she couldn't help the smile tugging at her lips. Just a little. Just enough.

Later that afternoon, Grandma dragged her to Annie's Café under the pretense of also getting groceries but really to showcase Ava like a prize chicken at the county fair. Annie had new help behind the counter. A teenager with blue hair and a nose ring, who mistook Ava for someone named Claire.

Ava tried to disappear into her too-large hoodie, sipping bitter coffee while Esther chatted about Ava's credentials with anyone who had ears.

Then, the door jingled.

"Hey, city girl."

Chap. Again. Because fate was apparently a stand-up comic.

He leaned against the doorframe like it was structurally necessary.

"Stalking me?" Ava asked, sipping.

"You wish. Meeting someone. But you're a better surprise."

She blushed. Because of course she did.

As Esther made her rounds in the café, Chap and Ava chatted. At first, awkwardly, about the coffee (too bitter), the weather (too wet), the engines (always finicky this time of year). But then they hit their rhythm.

Books.

Ava admitted to rereading *Persuasion* the week before the wedding-that-wasn't. Chap's eyes lit up. "Best of Austen," he said. "The quiet ones always carry the deepest heartbreak." She blinked, surprised.

"You've read *Persuasion*?"

"I've read everything Austen wrote. And Brontë. And a ridiculous amount of Melville because my dad thought it built character."

She laughed before she could stop herself. "You're a boat guy who reads Melville for fun?"

He grinned. "And *Woolf* when I'm feeling moody. Lots of time to read on the water."

He bought her a mocha with extra whipped cream. Didn't flinch when she licked the fluff from the lid. More points.

She told him about her final paper about Jane Austen and the betrayal in female narratives. He listened, really listened, nodding like her words were important, not indulgent. "Sounds like you were digging for truth," he said. "That kind of writing cuts close."

They didn't touch. Didn't flirt, at least not in the obvious ways. But something crackled in the air between them, subtle and electric.

They parted with a promise: a fishing trip, when she was ready.

Back home, she sat on the porch swing, letting the ocean speak in its slow, rhythmic language.

She wasn't whole. But she'd stopped falling apart in public.

Progress.

Chapter 4

Ava sat cross-legged on the bed, the spiral notebook balanced on her lap. Outside the window, the mist rolled in off the water, softening the edges of the world. She stared down at the blank page, pen hovering.

Dear William,

She scratched it out immediately.

She tried again.

Today I remembered that you hated the sound of seagulls. Said it reminded you of your childhood beach trips. The ones where your parents made you read The Economist instead of building sandcastles.

Another line drawn through the text. Another deep sigh.

She wanted to write him out of her system. Or write herself back into it.

Instead, she wrote:

You made me feel like too much and not enough. And I believed you.

She closed the notebook. Her chest ached in that dull, persistent way it had since the betrayal. Grief had moved in like a squatter. Uninvited, impossible to evict.

She wasn't ready to ask why she had so willingly given away pieces of herself out like party favors. Wasn't ready to admit how early she'd started dimming her light so he could shine a little brighter.

And the worst part? He never even asked her to.

That's the thing about losing herself. She didn't notice until she was halfway gone.

Or until your fiancé sleeps with your roommate and the universe hands you a very loud wake-up call.

But right now, it was easier to stay mad. Easier to tally his mistakes like receipts and ignore the quiet voice asking what she'd done to herself in the process.

Downstairs, Esther called up from downstairs. "Ava! Can you give me a hand in the kitchen?"

She tucked the notebook under her pillow and made her way down.

***

The kitchen smelled like brine and woodsmoke. Ava stood in fuzzy socks on the worn tile, eyeing the pressure cooker warily as it hissed and clattered. Esther moved around her with practiced, almost surgical precision. Gloved hands, sterilized jars, and an apron stained with the day's labor.

The air was thick with steam and the sharp tang of saltwater and fish.

"Don't just stare at it," Esther said, handing Ava a pair of tongs. "Start loading those jars. And watch those rims, or the seals won't take. That's a sin I won't forgive."

Ava obeyed, reaching for the glass jars lined up like soldiers on the counter. Each one held chunks of fresh-caught salmon, pink and glistening, flecked with peppercorn and dill. The act of sealing something so raw, so fleeting, into permanence felt strangely poetic. And unsettling.

Her grip faltered for a second. Maybe from the heat. Maybe from the memories flooding back.

Esther explained that Ava's mother had learned the recipe years ago from a Tlingit woman down the street. It had been passed down like stories, sealed tight in mason jars and memory.

Ava pictured her mom at the very same stove, stirring with the same wooden spoon, steam fogging her glasses, the smell of sugar and vinegar clinging to her hair for days.

It was muscle memory wrapped in love. A kind of inheritance that didn't need a will.

"She used to sing while we did this," Esther said, as if plucking the thought straight from Ava's mind. "Some terrible pop song. What was it? 'Maneater'?"

Ava chuckled. "Seriously?"

"Swore it helped keep rhythm. I think she just liked annoying me."

The pressure canner clanked. Ava twisted the lid tighter, more carefully now. "I miss her."

Esther didn't answer immediately. She pulled her gloves off and wiped her hands on her apron. "Yeah. Me too."

They stood in silence until Esther handed Ava a set of tongs. "Let's not screw up her recipe."

***

Later that morning, Ava pulled on her hoodie and XtraTuf boots, deciding to swing by Annie's for a coffee before picking up the canning supplies for Esther. It felt strange after years of drinking coffee made with home espresso machines topped off with oat milk. This was certainly not that. But something about this town made her crave the comfort of the familiar.

Annie's sat at the corner of the dock like it had always been there. Red shutters, a chipped sign, and a hanging basket of flowers that somehow never died. Ava pushed open the door and was hit with the scent of bacon grease, over-brewed coffee, and blueberry muffins.

Heads turned.

Not dramatically, not rudely. Just aware.

She stepped to the counter, hands in her pockets.

"Be right with ya, hon," called a tall woman with a graying ponytail and an apron that read *Brewed & Blessed.*

Ava nodded, feeling heat crawl up her neck. She heard snippets of conversations. Hot fishing spots, a car that wouldn't start, someone's cat pregnant *again.*

A chair scraped behind her, and someone approached the counter. An older woman with sharp eyes and a practical haircut.

"Well, I'll be," she said. "Esther's girl."

Ava offered a small smile. "Granddaughter. Ava."

"Right, right. I remember you. You were always reading in corners and correcting the preacher's grammar."

Ava's smile froze. "That sounds about right."

"I thought you were off in New York or some big city."

"Connecticut."

"Well, close enough. Welcome home."

Ava nodded, unsure how much to say.

The woman leaned closer. "Your mother was a spitfire. Loved her. She was … complicated. Like a summer storm."

Before Ava could respond, the woman turned and called over her shoulder, "Marge! Guess who's back!"

A voice replied, "That can't be Ava. I haven't seen you since you were a little girl."

She took her coffee to go.

As she stepped outside, the cool air hit her like a wake-up call. She caught the whispering almost immediately. Hushed voices behind cupped hands, glances that didn't quite look away fast enough. That didn't bother her. She expected it.

What stuck was how they talked about her mother: loud, wild, and unfinished.

Like a story that had been cut off mid-sentence.

She kept walking. Toward the general store. Toward the past. Toward something she wasn't ready to name yet.

Esther had sent her for more mason jars and sugar. Simple enough. But as Ava stepped onto the boardwalk, the wind curled around her like a living thing. The sea was loud. The sky was low and heavy.

Spruce Cove looked smaller than she remembered, and somehow bigger.

She took her time walking to the store, her boots squishing on the damp wood. The sea air clung to her like a second skin. She passed the marine repair shop with its peeling mural of a grinning octopus and a bench she and her mother used to sit on after long walks.

Inside the general store, she was greeted by the scent of cedar, motor oil, and peppermint gum. The checker, a man in his sixties with wild eyebrows and a thick Maine accent, gave her a slow nod as she placed her items on the counter.

"Looks like you're doin' some good ol' fashioned canning," he said, ringing up the jars.

Ava smiled. "Grandmother's orders."

He chuckled. "Ain't nothin' like homemade jam and canned salmon to make a house feel like a home, huh?"

"It's 'isn't anything,' technically," she corrected before she could stop herself.

The words hung in the air, heavy and sharp. The checker blinked at her, the smile dimming just a notch.

Ava's stomach sank. "Sorry. I didn't mean. Force of habit."

He nodded slowly and resumed scanning, smile gone. "You're George and Esther's girl, huh?"

She nodded. "Granddaughter."

"Haven't seen you since you were knee-high. Heard you went off to some fancy college."

"Yeah. Yale."

"Makes sense," he said, handing her the receipt. "Be careful out there. Boardwalk's slick."

Ava left the store with pink cheeks and the uncomfortable weight of her own misstep.

Outside, she nearly collided with someone.

"Whoa. You okay?"

Ava looked up into the face of a woman with messy blonde hair, black-rimmed glasses, and a flannel that looked like it had a thousand stories.

"Yeah, sorry," Ava said, stepping back.

The woman reached out and shook Ava's hand like she was trying to prove a point.

"You're Ava, right? Esther's granddaughter from Yale? I'm Liz, by the way. Editor and Publisher of the Gazette and unofficial town smartass."

Ava nodded, a little caught off guard. "Yeah. That's me."

"It's been a long time. Welcome back to Spruce Cove," Liz said, her smile crooked but not unkind. "It's not the Yale library, but we've got stronger coffee and better gossip."

Ava groaned softly. "I may have just corrected someone's grammar at the register."

Liz blinked, then burst out laughing. "You did *what?* Oh honey, that's a hate crime here."

Ava blushed, laughing despite herself. "That was supposed to stay in my head, but apparently my filter quit today."

"Force of habit, I get it," Liz said, lifting a brow. "But if you want to survive here, maybe try smiling and nodding when someone says 'irregardless.'"

"Duly noted."

Liz nodded toward her own cart. "If you're heading back toward the docks, I'll walk with you. Let's scandalize the town with our dangerous, intellectual energy."

They walked slowly, bags in hand, stepping over a cracked board in the walkway that Liz said had claimed three ankles and one tourist marriage.

"So, what's the real story behind that board?" Ava asked.

Liz grinned. "Legend says it gave out under a bridezilla from Portland who'd just bought a new pair of platform wedges. Her fiancé took it as a sign from the universe. Called off the wedding the next day."

They passed an older man hunched on an overturned bucket, swapping out hooks and checking his lures like he was prepping for battle.

"Morning, Liz," he said without looking up. Then his eyes flicked to Ava. "You're Esther's girl."

"Granddaughter," Ava said.

He nodded once. "Figured. You walk like your mother."

"That was Tim Lister," Liz said after they were out of earshot. "He once caught a crab with a plastic fork and claimed it was divine intervention."

They passed a pottery studio with a chalkboard sign that read *"Closed due to inspiration drought."*

"I haven't really met many people yet," Ava said. "Other than some guy named Chap. Ran into him on the dock. Not super chatty."

Liz glanced over, amused. "That'd be Chap Fisher. He helped build that dock. Quite talented with his hands."

Ava raised an eyebrow. "Is that a euphemism?"

Liz laughed. "Sadly, no. Though plenty have tried to make it one. He's one of the good ones. Doesn't date much."

"Everyone seems to know him."

"That's Spruce Cove," Liz said. "And Chap's the kind of guy who'd fix your furnace in a storm and leave a fillet of halibut in your fridge without sticking around for a thank-you."

Ava thought about the coffee he brought. The grease-stained forearms. The shy smile.

"So why emotionally unavailable?"

"Last girl who got close left town with a one-way ticket to Anchorage. Left him with a broken heart. He hasn't really let anyone in since."

They reached the corner where their paths split. Ava adjusted her hood against the drizzle.

"Thanks for the walk," she said.

"Anytime," Liz said. "Just remember, in a town this small no one's baggage stays packed for long."

Ava gave a small smile. "I'm carrying plenty of my own."

Then she turned and headed toward the docks, trying not to think too hard about how that smile of his had looked a little less shy this morning.

***

That evening, the house smelled like roasted chicken and rosemary potatoes. Ava helped Esther set the table, laying out mismatched plates and antique silverware.

George stepped in from the garage, wiping his hands on a rag. "Smells like you managed not to burn the place down."

"Careful," Esther called from the kitchen. "That mouth is awfully bold for a man who is always scrounging for my leftovers."

They sat, the sound of clinking silverware and glass filling the space where heavier words might live.

"This is amazing," Ava said. "I forgot how real food tasted."

"Your mom hated fancy food," Esther said. "She wanted burgers, pancakes and fried chicken."

"She used to make blueberry pancakes every Saturday."

George looked down. "She played music way too loud."

"She'd dance around the kitchen," Esther said. "Pretending the spatula was a microphone."

"She used to pull me in and make me dance with her."

"Your mom burned hot," George said. "Didn't always steer right, but she never cooled off."

"I wish I had some fire. I think I lost my spark," Ava said.

George set his fork down. "Nah. Fire doesn't go out. It just needs air."

"And maybe a little butter," Esther added.

After dinner, as Ava dried plates, Esther said, "You did good today. Went outside. Talked to someone new."

"I corrected someone's grammar in public."

"Well, nobody's perfect."

***

After dinner and dishes, Ava lingered in her room, aimless. The air was heavy with the scent of salt and the lingering warmth of roast chicken. She paced once, then sat on the edge of the bed. Her gaze drifted to the old bookshelf in the corner.

Tucked between an outdated Bali travel guide and a battered thesaurus was something that didn't belong. A small, dust-covered cedar box.

She pulled it out carefully. The lid stuck for a moment before it gave with a soft creak.

Inside, time had curled and yellowed the edges of everything. A faded Polaroid of her mother in a wetsuit, grinning and holding a seashell like a trophy. A tiny velvet pouch with a single silver charm inside. An anchor etched with initials. A hand-pressed flower between wax paper, petals still tinged with violet.

Ava's heart thudded as she picked up an envelope. Soft at the edges, sealed with Scotch tape that had yellowed like old teeth.

Her mother's handwriting sprawled across the front. Loose, slanted, unapologetically bold.

But it wasn't addressed to her.

Just a name she didn't recognize. A man's name.

Of course.

She turned it over, half-hoping for a note, a date, something. Nothing. Just that name and her mother's looping script like a ghost on the page.

Ava was disappointed but couldn't help but feel a small sense of relief, unsure if she was ready to know who her mother really was without her.

At least not yet.

She placed it back in the box, slid the lid shut, and stood.

The cedar scent clung to her like an old perfume. Her mother's presence: sharp, complicated, persistent.

Ava didn't cry. Didn't ache.

She just felt a little less sure of what she knew about her mother, about this place, about herself.

***

Ava went for a walk. She went farther than she meant to. The tide had begun to pull back, revealing scattered debris, seaweed, broken shells, and lengths of driftwood that looked like the bones of old stories left behind by the tide.

She was about to turn around when she noticed a man crouched near the rocks, stacking bits of driftwood into a teepee-like structure.

He was in his sixties, maybe older. Wiry, with skin leathered by years outdoors. His coat was two sizes too big, and a faded ATC cap

50

barely clung to his head. He muttered to himself as he worked, not noticing her at first.

When she stepped on a rock and it shifted, he turned sharply.

"Don't go sneaking up on people," he barked.

"Sorry," Ava said, holding her hands up. "Didn't mean to."

He squinted. "You're Esther's?"

Ava nodded cautiously. "Ava."

"Didn't think you'd come back. Thought you were city-bound forever like your mama."

"You knew her?"

He grunted. "Everyone knew her. Some more than others."

She waited for him to elaborate. He didn't.

Instead, he jabbed a crooked finger at the pile he'd made. "You see this?"

Ava glanced at the driftwood. "A sculpture?"

He shook his head. "It's a warning. This coast eats people. First their minds, then their hearts."

Before she could respond, he stood and brushed off his pants.

"Tell Esther that Earl says hi. She'll know."

And with that, he ambled off, his muttering carried away by the wind.

Ava stood there for a long moment, goosebumps rising on her arms.

She didn't know what unnerved her more. His strange words, or the idea that her mother might have once known a man like him.

The walk back to the house was quiet, except for the crunch of pebbles under her boots and the occasional screech of an eagle overhead. Ava couldn't shake the image of the man's crooked finger pointing at his driftwood sculpture, or the strange conviction in his voice.

She told herself he was just a local oddball, harmless and theatrical, but something about the encounter clung to her like damp fog. Still, as the porch light of the cottage came into view, a sense of calm began to settle in her chest. The kind that came with being somewhere familiar. Somewhere hers.

***

That night, Ava sat at the desk in the loft. The wind brushed the eaves outside like fingertips across an old piano. The house creaked gently, the way it always had when she was a child. Like it was exhaling, settling into sleep. Her lamp cast a soft cone of yellow over the desk, warming the worn wood and the edges of her spiral notebook.

She opened it and flipped backward.

A page from six months ago:

William wants to buy a condo. He says it'll be easier than renting, and besides, we're not kids anymore.

Another page.

He doesn't like that I cry after writing. Says it's indulgent. Dramatic. Said I was always chasing pain for sport.

Her fingers trembled slightly as she turned to the next.

My short stories are too emotional. "Nobody wants to read about women who feel too much," he said, pouring his second glass of wine.

She stared at the page until the words blurred. Her chest tightened, that familiar knot threading itself together again.

She closed her eyes.

And wrote:

William had a voice like honey and a mouth like a scalpel. I never knew if he was comforting me or cutting me. I told myself it was love because it hurt just enough to feel familiar. He made me smaller and called it protection. He loved me, I think. But only the version he edited first.

The words came faster now.

With William, I always felt like I had to earn my space. My silence was safer than my truth.

She paused, then started a fresh page.

Chap didn't flinch when I got awkward, or when I filled the silence with too many words.

He just smiled. Like he was amused, but not put off. Like maybe I wasn't what he expected, but not in a bad way.

He handed me coffee and sat beside me like we'd done this a dozen times. Like I hadn't just uprooted my whole life and crash-landed in his.

Green. That's the color of his flannel. His eyes too, maybe. Hard to tell in that light.

The ocean was behind him.

The feeling that maybe this is what starting over feels like: quiet, unannounced, and suddenly everywhere.

She looked across the room at the old bookcase. On the top shelf sat a photo album with a cracked leather spine. She hadn't opened it in years.

She pulled it down carefully. The pages whispered as she turned them, the paper worn soft with time.

Faces. Summers. People who no longer called or remembered.

Then, herself. Barefoot on a rock, age seven. Sunburned nose. Grinning like she owned the tide.

She smiled. Not sadly. Just surprised.

She turned the page and wrote:

I saw myself today. Not the woman with a broken plan, but the girl who didn't need one.

I forgot that girl existed. The one who smelled like salt and always climbed too high.

She paused, her pen hovering. Then added:

Maybe I'm not supposed to pick up where I left off.

Maybe I'm supposed to start exactly where I am.

Chapter 5

The morning mist clung to Spruce Cove like it had secrets to keep, and it probably did. Ava stood barefoot in the kitchen, arms crossed, and shoulders hunched against the chill that lingered despite the humming stove. The "Best Mom Ever" mug sat abandoned on the counter. Ironic if it hadn't come from a Juneau thrift store and been repurposed as a catch-all for paperclips, rubber bands, and loose change.

The cabin smelled like something mildly scorched. Ava glanced toward the toaster, which blinked back at her innocently. Esther, apparently, had declared war on it again. So far, the toaster had survived. The English muffin had not.

"You're up early," Esther said as she swept into the room like a force of nature wrapped in flannel. Her silver braid swung behind her like it had its own agenda.

Ava didn't answer right away. Mostly because it was 6:45 a.m. and her soul was still asleep.

"You've got bedhead and existential dread written all over you," Esther said, peeling a banana with the kind of enthusiasm most people reserved for winning the lottery.

"And you're very judgmental for someone who yells at appliances."

Esther ignored her. "Get dressed. We're going berry picking."

Ava blinked. "Berry picking?"

"What else would we be doing at 7 a.m. on a Tuesday? Salmonberries are ripe now."

"Sleeping. Crying. Googling revenge quotes for ex-fiancés."

That earned her a smirk. "You can cry in the woods. There's good drainage. Get moving."

Before Ava could argue, she was slipping on a pair of muddy XtraTufs. Esther was rummaging through the coat closet, muttering something about mosquito repellent and Ivy League blood probably tasting like filet mignon.

Fifteen minutes later, Ava was tripping over a root the size of a small child and trying not to spill her dented berry bucket. Her jeans were snug in that *why-didn't-I-size-up-after-finals* way, and her hoodie still bore the faded Yale logo.

The woods were what Instagram would call "enchanting." Ava would call "wet." Everything dripped. The trees dripped. The moss dripped. Even her thoughts dripped, one after another, pooling into the murky mess that was her current emotional state. So much for drainage.

Esther moved through the underbrush like a woman in a Land's End catalog shoot. Ava, on the other hand, looked like she'd lost a bet.

Crows cawed above them. One of them sounded like it was mocking her specifically.

She hated it here. She loved it here. She had no idea what she felt, which was basically her default setting these days.

Ava grumbled something best left off the record as she barely hauled herself over a mossy log. Her grandmother was a solid twenty paces ahead, moving like a woman half her age.

Ava suddenly paused and pointed to a wide paw print sunk deep in the mud.

"Okay. Is that from an unusually large dog, or should I start composing my 'eaten by bear' obituary now?"

"That's a bear."

"Oh. Cool. Totally fine. I'm sure it's vegan."

Esther forged ahead, swatting at branches like they were personal insults. Ava caught her toe on a root disguised as flat ground, nature's version of a practical joke.

"You'd think with all that schooling, you'd know how to step over a root."

"It's not my fault it hates me," Ava muttered, adjusting her hoodie. "It's probably in cahoots with that crow that dropped something on me earlier."

"That wasn't a crow," Esther replied without looking back. "That was a raven. They remember faces, so maybe don't badmouth them. One pooped on Mayor Tom's head three elections ago, and he lost the whole eastside vote."

Ava laughed in spite of herself. "Is that a real story?"

"You're in Alaska now. Everything's a real story if you believe it hard enough."

Esther paused to pluck a handful of red and orange berries, her fingers quick and confident. "First time I came to Spruce Cove with George, he tried to impress me by catching a fish with his bare hands. Slipped on a rock and landed flat on his back in the river. Swore the fish pulled him under."

Ava chuckled. "And you dated him?"

Esther shrugged. "I liked the way he didn't get mad about looking foolish. He showed up the next day with a pie and zero ego. Hard to say no to that."

They moved on, the canopy shifting overhead. Ava swatted another mosquito and cursed under her breath.

Esther glanced over. "Berry picking's a little like relationships. You have to reach for the good ones. You get scratched a little. But sometimes, you pick too fast and get a mouthful of sour."

"Sounds like a metaphor with dirt under its nails," Ava said.

Esther grinned. "Best kind."

Halfway down the trail, something stopped her. A smell, maybe. Or a shift in the light. Or memory.

She was nine again. Her mom was alive, laughing at something Ava had said, her cheeks berry-stained and her fingers sticky. They'd picked salmonberries until their buckets overflowed, and then they'd sat right on the forest floor eating them like candy. Her mom had woven a crown out of ferns and called her the Queen of the Tongass.

Her mother's laugh echoing through the old growth trees, a smear of berry juice across little Ava's chin. A makeshift crown of ferns. That was before Yale, before William, before the world cracked in two.

Ava had been chasing the sun through the forest, her mother just ahead with a recycled Folgers coffee can full of berries bouncing against her chest on a string.

One wrong step, and Ava stumbled straight into a patch of devil's club. All spines and regret.

She cried out, tears springing up fast as the sting bloomed across her arms and legs. Her mother turned, crouched, and kissed one scratched hand like she could steal the hurt away.

"You're tougher than you think," she whispered, gently plucking a spine from Ava's forearm. "From now on, keep your eyes on what's right in front of you. The rest will take care of itself."

She cupped her cheek, thumb warm against her skin.

At the time, Ava thought her mom meant the trail. The actual path through the woods, where you had to watch every root and pretend you weren't scared of bears.

But now?

Now she wasn't so sure.

Maybe it wasn't about the trail at all.

Maybe it was about paying attention to the details. Not to the map, or the plan, or the what-comes-next, but to that quiet voice inside you.

The one that whispers, *Here. Start here.*

She blinked hard. Focused on a juicy salmonberry almost out of reach. Picked it and proudly dropped it in the bucket like a prized possession.

They stopped on the top of a hill and admired the view. The kind that postcards would envy, overlooking a cove so still it could've been lacquered. Ava sank onto a downed tree that probably had been there since before she was born and wiped sweat from her neck.

Esther passed her a canteen. "Drink. You're turning the color of week-old guacamole."

Ava took a sip and immediately regretted it. The water had a taste. Not a *flavor*. A *taste*. Like something medicinal and moss-adjacent.

She stared at the ocean and wondered what it would feel like to float out there, far enough that nothing hurt. No Yale, no William, no wedding invitations she never got to mail.

"I had a plan," she said, surprising herself with the sound of her own voice. "Everything was lined up. I had fallen in love with the family we were going to create. It all made sense. Until it didn't."

Esther didn't interrupt. Didn't comfort. Just sat. Which, frankly, was the most comforting thing of all.

"I thought I was the lucky one," Ava added. "Turns out I was just the last to know."

The silence between them stretched, not empty but full of things said and unsaid. Of grief and resilience and that strange thing that lives between pain and possibility.

Finally, Esther offered a quiet, "Both can be true, you know."

That's when her phone buzzed.

William.

Her heart dropped into her boots … right next to her common sense.

Of course it was him. Like he could *feel* her finally exhaling, and couldn't resist pulling her back in.

She stared at his name, the way you stare at a ghost. Half afraid it might speak.

Esther caught the shift in the air and shot her a look. She didn't say a word.

Ava stood, walked a few steps away. Her thumb hovered. Then, slowly, she lowered the phone.

Not now.

***

The walk back to town was quiet. Esther didn't ask questions. Ava didn't offer answers.

They dropped the berries at home and Esther sent her to the general store for jelly supplies.

The boardwalk stretched out like a timeline Ava didn't recognize. Every creak of wood underfoot felt like a choice she hadn't made yet. The salty air carried the scent of fish and fir, a combination that shouldn't have been comforting but was.

She was rounding the last corner when she saw him.

Chap.

Leaning against a piling, laughing at something a kid had said, a crate balanced on his shoulder like it weighed nothing. The sunlight hit his hair just so, catching the glimmer of copper in his curls. He didn't see her.

And thank God, because she didn't have the energy to flirt or fence with the man who haunted her dreams like a character from a novel she wasn't sure she was brave enough to read.

A woman behind her whispered to a friend, "Funny, how the quiet ones always carry the heaviest stuff."

Ava didn't know if she meant Chap.

She walked on.

Her steps quickened without her permission, boots thudding too loudly on the planks. Before hitting the store, she ducked into Annie's Café. The bell over the door announcing her like a warning shot.

Inside smelled like cinnamon, bacon grease, and something she couldn't quite name. Comfort, maybe. Or the kind of home that came with good coffee and no expectations.

Martha looked up from behind the counter, glasses perched halfway down her nose. "You've got the look of someone heading somewhere fast but not entirely sure why."

"Just on my way to grab pectin from the store," Ava said, brushing a windblown strand of hair from her face.

Martha slid a to-go cup across the counter. "For jelly or just life in general?"

Ava managed a half-smile. "Still deciding."

As Ava headed out to the store, Martha whispered "whatever you're making, don't forget to leave a little space at the top. Things expand when they heat up."

Ava nodded, not sure if it was advice or just canning tips. But either way, she appreciated it.

Outside, Chap was gone.

Which was fine. Totally fine.

Except for the tiny, unreasonable part of her that kind of hoped he'd still be there, leaning against the railing with a half-cocked smile ready to volley some casual sexually charged banter like it was a team sport.

***

Later, back at the cabin, another call came in. William.

She almost didn't answer. Her thumb hovered over the red decline button, heart hammering against her ribs like it wanted out. But something, curiosity, weakness, unfinished business, won.

63

"Hi," she said, voice small.

"Hi," he breathed back, as if the word carried a thousand pounds. "I didn't think you'd pick up."

"I almost didn't."

There was silence. Long enough for the ocean outside the window to whisper its own opinion.

"I just needed to hear your voice," he said. "I know I have no right. But I can't stop thinking about you."

Her throat tightened. "You made a choice, William."

A soft breath. Then a sound, barely audible but unmistakable. He was crying.

"I made a mistake. The worst one of my life. I've regretted it every day since."

Ava closed her eyes. Images flickered. His hands on her waist. The first time he called her beautiful. Their takeout nights and book club arguments. How he'd once kissed her knuckles and promised to never be like her father.

"I thought we were real," she whispered.

"So did I. I panicked. I tanked everything in the worst way possible."

More silence. Just the sound of him breathing, uneven and congested. Like he was still trying to pull himself together.

"I love you," he added.

Ava took a deep breath, steeled her spine.

"I've already cancelled everything, William. The florist. The photographer. The hotel blocks. I'm done."

Except, that wasn't entirely true. She hadn't cancelled the venue yet. Or the minister. They were still on her to-do list, sitting like time bombs in her planner. A part of her had held off. Stubborn or stupid, she didn't know. Maybe it was hope. Or denial. Or just the understanding that once she said it out loud, it would be real.

With that, she hung up. Not in anger, but in ache.

Ava stared at the phone in her lap, fingers gone cold.

The shame came in waves. She still missed him.

Even after everything. After the lies, the roommate, the wreckage. Some part of her still missed the version of him she thought was real.

And maybe the worst part wasn't that he fooled her. It was that she still fantasized about the illusion.

She remembered the first night they met. A bookstore in New Haven. He'd been in the wrong aisle, looking for a Malcolm Gladwell and holding a book on grief instead. They'd argued about self-help versus memoir over coffee that turned into dinner, then dessert, then a slow kiss under a flickering streetlamp.

It had felt fated. Magical. Adult.

But it had never been safe. Not really. She'd spent so much time editing herself for him. Smiling when she didn't feel like it, biting back her opinions, shrinking to fit the shape of his dream.

And now, miles away, her body still wanted the comfort of what was familiar. The cadence of his voice. The ghost of shared plans.

But she couldn't go back. Not to someone who broke her trust with a girl who smelled like vanilla body spray and wedding cake.

She walked to the sink, ran cold water over her wrists, and stared at her reflection in the glass.

You're tougher than you think.

Her mother's words, echoing through the trees and into her chest.

She'd have to call the florist. Cancel the limo. Get her deposit back from the photographer if she could grovel hard enough. The venue still posted her wedding slot as unavailable; she'd checked the site last night, like a masochist. Their names were still there: Ava McCormick and William Hudson.

After the call with William, there was no more room for maybes. No sliver of almosts. She walked to the kitchen table, pulled out her phone again, and dialed the venue coordinator.

"Hi, yes. This is Ava McCormick. I need to cancel my July 20th reservation."

Her voice only cracked a little.

***

That night, Esther made soup and didn't talk much. Ava appreciated it.

After dinner, they sat on the porch, wrapped in mismatched quilts that smelled faintly of cedar and jelly. A candle flickered between them, its flame dancing in the breeze like it was listening. The tide whispered against the shore, the same way it had every night since Ava arrived. Persistent, soft, impossible to ignore.

"He called," Ava said, finally.

Esther nodded. "Figured."

"He cried. I didn't. Is that weird?"

"Nope."

Ava picked at the corner of the blanket. "Why do I feel so guilty?"

Esther sipped her tea, her eyes fixed on the dark water. "Because you're kind. But kindness doesn't mean you need to stay."

Ava let that sink in. She wanted it to feel like clarity, like a lightbulb, but instead it felt like an ache she couldn't quite name.

"I spent so long trying to be what he needed. The right kind of smart. The right kind of pretty. Like a job interview that never finished."

Esther hummed. "Sounds exhausting."

"It was. I don't even think he noticed. Sad thing is, I didn't notice."

Some men fall in love with the highlight reel," Esther said. "But when real life shows up, they act like someone changed the channel without asking."

They sat in silence until the sky turned lavender. A blue heron called somewhere out on the bay. A branch creaked. The air shifted colder.

Esther stood, joints popping like popcorn. "You need anything else, baby girl?"

Ava shook her head.

She eventually went upstairs, crawled into bed, and opened her phone. William's last text blinked like a wound: *I'm not giving up.*

She stared at it a long time, like it might rearrange itself into something easier.

Then she deleted it.

She rolled onto her side and faced the window. The sky was bruised violet now, the stars just beginning to poke through.

A red-hulled boat slipped past on the horizon.

Maybe it was Chap.

She didn't know. Then she realized that for the first time in weeks, she didn't feel like drowning.

The next morning, Ava woke before sunrise, her legs twitching with a kind of energy she didn't recognize. Nervous. Raw. Almost like hope. She pulled on leggings, a threadbare college sweatshirt, and laced up her sneakers like she knew what she was doing.

The air outside was brisk, biting just enough to wake her completely. The road to the harbor twisted downhill through stands of spruce and alder, and Ava let her feet find the rhythm, breath steaming, heartbeat pounding out its own mantra: *Keep going, keep going, keep going.*

She wasn't fast. Wasn't graceful. But something about moving forward, literally, felt like she was convincing the universe she wasn't stuck anymore.

She hit the gravel path near the docks just as the sky turned pink. The water shimmered with a sleepy kind of magic.

And that's when she saw him.

Chap.

On the *Malahini.*

He was crouched over a coil of rope, arms moving with the kind of ease people have when they know exactly what they're doing. A socket wrench sat next to him, a rag tucked into his waistband. There was a speaker clipped to the railing, playing something bluesy and low. He didn't see her.

But Ava stopped anyway. Just for a second.

Because there was something in the way he worked. Calm. Methodical. Focused. It made her chest ache. The way sunlight glanced off the curve of his shoulder and caught the flecks of copper-red in his hair.

He looked content. Solitary. A man in tune with his life in a way Ava had never quite managed.

She took a step forward. Then another. But the dock creaked beneath her foot and Chap glanced up.

Their eyes met.

Just for a breath.

Ava froze.

Chap didn't smile. Didn't wave.

He just looked at her like he wasn't sure if he should approach her.

But he didn't move. He didn't look away either.

His gaze held something quiet and restrained, like he was standing behind a wall he'd built himself. Like he wanted to cross it.

And God help her, part of her wanted him to.

Her pulse jumped. Not from fear. From the way his jaw tensed, the way his eyes flicked to her mouth for the briefest second and then back.

There was heat in it. Unspoken, unresolved, and definitely mutual.

She swallowed hard and gave a quick, awkward nod. It was the only move she could trust herself with. Then she turned away before she flirted her way straight into his berth.

She ran the long way home, legs burning, lungs tight. Not from the effort, but from everything she wasn't ready to say.

Back at the cabin, she poured herself a glass of water and leaned against the sink, heart still racing.

She wasn't sure if she wanted to kiss him or punch him for existing like that. So quietly alluring, so utterly unreadable.

But as her chest rose and fell, she realized one thing for certain. She was starting to want again.

Chapter 6

Ava stood outside the weather-worn offices of the Spruce Cove Gazette, the wooden sign above the door swinging slightly in the breeze. It had been nearly a decade since she'd been in a town this small and now she was about to write about it. What could there possibly be to report?

The inside of the newspaper office was a chaotic haven of yellowed newspaper clippings, old filing cabinets, and the faint scent of printer ink and sea salt. Liz Walker, the owner, editor, and unapologetic caffeine snob, looked up from her desk, clutching a steaming mug that read, "Death Before Decaf. But Maybe Tea First."

"You're late," Liz said in her best fake boss tone, without looking at the clock.

Ava stepped carefully over a stack of paper bundles. "You said ten-ish."

Liz raised an eyebrow, sipped her tea, and smirked. "And you thought I was being casual?"

Ava tried not to smile. "What's the dress code?" she asked, eyeing her own boots and sweater.

"If you're not covered in fish guts, you're overdressed," Liz replied. "Welcome to the glamorous life of small-town journalism."

Ava took in the cramped space, noting the corkboard plastered with push-pinned photos of fishing derbies, charity pie auctions, and an enthusiastic shot of Liz shaking hands with the governor. A rotary phone perched on one desk rang with a shrillness that suggested it hadn't stopped since 1987. A printer in the corner chugged out half a page, then whined and blinked an angry red light.

"That desk is yours," Liz said, nodding toward the rickety setup next to the heater. "And fair warning, the heater barks like a drunk sea lion when it kicks on. Don't take it personally."

Ava dropped her bag on the desk and tried not to look overwhelmed. "What exactly will I be doing here?"

"You're our new sports and features writer. Spruce Cove needs your Ivy League shine. You'll make Little League heroic and bake sales riveting."

"Do I get press credentials?" Ava asked.

Liz snorted. "You get a notebook, two pens if you're lucky, and a town that thinks your red hair means you're trouble. That's credential enough."

Ava chuckled despite herself.

Liz handed her a paper folder labeled "WEDNESDAY DEADLINE." Inside was a list: Little League game, library book sale, and an interview with a woman who claimed her cat had psychic powers.

"Start with the baseball game," Liz said. "Just don't get hit with a bat. The liability insurance lapsed in '19."

When Liz turned back to her own desk, Ava sat down at hers slowly. The chair creaked ominously but didn't collapse. Small wins. She pulled open each drawer one by one. A dried-up glue stick, two expired coupons for chowder, a cracked ruler, and a small bottle of ibuprofen with a single, suspicious pill left inside.

She laughed under her breath and began arranging her space. From her tote bag, she pulled out a small notepad, a pen she hoped wouldn't explode, and a well-worn photo of her and her mother standing outside a bookstore in Portland. She tucked it into the corner of the desk's corkboard.

Next came a little ceramic dish. Something she'd made at summer camp that would now hold paper clips. She peeled a sticky note from the top of her pad and stuck it to the monitor: "Observe. Absorb. Translate." Her old writing mantra.

For the first time in months, something that felt like pride flickered in her chest. Not the performative kind she used to chase at readings and launch parties. This was quieter, rooted. She was starting over, but she wasn't starting empty.

Liz glanced up, caught her looking around. "You nesting?"

"Maybe," Ava said. "Feels weirdly satisfying."

Liz nodded once, then returned to her editing with a grunt. Ava smiled. The Gazette office might have smelled like toner and seaweed, but for the first time since her wedding plans imploded, she felt like she had a place to be.

That morning, Ava had sat at the kitchen table, sipping the tea Esther placed in front of her like an offering.

"Chamomile for calm," Esther said.

"I'm not nervous," Ava lied.

"You're biting your lip."

"I always do that."

Esther smirked. "That notebook better be waterproof. You remember when you tried to interview the postmaster for that 'What I Did Over the Summer' report? You wouldn't stop asking questions and he spent the rest of the day drenched like a dishrag just trying to hand out mail."

"I was twelve," Ava laughed.

"And ambitious."

They shared a quiet moment before Ava grabbed her coat and bag. Esther called out as she left, "Write the truth, even if it's messy."

***

The stands told their own story. Mothers wrapped in fleece blankets, mugs of coffee or beer clutched close, chatting while keeping one eye on the field. Fathers in baseball caps and flannel swapped fishing stories, each tale larger than the last, their laughter rising like fog off the bay. A pack of kids raced behind the bleachers, ducking in and out of trees, climbing with the sure-footedness of goats, ignoring the game in favor of mud and mystery.

Out on the field, chaos reigned. Kids in baggy uniforms swung wildly at soft pitches. Parents shouted from the sidelines, each convinced they had a future pro on their hands. A 2-year-old escaped from the bleachers and toddled directly into center field before an umpire scooped him up, holding him like a bag of flour.

The snack shack ran out of hot dogs twenty minutes in, prompting a minor revolt from two dads who had skipped lunch. A rogue golden retriever named Chester interrupted the game twice. Once to chase a foul ball and once to steal a little girl's snow cone. No one seemed terribly upset.

Ava's borrowed pen exploded halfway through the third inning, leaving an inky splotch on her notes and a blue smear on her thumb. She muttered a string of quiet curses, pressing her notepad against her jeans to wipe it clean.

She barely noticed Chap until he was beside her, crouching to free a baseball wedged underneath a chain-link fence.

"You clean up nice," he said without looking up.

"I'm not here for you," Ava replied, her eyes narrowing.

He stood, smirking. "Didn't say you were."

Ava's notepad began to flap in the wind. A seagull shrieked overhead. Startled, she started to lose her grip. Chap grabbed it mid-air and handed it back without ceremony.

"This sure is a long way from New Haven," he added.

Ava turned toward him. "From Ivy League to Little League. Living the dream."

Chap chuckled and nodded toward the field. "You ever play?"

"I was more of a track girl," she said. "Straight lines. No balls flying at my face."

Chap raised an eyebrow, just enough to make her wonder if he caught the double meaning.

"Pity," he said, voice low. "You strike me as someone who could handle a curveball."

Ava didn't miss a beat. "Only if I see it coming."

She caught a flicker of a grin tugging at his mouth, slow and deliberate, like he was letting her have the last word on purpose.

Before she could decide if that was a compliment or a flirtation, Chap walked off, joining a group of fishermen leaning against the fence. She scribbled a final thought in her notebook: "Small towns are never quiet. They're just noisy in a different pitch."

After the game, Ava approached the team's pint-sized captain, Owen Macready, age nine. He wore his baseball cap backward and had a missing front tooth.

"How do you feel about today's game?" Ava asked, kneeling to his level.

"We lost," Owen said solemnly. "But I caught a pop fly, and Chester didn't pee on the dugout this time, so I call that a win."

"Solid logic," Ava said, scribbling quickly. "What's your favorite part about playing?"

"Snacks," Owen said without hesitation. "And Coach lets us swear once per inning if no moms were around."

Ava raised her eyebrows. "Sounds like you've got a good coach."

"The best," Owen nodded. "He taught me to spit right."

She jotted down his quote with a grin.

***

Ava then hurried to the Spruce Cove Library's annual book sale. A white tent sagged slightly over rows of battered folding tables, all stacked with used paperbacks. She wasn't expecting much, maybe a few quirky locals. But halfway through snapping photos, she ran into Mabel Kinney.

"You're Ava," Mabel declared, holding a teetering stack of romance novels.

Ava hesitated. "Yes?"

"I knew your mother. She used to write poems in the margins of the gardening section."

Ava blinked. "She did?"

Mabel nodded. "Still have one. About moonlight and fireweed. Lovely stuff. You favor her in the eyes."

Ava smiled, surprised by the ache that crept in as she imagined her mother scribbling poems in the newspaper margins?

So why had she acted like writing wasn't something worth chasing?

Why tell Ava to get serious, get practical, get real? When she'd once written about moonlight and fireweed?

Before Ava could ask more, Mabel waved her off. "Liz says you are going to come see my cat sometime. She knows things."

Chap appeared beside the table, holding a battered copy of Moby Dick. "You're following me now, aren't you?"

Ava shook her head, smiling. "I think you're following *me*."

"Not my style," he said, placing the book gently on the checkout pile.

She crossed her arms, mock-serious. "I took this reporting gig because the only other option was working as Grandpa George's deckhand. And between you and me, I don't do well with fish guts before noon."

He laughed, a real one that crinkled the corners of his eyes. "Smart choice. George doesn't take kindly to slacking."

***

As the sun dipped lower over Spruce Cove, Ava found herself at the town's weekly Friday fish fry, held at the American Legion. The whole space buzzed with laughter, clinking plates, and the smell of fried halibut.

Rows of folding tables were covered in mismatched checkered tablecloths. Someone had tied balloons to a chair, and a child was guarding them like they might float away. Ava grabbed a paper plate and slid into line behind a woman debating coleslaw versus potato salad like they were competing suitors.

"I hear you're the new Gazette reporter," the man at the fryer, handing her a steaming filet with tongs. His name tag read *Ken* and his apron said *Cod Squad.*

"I am. Hoping to survive my first deadline."

Ken winked. "You will do fine. Write about this fish and you'll win the town over in no time."

Ava smiled and moved to the end of the table, balancing her plate. She found an open seat next to a group of older women in thick knit sweaters, all playing bingo between bites.

"It's Ava McCormick," one of them said, eyeing her. "Margaret's girl. You've got her nose."

Ava blinked. "You knew my mom?"

"Everyone knew your mom. She won the bake-off three years running and nearly set the community center on fire doing so." They all laughed like it was a fond memory.

Someone strummed a guitar in the corner. Kids darted between tables. A couple slow-danced by the drink station to a song Ava didn't recognize.

She sat back in her chair, her plate nearly empty, and felt the warmth of it all settle into her bones. The laughter, the fish, the way everyone knew each other.

For the first time in a long while, she didn't feel like she was chasing a story. She was inside one.

****

The next morning, Ava followed a handwritten address from Liz's file to a weathered house tucked behind a row of wind-bent pine trees on Gull Point Road. The porch sagged slightly under the spruce of tangled buoys and a milk crate overflowing with old newspapers. A ceramic plaque beside the door read:

Mabel Winthrop, Retired Librarian (Also Home to Princess, the Cat Who Knows Things)

Before Ava could knock, the door creaked open.

"You made it," Mabel said, excited for her moment in the sun.

Ava stepped inside, brushing wind from her hair. "I need to meet this cat that everyone keeps talking about."

"Welcome," Mabel replied, stepping aside.

"That's Princess," Mabel said, gesturing Ava toward the couch. "Locals say she's psychic. I say she's just been watching long enough to know how stories tend to turn out."

Ava opened her notebook. "Tell me about her ... abilities."

Mabel poured tea into a mismatched mug and passed it over. "Well, she meowed the morning the harbor ferry engine gave out. Wouldn't go near it. Hissed at a councilman before he got caught padding invoices. And she once sat on the lap of a woman the day before she got proposed to."

"She ever wrong?"

Mabel shrugged. "Not yet."

They talked for nearly an hour. Ava scribbled notes about Spruce Cove folklore, Princess's local fan club, and the cat's aversion to tourists with Bluetooth headsets.

Eventually, Ava leaned forward, her pen pausing mid-air. "Okay, humor me. If I asked her a question, how does it work?"

Mabel smiled without answering. Princess stood, stretched like she'd been waiting for the cue, and walked over to sit directly in front of Ava, tail curled neatly around her paws.

Ava cleared her throat. "Will I end up back with William?"

Princess blinked. Looked left. Let out a quiet meow.

Ava stared. "That's a yes?"

Mabel sipped her tea. "That's a yes."

Ava laughed, half-nervous, half-defensive. "Well, that's disappointing. I was hoping for 'absolutely not.'"

"She doesn't deal in wishful thinking," Mabel said. "Only truths."

Ava, asking herself why in the world Liz would give her this assignment, shut her notebook a little harder than she meant to. "That's not something I'm ready to believe."

"Then don't. Belief has nothing to do with it."

Ava glanced down at her lap. "The other day, you told me you knew my mom."

"I did," Mabel said, her voice gentler now. "Margaret used to come by with a grocery bag full of returns and a notebook tucked under her arm. She never said much about what she was working on. But she always looked like she was writing to make sense of something she hadn't said out loud yet."

Ava hesitated. "She didn't want me to write. Not really. Told me I needed something solid. Something practical."

Mabel looked at her for a long moment. "Sometimes we push our kids away from the very thing we wish we'd had the courage to do."

Ava stood, brushing a thread from her jeans.

"Thanks for the tea," she said. "And the ... prophecy."

"Anytime," Mabel said. "Just don't say she didn't warn you."

Outside, the wind had picked up. Ava paused at the edge of the porch and looked back through the window. Princess was still there, still watching.

She jotted one last note: *We build our parents out of memories. Turns out, some of the pieces never belonged to us.*

***

Later, after submitting her story and changing back into her boots and hoodie, Ava took her notebook down to the dock. It was quiet, fog curling at its edges like the hem of an old robe. Wooden planks creaked underfoot with every step, a rhythm she hadn't realized she missed. Seagull cries echoed across the harbor, and the water lapped gently against hulls rocking in their slips.

She sat on the bench where her grandfather once taught her to tie a slip knot. She could still see the rope worn smooth from years of calloused hands. This was the same bench where she'd once watched the boats return from sea, squinting into the sun to catch a glimpse of Grandpa George waving from the bow.

The tide was coming in now, slow and certain, like breath.

Opening her notebook, Ava stared at the blank page. Then, the pen moved. She wrote about the fish fry, about Owen's missing tooth and love of snacks, and about Mabel's psychic cat. She wrote about Chap's smirk, the smell of woodstove smoke and sea salt that made her ache without knowing why.

Her writing felt clearer here. Less performative, more honest. She wasn't trying to prove anything.

For once, her world wasn't about William anymore. It wasn't about what she'd lost. It was about the quiet cadence of a town where there were boys named Owen and old men who told fish tales. A place where she wasn't anonymous, or famous. Just Ava.

***

At home, the kitchen smelled like roasted salmon, fresh dill, and something buttery that made Ava's stomach growl. Esther stood at the stove, her silver hair twisted into a loose bun, humming off-key to an old Patsy Cline song drifting from the radio. George hunched over a half-finished jigsaw puzzle at the table, tongue peeking from the corner of his mouth in concentration.

"How was your interview with Mabel?" Esther asked without turning.

Ava dropped her notebook on the table and slid into a chair with a groan. "The cat might be the most emotionally intelligent being I've met in this town. Including the humans."

George grunted. "Cats usually are."

Esther smirked. "Did she predict your future?"

Ava raised an eyebrow. "She meowed after I asked if I'd end up with William again. I think I'm supposed to take that as a sign. For the record, I am not."

Esther set a mug of chamomile in front of her. "That cat once hissed at Mayor Stu's wife. Three months later? Divorce papers. So tread carefully."

Ava wrapped her hands around the cup. The steam curled between them like something sacred. "I don't know. It was strange. Mabel talked about mom. She sounded like someone I didn't know."

Esther sat down with her own tea. "Your mother was a lot of things. Some of them even she hadn't figured out."

Ava hesitated. "She didn't want me to be a writer. But then, she wrote poems."

"I think she was scared for you," Esther said. "But that's not the same as what she was hoping for."

Ava stared into her mug. The tea smelled like honey and childhood. "Mabel says Princess is never wrong."

George snorted without looking up. "That cat told me I'd win the fishing derby three years in a row. Haven't caught anything but seaweed since during the derby."

Esther chuckled. "Maybe she meant emotional victories."

"Anyway, are you having fun?" she added gently, switching tones like only grandmothers can.

Ava exhaled. "Maybe. I like observing people. Writing about them."

"This place. It gets into your blood. Whether you want it to or not," Esther said.

Ava gave a small smile but kept her eyes on the mug. "It's charming here, but you know I'm not staying, right? I needed a reset, not a re-rooting. There's still so much I want to do. Places to see. Stories to chase."

Esther's smile faltered, just a little. "Of course. Just like your mother."

Ava paused. "She left to grow, didn't she?"

"No," Esther said softly. "She left to breathe. But she carried this place with her. Sometimes I think she never really left."

From the other side of the table, George slid a puzzle piece into place with a triumphant "hah!"

"Finally found the sky," he muttered. "Been looking at blue for an hour."

Esther didn't look up. "Try finding the patience to live with him."

George grinned. "She married me for my charm."

"She married you for your boat," Esther shot back.

Ava smiled. "You two are ridiculous."

"We're rooted," Esther replied. "There's a difference."

Outside, the wind shifted. The ocean hummed its constant lullaby, and somewhere in the dark, a bell clanged in the wind like a heart finding its rhythm again.

For the first time in a long while, Ava didn't feel like she was passing through.

She felt still. Present.

Maybe not whole but getting there.

And for the first time she was asking if, when the time came, she would want to leave at all.

****

That night, Ava couldn't sleep. She pulled on an old hoodie and slipped out the front door, the screen creaking like it remembered her. The streets were empty, the sky above a velvet dome with scattered stars.

Spruce Cove at midnight was different. Quieter, yes, but also more itself. Porch lights glowed like lighthouses. Somewhere, a wind chime played a lazy tune. She wandered past the Gazette, its windows dimmed, then paused when she saw a back light still burning.

She knocked lightly on the glass.

Inside, Liz sat cross-legged on the floor with a half-eaten cookie in one hand and a stack of page proofs spread around her. Her hair was piled into a messy knot, glasses slipping down her nose.

"I thought you were going home," Ava said through the door.

Liz blinked, then waved her in. "I lied. I forgot to edit an obit."

Ava stepped inside. "Do you live here?"

"Only emotionally," Liz muttered, brushing crumbs off her sweater.

They sat in silence for a moment, the quiet kind that feels earned.

"You did good today," Liz said finally. "That column? It read like you gave a damn."

"I did," Ava admitted.

"Keep doing that," Liz said. "Don't write safe. Write like it matters."

Ava nodded, not trusting herself to speak.

As she left, Liz called out, "And next time bring snacks. I'm running on peppermint candies."

***

At 10:43 p.m., Ava's phone buzzed.

Liz: Your stories are live. Don't let it go to your head.

Liz (2 seconds later): Also, good job.

Ava stared at the screen and smiled. She saved the messages before shutting off her phone and sliding into bed.

Chapter 7

Ava walked the length of the boardwalk with her hands tucked into the sleeves of her sweater, letting the gentle morning sun warm her face. The ocean stretched out beside her like a vast sheet of silk, shimmering in hues of blue and silver. Spruce Cove was quiet today. Quiet in a way that didn't feel heavy, for once. Just calm. Content. And, unexpectedly, so was she.

She paused near the harbor where a group of sea otters floated lazily on their backs. One cracked a clam shell against a rock balanced on its belly, oblivious to the bits of shell flying into the water. Another swam in a lazy circle, grooming itself with the kind of focus only sea mammals and retirees seemed to manage.

"They are cute, aren't they?" came a voice beside her.

Ava turned and found herself looking at a man with weathered features, a trimmed gray beard, and eyes so familiar they startled her. He looked like a man who'd seen decades of sunrises, sea storms, and stubborn fish.

He gave a wry chuckle. "They're also eating us out of house and home. Town's been grumbling about them for years. Used to be you'd drop a crab pot and come back with dinner. Now? Nothing but busted dreams and seaweed."

Ava blinked, then laughed. "I didn't realize they were so destructive."

"Oh, they're a menace in a fur coat," he said. "But you can't exactly chase 'em off. Bad PR. And the Feds protect them. No one wants to see a guy take out something with a whiskered smile cracking shellfish."

She grinned. "Fair."

He extended a calloused hand. "Jack, by the way. I run one of the charter boats out of South Harbor."

"Ava," she said, shaking his hand. "I'm staying with my grandparents George and Esther McCormick."

His expression shifted, just a flicker, then settled into a nod. "Good folks. Haven't seen George at the docks in a while. Boat still running?"

"She's more stubborn than seaworthy, but we're working on it."

Jack chuckled. "Sounds like half the people in this town. Held together by routine, duct tape, and pure spite."

They stood quietly for a few moments, watching the otters float and snack as the tide lapped at the pilings below.

Then, almost casually, he said, "I remember Margot."

Ava blinked. No one called her mother that. Not unless they'd known her before she was a mother.

"Red hair like fire, a laugh that could startle seagulls. Hard to forget a presence like that." His voice softened, his eyes not quite meeting hers.

Something in the way he said her name caught Ava off guard. Not *Margaret. Margot.* A name wrapped in memory, not formality.

He paused, watching her face. There was a gentleness in it. Tempered curiosity, like he was searching for something he wasn't sure he had the right to find.

"She was unforgettable," he said carefully, as if about to add more, then stopped himself. "Anyway, enjoy the otters."

"Bye," Ava replied, and watched as he walked off toward the docks. Something about the set of his shoulders, or the way his voice had a rasp she almost recognized. It stuck with her.

She lingered a moment longer, eyes drifting back to the otters. They really were adorable. Soft and round, like little aquatic teddy bears. Cracking open shells with their tiny hands. Looking like they knew exactly how charming they were.

And yet, apparently, they were also quietly ruining everything. Wreaking havoc on the ecosystem, one bite at a time.

It reminded her of William.

He'd been charming, too. Adorable, even. He wasn't exactly handy, but he tried. Watching YouTube tutorials before fixing a leaky faucet, holding doors like it was his mission, and showing up with her favorite candy when she'd had a rough day. But underneath the glossy surface, he'd been casually and thoroughly dismantling the things she valued most. Her confidence. Her ambition. Her gut instinct.

Like the otters, William never meant to destroy anything. He was just hungry. For praise. For control. For the version of Ava that stayed small enough to make him feel big.

She looked at the otters again, now with a faint smirk.

"Cute," she murmured. "But nope. Not falling for it this time."

The sea breeze brushed her cheek, and beneath it came the rhythmic *crack, crack, crack.* The otters, still working away at their shells with innocent delight. Destruction, dressed in darling fur coats.

She shook her head, turned, and headed for Annie's Café.

***

The bell over the café door jingled with the usual cheer.

"There she is," Martha called from behind the counter. "I was about to put your face on a milk carton."

Ava grinned. "You'd miss me that much?"

"I'd miss your tips. And your taste in muffins. Blueberry?"

"Always."

Martha slid a steaming cup across the counter. "Rough morning?"

"Actually, no," Ava said. "I saw sea otters. I might've communed with nature."

Martha grinned. "Careful. You let your guard down and next thing you know, you've adopted a sea otter and named him Theo."

Ava laughed and stepped aside to let the next customer order, carrying her muffin and coffee to a stool at the end of the counter. A couple of locals were already there. Older men in flannel, a woman knitting something purple and fuzzy without looking down.

"Morning, Ava," one of them said. "How's George's boat treating you?"

"Like it resents my existence," she replied.

They chuckled, and she found herself smiling for real. Conversation bounced around from crabbing season, the new guy running the post office, to someone's dog being chased by a deer.

Martha leaned over the counter a few minutes later, drying her hands on a towel. "Hey, when you get a sec, think you could sweet-talk your grandma into giving me her blueberry pie recipe? The one with the sugar crust on top?"

Ava raised an eyebrow. "I'm pretty sure that recipe is stored in a vault, guarded by sea lions."

"Worth a shot," Martha said. "I'd trade my left pinky toe to make a crust like Esther's."

One of the older men leaned in. "Esther always said it's about the butter. And attitude."

They all laughed, including Ava.

For the first time in a long time, she didn't feel like she was faking the smile.

She took a sip of coffee and said lightly, "Careful. You're all making this place dangerously likable."

The bell above the door jingled.

And just like that, her anxiety relapse arrived.

"She's back. Brace yourself." Martha nodded toward the door.

Ava turned. There she was.

Amelia Colburn stepped into the café like the morning belonged to her. Her blond waves were pulled into a loose braid over one shoulder, and she wore snug, high-rise jeans with a white tank top peeking out beneath a fitted flannel shirt; sleeves rolled, buttons left casually undone at the collar. Her Xtratufs hit the floorboards with a confidence that echoed. There wasn't a speck of makeup in sight, and she didn't need it.

The conversation in the café dimmed just a touch, not with hush but with interest. Three men at different tables subtly straightened in their seats. One of them actually tilted his head.

Ava noticed.

No one straightened when *she* walked in.

She sipped her coffee and braced herself as the woman made a beeline for her.

"You're Ava, right?"

The voice was friendly, with a sharp undertone wrapped in velvet. Ava watched the tall woman with a braid and sharp eyes approaching.

"I'm Amelia," she said, offering a hand. "Colburn."

Ava shook it, unsure who she was. "Nice to meet you."

Amelia's smile was practiced and polite. Just wide enough to pass.

"I've heard so much about you."

There was no warmth in it. No context. Just the suggestion that *whatever she'd heard*, it had been discussed more than once and likely with raised eyebrows.

"Hopefully good things," Ava said, attempting lightness.

Amelia just smiled again. No answer. Just an echo.

"Welcome to Spruce Cove," she said. "We're small, but we've got personality."

Ava gave a half-smile. "Yeah. It's quieter than I remember. Or maybe louder now."

"See you around."

She turned and strolled toward the counter, boots echoing with each step. Heads followed her. Not dramatically, but instinctively.

Several patrons had watched the interaction with thinly veiled interest. One woman near the window raised her brows meaningfully at her companion. Another gave Ava a small, knowing smirk before returning to her Sudoku.

Ava could feel it. Attention curling around her like smoke. Not the kind that warms, but the kind that chokes.

She sipped her coffee, suddenly aware of how hot her cheeks felt.

Without a word, she turned and walked out the door, the bell chiming behind her. She didn't know exactly what had just happened, but she was certain it hadn't been a welcome.

***

As she walked away from Annie's, Ava let the scent of salt and kelp linger in her nose, a briny calm that had started to feel oddly comforting. The boardwalk creaked beneath her boots, and a pair of seagulls bickered overhead like bitter roommates.

She passed two older men hunched over a weathered tackle box on a bench near the docks, voices rising above the hum of the harbor.

"No, no. Flash-Rite green with a silver stripe," one said, jabbing a finger toward a laminated package.

"You're outta your mind," the other grumbled. "Nothing beats the OG Hoochie Mama in UV pink. The cohos go nuts."

Ava smirked, slipping past unnoticed, making a mental note to Google "Hoochie Mama" later to make sure it wasn't something NSFW.

She slowed near the harbor, where Chap stood shirt-sleeved in the chilly morning, knee-deep in coiled rope and mechanical frustration. He looked up briefly, sensing movement and saw her.

For half a second, something passed across his face. Not surprise. Maybe confusion. Or disappointment.

She hesitated, one hand lifting in a wave she aborted halfway through. He gave a small nod. That was it.

The moment felt thinner than it should have. Ava turned away first, feeling like she'd just fumbled a line in a scene she didn't know she was in.

She kept walking, the cold creeping in a little faster than before.

What was that?

She walked faster than she needed to, heat creeping up her neck despite the cold. It wasn't like she expected him to come running over. But something. A smile? A wave? Recognition beyond a brief flicker?

Maybe she'd imagined their connection. Maybe it was just proximity and fresh paint fumes and shared coffee in a town that recycled stories faster than its newspaper.

Or maybe she was being ridiculous.

Still, the way he'd looked at her. Like she was someone he barely remembered, lodged in her ribs.

Was he mad? Did Amelia have something to do with this? Had he heard some twisted version of her love life at the café?

She sighed. This was ridiculous. She didn't even know him that well. One cup of coffee and a few casual conversations did not equal a romantic connection.

And yet, there it was. That dumb ache in her chest, like she'd been benched from a game she wasn't sure she'd agreed to play.

She shook her head, nearly laughing at herself. She was not here to spiral over broody boat guys with good shoulders. She was here to write. To rest. To fix her damn life.

Still, her feet dragged just a little as she turned the corner toward the newspaper office, like she was hoping, just maybe, he'd call out after her.

He didn't.

***

By the time she made it to the Gazette office, Ava had run through at least six imaginary comebacks and discarded them all for being either too passive or too violent.

Liz barely looked up from her desk. "You've got that look."

"What look?"

"The one where you either just got hit on or hit by a truck. Possibly both."

Ava dropped her bag with a huff. "I met Amelia."

"Oh," Liz said, drawing the word out. "So a truck, then."

Ava slumped into her chair. "She introduced herself like I was a transfer student in a high school movie. Said she'd heard *so much* about me. Then gave me a look that made me want to check if there was toilet paper stuck to my shoe."

Liz spun slowly in her chair. "Welcome to Spruce Cove's version of a background check."

Ava leaned forward. "What's her deal?"

"She's smart, local, terrifying in a weirdly elegant way. Think small-town prom queen who could probably dress a deer. And then there's the thing with Chap."

"Chap?"

Liz raised her brows. "They have a history. Complicated. Depends on who you ask. They dated for a long time. Until they didn't."

"Do they still? I mean, is she still into him?"

"Define *into*. This town only recycles three things: plastic, gossip, and romantic tension."

Ava blinked. "That might be the most Alaskan thing I've heard."

Liz smirked. "You haven't heard the town debate over bear-proof trash cans."

Ava sat back. "It's just weird. I didn't expect to feel like I crashed someone's party."

"But Amelia's used to being the loudest voice in the room. And you didn't need volume to be noticed."

***

That night, Ava sat at her desk with her laptop open, staring at a blinking cursor and wondering if she could somehow assign the Little League feature to the cat.

Her journal lay open beside her. She picked up her pen, hesitated, then scribbled:

I came to Spruce Cove for silence. I got an emotionally constipated fisherman, a deeper caffeine addiction, and public speculation. Still ... not the worst trade.

She smirked.

Then, below it:

I didn't come here to fall in love. But I also didn't come here to stay broken.

She stared at it for a long moment, then shut the journal.

***

That night, Ava lay in bed, wrapped in a quilt that smelled faintly of cedar and whatever laundry soap Esther used. It was gentle, old-fashioned, and a little lemony. Outside, the wind whispered through the trees, and branches tapped occasionally against the side of the house. A dog barked in the distance, then fell quiet.

Through the floorboards, she could faintly hear the television murmuring from downstairs, and the familiar rumble of Grandpa George snoring in his recliner. The sound made her chest ache. Not with sadness, exactly, but with something warm and worn. Safety, maybe. Or the illusion of it.

She didn't bother reaching for her phone. For once, she didn't need digital noise to drown out her thoughts.

The day had been good. Objectively. Sea otters, coffee, actual laughter. People knew her name now, and not just because she was Esther and George's granddaughter. She was writing for the paper. Thanks to Amelia, she was a point of discussion. Her presence had shifted, and she wasn't sure if that felt like progress or intrusion.

She stared at the ceiling and thought of Chap. Of his brief nod. The quiet in his eyes. That look. What was it?

Then Amelia's smile surfaced in her mind again. That perfect, razor-edged smile. Ava wasn't used to other women making her feel small. Back in New Haven, she had her footing. She could handle tenured professors who mistook arrogance for brilliance and trust-fund students who thought deadlines were optional. But Amelia had dismantled her confidence in under two minutes, using nothing but suggestion and hair that didn't frizz in coastal humidity.

She reached for her journal and flipped past scribbles and half-finished story notes. She stopped on a blank page and wrote:

What if healing isn't quiet? What if it's messy, awkward, loud and wears flannel?

She paused. Then under it:

What if I don't want to be healed? What if I just want to be left alone.

She stared at the words for a long time. Then added:

I didn't come here to be seen. I came here to disappear. But maybe …

She didn't finish the sentence. Just capped the pen and closed the journal.

Maybe was enough for tonight.

***

After forty minutes of tossing and re-fluffing her pillow with increasing aggression, Ava gave up. She pulled on socks and padded softly down the creaky stairs, the familiar scent of woodsmoke and old linoleum greeting her in the dark.

The kitchen was lit only by the stove light, casting a golden puddle on the tile. Esther sat at the table in her robe, barefoot, flipping through a dog-eared magazine with her readers perched low on her nose. A steaming mug sat in front of her.

Ava paused in the doorway. "Can't sleep?"

Esther looked up without surprise. "Didn't even try. My joints tell me when a storm's coming."

Ava opened a cabinet and pulled down a mug. "Mind if I join you?"

"Please do. There's peppermint in the blue tin."

Ava filled the kettle and leaned against the counter. "It's quieter here than I thought it would be."

"People mistake quiet for peace," Esther said. "They're not the same thing."

Ava smiled. "That's very fortune-cookie of you."

Esther took a sip of tea. "You had a day?"

Ava nodded. "Amelia introduced herself. It wasn't the friendliest of introductions."

Esther didn't say anything for a moment, then: "That girl was born with her claws filed."

"I couldn't tell if she was being polite or threatening."

"Probably both. Amelia's always been polished. She remembers everything. She doesn't forget slights, real or imagined."

Ava poured hot water into her mug. "Were she and Chap really a thing?"

"For quite a while. She liked having the upper hand."

Ava stirred her tea. "She still does."

Esther looked at her over the rim of her glasses. "Let her think she knows who you are. You just keep being you."

Ava took her mug and sat down. "That's your advice? Out-sincerity her?"

"I'm saying, don't play a game you're not interested in winning. This town loves a good rivalry. But it loves a good comeback more."

They sat for a moment, the kettle clicking as it cooled.

Ava exhaled slowly. "I didn't come here to fight over a man."

"I know," Esther said. "But that doesn't mean you won't."

Chapter 8

Spruce Cove had a way of hiding things in plain sight. Truths tucked behind lap siding. Histories folded into casserole recipes. Entire heartbreaks buried under smiles exchanged at the grocery store. Ava McCormick was learning that the hard way.

There were certain sights she had learned to brace herself for in Spruce Cove like a bear cub on the boardwalk or her grandmother wielding a splitting maul before coffee. But nothing prepared her for what she saw that breezy Wednesday evening.

Chap Fisher, sitting shoulder-to-shoulder with a woman on the dock. His hand pressed to her back, moving in small, steady circles.

Ava stopped so fast her breath went shallow. The smell of kelp and diesel, wet rope and cold metal rushed at her like a wave. Ava could hear the soft hiccup of the woman's crying even over the seagulls. Chap's thumb kept tracing that familiar path, like he was soothing a crease out of a shirt he'd ironed a hundred times.

She didn't need the woman to turn her head.

Amelia.

The name dropped through her like a stone through water. Fast, inevitable, leaving rings of ache. Ava eased behind a stack of crab pots. She had no right to watch. She knew that. But leaving felt impossible, like someone had glued her boots to the dock.

Amelia didn't look like the storm Ava had found herself dreading since their first meeting. No sharpened smirk. She looked soft. Unraveled. Her hair was windblown, her hands clenching the edge of Chap's jacket, her cheek tucked into the space where a shoulder meets a neck. The spot that felt like home when you were in love or used to be.

It wasn't jealousy Ava felt. Not exactly. Envy, maybe, but more than that. A bleak little slice of recognition. She'd read the map wrong. While she'd been sketching a maybe-future in her head, Chap had been walking a road with well-worn footprints. And Amelia? She still knew that road in the dark.

A boat horn echoed across the harbor, low and mournful. Chap dipped his head to hear Amelia better, hair falling into his eyes. That hair. That stubborn cowlick. Her chest pinched; the feeling was so swift she had to look away.

Ava took one step back. Then another. The wind whipped her hair across her face, as if the universe was belatedly trying to shield her. The dock boards creaked under her weight. Treacherous, tattling things.

She turned then, carefully, and threaded herself through the maze of stacked pots and coils of line. Near the end of the dock, she nearly collided with Hank, the harbor assistant, who was carrying a rusted bucket and humming off-key.

"Whoa there, slow your roll," he said, hopping back.

"Sorry," she mumbled, focusing on the gap between his elbow and a piling like it was a finish line. She couldn't look at a human face right now, not even Hank's kindly one.

"You alright?" he asked, because Spruce Cove asked, even when you clearly weren't.

"Wind," she said, patting her hair with a brightness that felt like a lie and a scream.

Hank nodded, buying it, or pretending to. "Blows the truth out of people," he said sagely. "Careful out there."

Too late, she thought, and kept moving.

***

Instead of home, she cut down to the beach. Low tide had left slick ribbons of seaweed and tide pools winking like tiny mirrors. Her boots found the surest ground by instinct. She'd spent enough summers here to know which rocks wobbled and which ones held their ground.

Seagulls wheeled and scolded like an old chorus that knew everyone's business and wasn't afraid to sing.

She tried not to replay the scene at the dock. But the body remembers what the mind refuses to acknowledge. Her shoulders remembered the curve of Chap's hand, even though it had never held her that way. Her stomach remembered the tilt of his smile, the one he wore when he was trying not to smile.

At the far end of the beach, she climbed onto a flat rock and sat, knees up, arms looped tight. Across the water, the horizon was a gray line stitched between ocean and cloud. She wished she could unzip her chest, let the wind air it out, snap herself back into place with salt and cold.

Her mother used to say, during their summers in Alaska, "Some things break smooth if you let the ocean do the work." Back then, Ava had rolled her eyes, impatient with metaphors and bored with melancholy. Now she understood. Enough waves and even glass turned harmless. The edges wore down until they couldn't cut you anymore. Until you couldn't even tell what the thing had been before it got tossed and tumbled.

Maybe that was Chap and Amelia. Worn, smoothed, stubbornly still together in some shape, even if the original had shattered long ago. Maybe Ava had mistaken something polished by years for something new and bright that might belong to her.

She sat until numbness crept into her thighs. The tide inched closer. When the water licked the base of her rock, she finally stood and climbed down, stepping carefully until sand replaced stone and the ache quieted to something she could carry.

***

The house smelled like something roasting. Esther believed food could fix ninety percent of life's problems; for the other ten, she recommended hot tea and not reading the comments section. She was at the stove when Ava slipped in, humming a Johnny Horton tune and wielding a wooden spoon like a conductor's baton.

"You look like you got home two hours later than you actually did," Esther said without moving from the stove.

"What does that even mean?" Ava asked, leaning on the doorway because her legs didn't trust her yet.

"Means your face says, 'I ran a marathon,' and your hair says, 'I lost a fight with a gale.' Sit. Taste this potato. Tell me if it needs more salt."

Ava sat. She tasted. She nodded. "Perfectly seasoned."

"Ha." Esther thumped a pot lid back into place, then finally looked over, eyes crinkling. "You've got the look."

"What look?"

"The one you had when you realized Santa wasn't real, and again when you found out William was."

Ava huffed a laugh that wasn't quite one. "It's nothing. I just saw something I can't unsee."

Esther didn't press. She had learned long ago that some truths were like sourdough. You couldn't rush the rise. "Then you should open that box I put on your bed. Found it while cleaning out the attic," she said instead, nodding toward the hallway. "If your head's full of ghosts, best to invite the loudest of them to speak first."

Ava wanted to argue. To claim she was done letting the past set her day's agenda. But instead, she stood, kissed Esther's cheek, and carried a bowl of roasted potatoes up to her room. They were something solid in a world that wasn't.

***

Ava opened the shoe box Esther had left on her bed. Within a half hour, her bedroom floor had become an archaeology site of one family's forgotten language. Ticket stubs from the ferry. A library card stamped *Spruce Cove Municipal,* the name MARGOT MCCORMICK written in a teenage bubble handwriting. A grocery list in blue ink: *eggs, flour, sugar, berries (if cheap), forget the butter. Mom always has butter.*

And a photo.

Her mother, barely older than Ava was now, leaning into a man whose face had been half lost to time. The man's arm slung casual over her shoulders. The posture said practice. The smile said secrets. On the back, Margot's handwriting, loopy, decisive: *Dad can never know.*

Ava's chest pinched the way it had when she'd watched Chap's hand move across Amelia's back. This time caused by the feeling of being late to your own history.

Why write it down at all if you didn't want someone to read it?

She laid the photo flat and angled the desk lamp closer, as if light could coax the blurred half of the man's face back into being. If she squinted, she could make out the line of a cheek, the shadow where a smile might live. He wore a jacket with a high collar, the kind men in town wore to look like they didn't notice the rain.

A ferry ticket slid loose from between two clippings. *Sitka → Spruce Cove.* It was from the same summer Margot had vanished for a week. Esther had told that story once: your mother got quiet, she'd said. Sad in a way that didn't have a sound. Then, one morning, she was gone for a week and came back with her hair hacked short and a new laugh that nobody trusted.

Ava traced the back of the ticket and felt the pull of two currents at once. Toward the man in the photo, and toward the interview she was supposed to be preparing for.

As if cued, her phone buzzed.

Liz: Ellery at 10 a.m. Don't be late or charming.

Ava smiled despite herself. Liz believed in clear instructions.

She slid the photo back into the box but didn't close the lid. She left it open like a question.

***

Spruce Cove High had the tired optimism of every public school in a small town. Someone had stapled construction-paper stars around a laminated poster that read, WORK HARD. BE KIND. A trophy case held more middle-school participation medals than actual trophies. The gym roared with adolescence: sneakers skidding, a ball clapping the backboard, laughter too loud for the hour of the morning.

Coach Connor Ellery was center stage, tall and fit and radiating the kind of authority that made teenagers move without thinking about it. He blew his whistle and two boys in mismatched shorts froze like strings had been yanked somewhere in the rafters.

When he saw Ava, he jogged over with a smile that landed in the quadrant between charming and calculated.

"You must be Ava McCormick," he said, offering a hand. "Liz says you're the kind of reporter who makes people interesting even when they aren't."

"So, you're saying I've got my work cut out for me?" she countered, taking his hand. Firm shake. Calluses. Warmth.

"Only if you catch me on a day when the shot percentage is honest." He gestured to the sideline. "Walk with me?"

They paced the perimeter of the court while boys ran a layup drill that sounded like a drum line trying to find a rhythm. Ava clicked her pen and pitched her softballs. How long have you been here, what's your philosophy, which kid's going to make you look like a genius this year?

He answered like a man who'd done this before. "We build men here," he said. "Accountability. Brotherhood. Show up for each other. Half these guys don't have a male role model. This team fills a hole."

It sounded good. Too good. The cadence of a stump speech he'd trimmed the fat from years ago.

"You coached in Juneau?" she asked, making her voice idle. "Before that Anchorage?"

"Right," he said. "Always go where I'm needed. Might be my flaw." He grinned.

"A flaw that photographs well," she said, and he laughed like she'd given him a line he could use later.

They stopped near the bleachers. A cluster of girls sat with notebooks on their knees, half-watching, half whispering. One with a ponytail, chipped purple nail polish looked at Ellery with a mix of awe and something Ava couldn't name. The girl's gaze flicked to Ava and away, guilty as a cat on a counter.

"You coach girls' teams too?" Ava asked, still casual.

"Just fill in when needed," he said. "But boys' ball is my focus. It's where I connect."

"Why's that?"

He glanced at her, then at the court. "Teenage boys can go one way or the other. You give them a net that isn't just nylon? You change a life."

Another good answer. His clipboard tapped a slow beat against his thigh. A ball rolled their way and he stepped into Ava's space to block it, hand brushing her elbow as he stopped the spin. The touch was nothing. Polite, incidental. Then it wasn't. It lingered just long enough for her to feel patronized.

She stepped back and smiled with her teeth.

"Sorry," he said. "Reflex." His eyes did a quick scan that felt like a box being checked. "So you're not from here?"

"I visited summers," she said. "I know enough to duck when someone shouts 'heads.'"

"You planning to stay?" he asked, too lightly.

"Planning is generous."

He grinned. "I'll look for your byline either way."

He blew the whistle and shouted at a kid named Wyatt to follow through. His voice was warm but carried iron underneath. A new boy fumbled a pass and winced. Ellery's hand was on his shoulder in a flash, gentle enough to soothe, firm enough to direct. The kid straightened like the touch had a spine in it.

"Thanks," Ava said a few minutes later, snapping her notebook closed when her tolerance for charm had hit its limit. "You're easy copy."

"Be kind," he said with a half-salute. "Or at least be fair."

"Fair is my middle name," she deadpanned, and he laughed, a beat too long.

In the hall, a bulletin board sagged under flyers. Bake sale, fishing derby, a lost cat named Moose with a snaggletooth. On the edge, half hidden, a faded poster for a Juneau invitational from two years back. She wandered closer. There was a roster paper-clipped to it. The names were smudged, the ink bled. Nothing to see.

***

The Gazette office lived in a building that had once been a canning warehouse and still smelled faintly of brine when the heat kicked on. It was both less and more than a newspaper office with two desks, a mismatched set of filing cabinets, a list of advertisers taped to the wall, a coffeemaker Ava suspected had tenure.

Liz Walker loved this place with a ferocity that made Ava want to be braver. She was bent over the copier when Ava arrived, thwacking its side and muttering, "Do not test me, demon."

"It prefers flattery," Ava said, lifting the top and adjusting the paper like she'd learned on day three.

"I prefer a budget," Liz said, swatting her hand away and jamming the Start button. "Well?"

"He's a soundbite factory in sneakers," Ava said. "Polished. Posed. Jawline that could sell nonprofit gala tickets."

Liz blew a strand of hair out of her eyes. "Did he touch your elbow?"

Ava stilled. "Yes."

"He pulled the same thing with the *Sitka Sentinel* reporter last spring," Liz said. "She called it 'command presence' in print. I would have told him this is a puff piece, not a Senate run.'"

Ava snorted. "You're impossible."

"I am editorially allergic to golden boys," Liz said, handing over a manila folder. "And you, my dear, are about to tell me whether my rash is justified."

"What's our angle?" she asked. "For Ellery, I mean."

"The one that keeps us in business," Liz said. "Profiles that play well next to ads for propane and paper towels."

Ava thought about the elbow touch and the lingering and the practiced smile. She compared that to Chap's hand on Amelia's back and how familiarity could look noble from a distance and like something else entirely up close.

They worked in companionable silence for an hour. Liz puzzled over ad placements and Ava shaping her notes into sentences. The office hummed with the printer's stubborn rhythm and the distant thud of someone dropping something heavy on the sidewalk out front.

When the draft was passable, Ava leaned back and let her gaze drift to the corner where a milk crate held old issues. The top paper was from the year her mother had left Alaska. A photo on the front page showed a Fourth of July parade. Kids with streamers on their bikes, a dog in a bandana, a woman on the curb with red hair that caught the light just so.

It could have been Margot. Or it could have been a stranger with the same haircut and a trick of the sun. That's how memory worked in a small town: it blurred strangers into family and family into myths.

"Go home," Liz said without looking up. "Before your grandmother decides you're spiraling and shows up with three dozen oatmeal cookies."

"She already did," Ava said, standing to stretch. "They're in the freezer labeled 'For Emotional Emergencies Only.'"

***

Evening slid in on quiet feet.

Dinner consisted of venison from the freezer, a salad that tried to pretend lettuce was exciting, and pie because George had apparently manifested it. The house hummed: the refrigerator kicking on, Esther singing, George whistling something tuneless as he turned off outside lights.

In her room, the box waited with the patience of inanimate things that somehow know what you owe them.

She sat cross-legged on the rug and pulled the contents closer. The ferry ticket again. The grocery list. A schedule from the cannery with Margot's name under a block of days and then a sudden gap where she hadn't worked. A receipt from the hardware store for a lock and a length of chain.

"What were you guarding?" Ava murmured, though there was no one to answer.

She lifted the photo again. The stranger's arm curved around her mother with a possessive ease that made Ava's jaw tighten. She turned the picture over and traced the words like a prayer that had never helped anyone: *Dad can never know.*

Why write it at all unless you wanted someone someday to find it? Maybe secrets were only bearable if they came with an escape hatch.

Her phone buzzed on the bed. A text.

Liz: Headline idea: 'Coach Ellery: Building Men, Bending Knees (in Prayer, Calm Down PTA)'

Ava smiled and typed back: Try: 'Coach Ellery and the Art of Perfect Answers.'

Liz: Too Spicy. We're still charging local businesses for ink.

Ava: I'll write it soft. But my gut is humming.

Liz: Then hum and watch. Also, you left your sweater. If I keep it, it becomes mine in 48 hrs per newsroom law.

Ava smiled, and some of the heaviness slid off its hook.

She wrote for a while. Enough to feel like she'd earned sleep. The profile was fair, even warm. Ellery came off as committed, articulate, a man who understood what a town needed from a coach and how to deliver it. None of that was untrue. That was the trick about truth; it was only as honest as the edges you framed.

When she was done, she saved the file and slid the laptop shut. The house had gone quiet in that Alaska way she was still getting used to. No sirens, no horns, none of a city's constant hum. Just wind rattling the trees and the ocean keeping its own secrets in the dark.

She padded to the porch with her mug of tea and sat on the swing, tucking her toes under the throw blanket Esther had left there precisely for this purpose. The boards creaked a familiar rhythm beneath her. The dark smelled like rain and cedar.

Down on the water, a bell buoy clanged, a lonely sound that still managed to comfort. Ava wrapped her fingers tighter around the mug and let the heat seep into her hands.

She thought about the way Amelia had leaned into Chap and the way Chap's hand had found its path without needing to look. She thought about a coach whose answers slipped into place like puzzle pieces you didn't realize had been shaved to fit.

She thought about her mother's note on the back of a photo and the ferry ticket.

Spruce Cove hid things in plain sight. Today, she'd finally seen that as a challenge instead of a charm.

The tea went cool in her hands. The tide kept its appointment with the shore. Somewhere in the house, Esther coughed and turned in her sleep. Somewhere in town, a girl texted a secret she might later try to forget. Somewhere on a dock, a man steadied someone he used to love.

Ava set her mug down and let the swing move. Forward, back, forward. Until her mind found the quiet center you get to only when you've exhausted all your worry.

She wasn't sure who the stranger in her mother's photo was. She wasn't sure who Chap was to Amelia anymore, or who he might be to Ava someday. She wasn't sure what, exactly, felt off about Coach Ellery beyond a whisper in her bones.

But she knew how to do one thing: pay attention. And she knew what stories did when you paid attention to them. They unfolded.

Chapter 9

The sun hadn't yet burned off the morning mist when Chap knocked on the door with two steaming thermoses and a grin that said he was up to something.

"Hope you're not busy," he said when Ava opened the door in her socks and hoodie. "I've got a boat, a couple of rods, and a hunch the salmon are biting."

Ava blinked at him, bleary-eyed. "Is this your way of luring me out of bed? With caffeine and fish?"

"It's working, isn't it?" he said, handing her a thermos.

Behind her, Grandma Esther poked her head around the corner. "Fishing, huh? Hold on. I'll scramble you two some eggs. No need to go out there on an empty stomach."

Before Ava could protest, Esther had disappeared into the kitchen, already humming and clattering pans like a one-woman breakfast brigade.

Ava gave Chap a look of apology. He just grinned. "The fish can wait. Not gonna say no to eggs."

Ten minutes later, the three of them sat around the kitchen table. Esther served up scrambled eggs with chives, thick sourdough toast, and jam that tasted like summer.

"Do you always show up with bait and no breakfast plans?" Esther teased, sliding a plate in front of Chap.

"Only when I'm trying to impress someone," he said, shooting a quick glance at Ava.

Esther raised her eyebrows but said nothing. Ava pretended to focus very intently on her toast.

"So, where are you two heading?" Esther asked, pouring herself a fresh cup of coffee.

"Thinking of trolling off Seal Point," Chap said. "Kings are running thick right now."

Esther nodded. "Good spot. Hal caught a monster out there last week. Forty-seven pounds if you believe him. He said it fought for an hour."

Chap chuckled. "If Hal said it, I'll shave off five pounds and still be impressed."

Esther smiled and sat down with her coffee. "Nice morning for fishing. Nothing like the water to clear your head."

Chap nodded. "That's the plan."

She glanced between them, then added lightly, "Even better with good company. Makes the coffee taste sweeter."

Ava didn't meet his eyes, but she felt her cheeks warm.

The room quieted for a moment. Ava felt the warmth from the eggs, the hum of the kettle behind her, and something else. A thread connecting the three of them.

As they finished eating, Ava felt a strange warmth in her chest. Not just from the eggs or the coffee, but from the ease of it all. The normalcy. The sense that maybe, just maybe, she was allowed to enjoy a morning like this without questioning it.

***

Twenty minutes later they were on the dock, loading Chap's boat. They were just about to untie when a sharp voice cut through the salt air.

"Chap?"

Ava turned to see a man stepping out from a parked pickup, dark ballcap tugged low, raingear prepared for any weather. Something about the tight set of his shoulders told her this wasn't a friendly greeting.

"Hey, Mason," Chap said, his posture shifting. Not defensive, but careful.

Mason was in his mid-thirties, same jawline as Chap and had a perpetual scowl. He approached with a half-laugh that didn't reach his eyes. "Didn't expect to see you out here this early. Let alone with company."

Chap gave a small nod. "Just taking the boat out. Need to fill the freezer."

Mason's eyes flicked to Ava and lingered. She smiled, unsure. He didn't return it.

"You two heading out to Seal Point?"

"Thinking about it," Chap said easily.

"Huh." Mason rubbed his jaw. "Funny. Amelia always said you'd never find someone who liked fishing."

Ava stiffened.

Chap's mouth tightened. "Things change."

"Guess they do." Mason gave Ava another long look. Observing. Calculating.

He turned and walked back to his truck, gravel crunching beneath his boots. No goodbye.

Ava watched him drive off, unease prickling her neck. "That was?"

"Amelia's brother," Chap said simply. "Mason's got opinions. Most of them outdated."

She stared at the horizon a moment before speaking. "Our fishing trip is gonna be around town in an hour, isn't it?"

"More like thirty minutes," Chap said, giving her a wry smile. "Fifteen if he stops by the café."

They finished loading in silence, the weight of Mason's presence still hanging in the air. Ava tucked her bag under the console and opened it to grab a drink.

Chap leaned over to check the cooler, then froze.

"Is that a banana?"

Ava looked up. "Yeah. Why?"

Without a word, Chap snatched it from her bag and hurled it into the bay. It hit the water with a soft *plunk*.

Ava blinked. "Did you just throw my snack overboard?"

He pointed a finger at her, mock-serious. "Bananas are bad luck on a boat. Total curse."

"You're joking."

He crossed his arms. "Do I look like I'm joking?"

She stared at the floating banana skin drifting away. "I'm sorry, is this a maritime law?"

"It's a maritime fact. Look it up. You bring a banana, you catch nothing. And possibly die."

She gave him a look. "You owe me a protein bar."

He handed her a granola bar from the glove box with dramatic ceremony. "For your safety. And mine."

***

Soon they were skimming across the water in Chap's Bayliner, the early light painting the surface with ripples of silver. Ava sat near the bow, wrapped in one of Grandpa George's spare jackets, inhaling the sharp, clean air. The town faded behind them, and with it, her anxious loop of overthinking.

The boat bounced lightly over the waves, passing kelp beds and rocky shores. A bald eagle soared above them, casting a fleeting shadow across the deck. Chap whistled softly as he steered, one hand on the throttle, the other cradling his thermos.

"Alright, lesson one," Chap said as he stopped the boat and fired up the kicker. "You want to clip the line into the downrigger like this" He showed her, hands confident and practiced. "Then we drag the bait nice and slow. The fish can't resist."

"Is that the secret? Slow and steady wins the salmon?"

He winked. "That, and my not-so-secret weapon. Dunking the bait in coffee. Swear it drives the salmon wild."

Ava watched in disbelief as Chap uncapped his thermos and dipped the baited herring into it.

"You're joking."

"Dead serious. Coffee-marinated bait. Fish love it. Might be the caffeine. Or the fact it masks human scent. Either way, it works."

"That's weirdly brilliant."

He shrugged. "Fishing's half science, half superstition."

They settled into silence, the kind that came not from awkwardness but from the rhythm of water and waiting. The rods bobbed gently with the motion of the boat.

"Amelia always hated this part," Chap said, after a while. "The waiting. Said it was dreadfully boring."

Ava glanced at him, sensing the shift.

"We were together four years. Got together during a really stormy time in my life. She made it clear from the start that boats and rain and fish guts weren't her thing. I kept thinking I could keep fishing and keep her happy. Turns out, you can't be two people at once."

Ava nodded slowly. "I know that feeling. William, my ex, I think he wanted this perfectly curated version of me. I dyed my hair the way he liked it. Didn't dare compete with his goals."

"You still dye it?"

She shook her head. "Not since I got here. This is the real red."

He smiled, quiet and approving.

Suddenly, Ava's rod jerked down hard.

"Oh! Oh God. What do I do?"

Chap was already at her side. "SET THE HOOK!"

"Set it where?!"

"Yank it up! Firm! You've got a keeper on!"

Ava flailed, trying to pull back the rod. Her line screamed off the reel. Chap reached around her, adjusting her grip.

"No, like this! Keep the tip up! Keep the tension!"

As he helped guide her hands, his own rod gave a violent tug.

"You've got to be kidding me," he muttered. "Double header!"

Now both were reeling, yelling, trying not to trip over the tackle box or each other. Ava's reel handle jammed; Chap's line crossed over hers in a tangled mess.

"We're crossing! We're crossing! Lift yours, move left! No, the other left!"

"Why do you have two lefts?!"

They danced around each other, lines tangling more. A minute later, both rods went slack.

Ava stared at the water, panting. "We lost them."

Chap dropped his head back and groaned.

Silence fell.

Ava looked at the empty water, then down at the rod in her hand. She wondered, *was that a sign?* She shook the thought away before it could settle.

Chap cracked open a fresh thermos. "Next time, I'm bringing a referee."

She laughed, breathless. "And maybe a manual."

***

Later, after the lines were re-rigged and the water calmed, Ava felt a slow, steady pull.

"Got another one," she said, more calmly this time.

Chap helped guide her through it. No shouting, no crossed lines, just patience. And this time, they landed it.

A shimmering king salmon, gleaming and feisty. She beamed.

"Dinner," Chap said. "Redemption."

They drifted a while longer, and Chap opened the cooler to reveal smoked salmon sandwiches wrapped in wax paper. "You've earned lunch," he said, handing one to her.

Ava took a bite, surprised. "This is really good. Did you make this?"

"I fish. I read. I cook. Soon enough you'll realize I'm basically a catch," he said with mock pride.

She rolled her eyes. "Well, this kind of makes New Haven brunch look tame."

Chap smiled. "So, what did you like about living in New Haven?"

Ava considered. "The cafes. The bookstores. I used to walk the old campus paths and pretend I belonged to every century at once. But it always felt like I was playing a part. Here, I'm not sure who I am yet. But it feels real."

He nodded, watching the horizon. "That's something."

"Yeah. Four years at Yale. It was fast and ambitious and so far from how I grew up. Certainly, different than this place. I sometimes forgot what quiet sounded like."

Chap nodded, chewing. "Quiet can be the loudest thing when you've been drowning in noise."

Ava's mind drifted off. She imagined Chap and Amelia bobbing in the ocean together. Amelia bored, maybe scrolling her phone, and Chap doing what he loved, quietly hoping she might learn to love it too. The image ached in a way she hadn't expected.

Did I ever try that hard for William? Or did I just keep tailoring myself, hoping to fit?

She glanced at Chap now, his profile etched in light and sea spray. He didn't seem like someone trying to be anything but who he was.

Something inside her stirred. Longing, maybe. Or the first flicker of honesty in a long time.

"Do you ever miss her?" Ava asked softly.

Chap looked down at his sandwich. "Sometimes. Not in the way you'd think. I miss who I thought I could be with her."

Ava was quiet, letting that sink in. "That's the part that's hardest to mourn, isn't it? The version of yourself that only existed for someone else."

They both looked out at the ocean.

Eventually, Chap started reeling in the lines. "Alright. We've tempted fate enough for one morning."

As Ava helped tidy up, she opened the glovebox and found a paperback copy of *The Old Man and the Sea*. She grinned.

"Seriously?"

Chap glanced over and shrugged. "It's a classic. I keep it for luck."

"You read Hemingway on the water?"

"Only when I'm not reeling in chaos."

They both laughed.

Just as she stepped off the boat, a seagull swooped overhead and promptly relieved itself. Right onto Chap's shoulder.

Ava doubled over, wheezing with laughter. "That is cosmic timing."

Chap wiped his jacket with a rag from the boat. "Guess I had it coming."

When they docked, Chap handed her a bag full of salmon fillets from the cooler. "Dinner. Or proof we're not completely useless."

Ava took it, smiling. "Dinner, definitely."

She walked back up the dock, boots echoing on the planks, warmth rising in her chest. The mist was gone now. The town ahead was quiet but not heavy. Behind her, Chap watched her go, arms crossed, that quiet half-smile tugging at the corner of his mouth.

Maybe not a sign.

Maybe just a beginning.

***

That evening, Ava returned home from the fishing trip with a Ziplock full of king salmon. She found George in the backyard poking at the grill, a "License to Grill" apron tied over his T-shirt like he was hosting a Fourth of July cook-off.

"Well, well," he said, peering over his readers. "You bring that sea beast home yourself?"

Ava held up the fillet with a proud smile. "Reeled in by me. More or less."

George took it reverently and set aside the burgers he was about to toss on the grill. "This one's a beauty. Clean cut, nice fat cap. I'll get the cedar plank."

Esther came out with a bowl of lemon wedges and a side of knowing. "So," she said casually, "how was the fishing trip?"

"Successful," Ava replied, brushing past her with a wink.

"Successful," Esther echoed with mock disappointment. "Not exactly the juicy postmortem I was hoping for."

George snorted. "Leave the girl alone, Essie. All I need to know is that the fish made it here in one piece."

"Well, that and whether he used his famous coffee bait," Esther added.

Ava blinked. "You knew about that?"

"Oh, honey." Esther grinned. "That man's been dipping bait in coffee since he was old enough to hold a fishing pole."

They ate out on the porch as the light softened, the salmon flaking perfectly under George's touch. Ava said little, but not for lack of feeling. Her head was still somewhere out on the water, tangled in sunlight and tension and the quiet thrill of being seen.

After dinner, Ava carried dishes in from the porch, stacking them by the sink and starting to scrub. Esther joined her, sleeves rolled up, the corners of her mouth curled with something that looked dangerously close to satisfaction.

"I can tell you were laughing today," Esther said as she rinsed a plate.

Ava kept her eyes on the soap bubbles. "I laugh."

"Not like that," Esther replied, quiet but sure. "That was the kind that comes from your chest. From being seen."

Ava paused, sponge mid-air.

"I just …" She exhaled. "I forgot what it felt like. To feel happy."

Esther bumped her shoulder lightly. "Doesn't mean it's love. But it's something. And you deserve something."

They finished the rest in companionable silence.

Later, as Ava stepped into her room, she caught her reflection in the window. Boat hair, cheeks pink, eyes clearer than they had been in months.

She reached for her phone, half-expecting another dig from William.

Instead, she found a new message.

Chap: George has got grill skills. I bet the salmon was perfect. Thanks for today.

Ava stared at the screen, smiling before she could stop herself. She didn't reply.

She didn't need to.

Later, inside, Ava curled into her favorite chair by the window, a mug of chamomile cradled in her hands. Her phone buzzed on the armrest.

Her phone buzzed again.

William: Saw the photos of your fishing trip on Facebook. Glad you're smiling again. I hope it's real.

She stared at the screen. There it was. His signature blend of polished regret and subtle guilt-tripping. Carefully worded. Just enough sweetness to make her doubt her anger, and just enough pity to make her question her joy.

For a long moment, she didn't move.

Then she locked the phone, set it screen-down on the table, and exhaled.

Outside, the wind stirred the porch swing. Distant waves rolled like memory.

And still, she thought about that laugh. Hers. On the boat. Real.

***

That night, Ava lay in bed with the quilt pulled high and the scent of salt and grilled lemon still lingering in her hair. But her body hadn't quite returned to land.

She could feel the ocean in her bones. The subtle, phantom rocking that made her toes curl against the sheets. As if the bed were still floating beneath her, the mattress rising and falling on some invisible tide.

She closed her eyes and let it carry her.

Her thoughts slipped back to the boat. The way Chap had stood beside her, steady and calm. The way his hand had brushed hers when he passed the rod. The sound of his laugh when the lines crossed.

That lopsided smile when he tossed the banana overboard like he was protecting them from a curse.

There had been a moment, brief but unmistakable, when she'd caught him looking at her. Not like she was a puzzle or a project or a prize, but like he was just glad she was there.

Her breath hitched slightly.

Her skin was tight from the sun and wind, but now something deeper stirred beneath it. A slow, spreading warmth that wasn't just leftover adrenaline. It felt heady. Unexpected. Like the edge of something she hadn't dared to want in a long time.

She shifted on the mattress, sighing quietly.

And then, a memory flickered.

Another boat. Another body of water.

William's parents had a lake house in Vermont. Polished wood decks, a dock with faded striped cushions, and a gently bobbing canoe tied to cleats like shoelaces. One summer, he'd surprised her with a weekend trip, complete with rosé and matching linen shirts. She'd felt glamorous then, glowing and curated, like something out of a lifestyle shoot. There had been laughter and sleek sunglasses and soft kisses under the sun.

It had been a beautiful weekend.

So different from today.

Not better. Just different.

Chapter 10

Spruce Cove only had two speeds: slow and slower. But on the day of the annual Fireweed Festival, the town pulsed with unexpected energy. Bunting made from old fishing nets flapped in the breeze above the boardwalk. Homemade booths lined downtown like crooked teeth, each one stacked with hand-knitted goods, smoked salmon, and jars of huckleberry jam. The air buzzed with fiddle music and the mingling scents of fry bread, kettle corn, and woodsmoke.

Ava walked beside Liz, feeling unexpectedly at home. They wove through a crowd of now-familiar faces. There was Joe, a freelance photographer from the Gazette office who wore a constant squint and camera slung around his neck; Sara from the general store, handing out candied salmon skewers; and Benny, the lanky cannery superintendent with stories longer than the tide line. Dogs zipped between festivalgoers, chasing toddlers who squealed with delight. Instead of whispers or second glances, she got nods, smiles, and the occasional, "Hi Ava." Not George and Esther's granddaughter. Just Ava.

She'd expected to feel awkward. Instead, she felt anchored.

"Smells like a fair and a fish market had a love child," Liz muttered, sipping her lemonade slushie.

Ava swirled an invisible glass. "I'm getting moss and a lingering hint of pride."

The two wove through the crowd toward the judging tent. Esther's famous huckleberry pie sat under a glass dome, its crust perfectly browned. Ava had helped crimp the edges and added the extra cinnamon. Esther had deemed her crust-crimping "passable," but later Ava caught her humming in the kitchen. Off-key and content, the way someone hums when they're pleased and don't want to admit it. It wasn't a compliment exactly, but it felt like one.

When the blue ribbon was placed next to her pie, Esther's eyes sparkled and her chin lifted just slightly. She turned to Goldie, who'd held the title two years running, and offered a smile as sweet as her berry filling.

"Your peach was lovely, dear," she said, voice warm and even. "That hint of cardamom? Inspired."

Goldie nodded, polite, and gave a forced half smile.

Esther patted her arm gently, then turned back to Ava with a twinkle in her eye. "Nice to know the old girl's still got it," she murmured, barely audible over the crowd.

She gave Ava's shoulder a light squeeze before gliding back to her station at the cotton candy booth, her pride practically steaming from her pores.

She'd tested recipes for two straight years, two long summers of almost, and today Esther took her crown back.

Nearby, cheers erupted from the harbor. A crowd had gathered at the edge of the dock, where a narrow log, lathered in dish soap and suspended over the bay, jutted out like a dare. A wrinkled $100 bill was taped to the far end, fluttering in the breeze.

"Greasy pole," Liz said. "Local tradition. Also, a favorite way to pull hamstrings."

Ava laughed as kids, teens, and grown men lined up barefoot, stretching and sizing up the log. Chap stood among them. Curls already damp from what she assumed was at least one theatrical wipeout, grinning like he had something to prove.

Chap peeled his t-shirt off in one practiced motion, and Ava's brain short-circuited for a second. His chest was sun-warmed and unapologetically solid. The kind of tan you earned stacking crab pots, not booking beach vacations. She tried to look amused. Tried to smirk like this was all just charming local color. But her pulse had other ideas. She folded her arms a little too tightly across her chest and watched him jog barefoot to the edge of the dock, muscles shifting like a secret he hadn't quite decided to share. Or maybe he already had and she'd just started paying attention.

He glanced back at her, shot her a wink, then stepped onto the slick log like he was born for it.

He moved with easy balance, arms outstretched, toes gripping the beam. The crowd leaned in. Ava's heart beat faster than she wanted to admit. Four steps in, he started to slip, drawing a collective gasp. Then, righted himself with a dramatic flail, only to lunge and grab the soggy $100 bill just before a spectacular splash into the icy water.

The crowd roared.

Chap surfaced seconds later, laughing, triumphant. Water streamed from his curls, plastered to his forehead. He put on his t-shirt, which now clung to his torso and outlined every muscle and line. Ava swallowed hard. He looked like he belonged in the sea, mythic and maddening.

He made a beeline for her, drops glinting on his lashes like flecks of sunlight.

"You owe me a dance later," he said, holding up the crumpled, soaked bill like a trophy.

"You're just fishing for attention," she said, trying to sound unimpressed.

"Worked, didn't it?"

She rolled her eyes, but her cheeks burned, and the corner of her mouth curled before she could stop it.

Nearby, kids shrieked with excitement. A long wooden board sat on sawhorses, smeared with wet leaves and lined with tape marks like a tiny Olympic track.

"Slug race," Liz said. "Highly scientific. Some folks place bets. Others just name their slugs and hope for the best."

Ava leaned in as a boy in a Spider-Man hoodie shouted, "Go, Slime Machine!" A girl beside him yelled for "Captain Gooey."

The slugs inched forward at glacial speed, leaving shimmering trails. Parents laughed. Teens jeered. A small dog barked like it was personally offended.

Then someone bumped into Ava's shoulder.

"Careful," Chap said, grinning as he steadied her. "Wouldn't want to interfere with peak slug performance."

"You're here for the sport?" she asked.

"I'm here for the drama," he replied. "These mollusks are cutthroat."

"This is possibly the weirdest thing I've ever seen," Ava whispered.

"And yet, oddly captivating," Liz replied.

They watched as "Captain Gooey" made a surprise surge and crossed the finish line to triumphant applause.

***

Just past the smoked salmon booth, a ring of lawn chairs had been cleared for what a handmade sign called the "Spruce Suds Showdown." Locals hooted, a bell clanged, and a burly man in overalls carried a crate of sweating bottles onto a wooden table.

Ava paused with Liz. "What is this?"

"Amateur beer-drinking contest," Liz said. "Unofficial. Totally absurd. Highly entertaining."

"Do they win anything?"

"Just glory. And indigestion."

"George McCormick!" someone hollered. "We need a real competitor!"

George, already loosening his belt, ambled forward to applause. "Someone's gotta show these young bucks how it's done."

Ava laughed as a group of teenagers shoved towards her grandpa. "What about Fisher?"

Chap held up his hands. "All right, all right." Then, catching Ava's eye: "Apparently, I'm in it for the glory."

"And indigestion," she called back.

He grinned. "Might be worth it."

The rules were shouted by a guy in a rain slicker and Crocs: "First to finish four cans wins. No puking. No cheating. No whining."

Ava leaned on Liz's shoulder, watching George roll up his sleeves and Chap crack his neck with exaggerated bravado. The tension was faux-serious, the kind of theater only a small town could pull off.

"Begin!"

Cans were crushed. Foam splashed. George drank with slow, methodical gulps. Chap tilted his can and went fast, steady, but not reckless. His Adam's apple bobbed with each swallow. Ava found herself staring.

By can three, the crowd roared. Chap burped once, loud and theatrical. George burped back, one octave lower. They high-fived mid-gulp.

By bottle four, they were neck and neck. Chap slammed his bottle down milliseconds before George.

"Victory!" he yelled, arms wide, breathless and grinning.

George clapped him on the back. "You cheated. You're young."

Chap looked at Ava. "I was motivated."

The crowd hooted. Ava rolled her eyes, but her face flushed.

Later, as the crowd dispersed and George returned to a cheering Esther, who handed him a ginger ale and made him sit down. Chap wandered over to Ava.

He smelled like sweat, hops, and woodsmoke. His smile was lazy and loose.

"You enjoy the show?"

"I'm still deciding if I should be impressed or mildly concerned for your liver."

"Maybe both?"

Liz glanced between them, then took a subtle step back. "I should probably go check on the pie auction. They were down to the last slice of Esther's huckleberry and things were getting violent."

She gave them both a knowing glance. Equal parts encouragement and amusement. Then, turned on her heel and disappeared into the crowd. Chap leaned closer. "She always that subtle?"

"No. That was her being obvious."

His smile curved. "Good."

***

As the sun dipped lower, the band struck up a waltzy folk tune. Something with fiddles and long vowels. A few couples drifted to the makeshift dance area near the bonfire pit. Married couples moved like they'd been dancing together for decades, because most had. Teenagers spun too fast, bumping elbows and laughing too loudly. Not because the music called for it, but because they could. And in the middle of it all, Ava stood still, taking it in and wondering when this strange little town had started to feel like home.

Chap held out a hand. "You owe me a dance, remember?"

Ava arched a brow. "From the greasy pole? I thought that was nullified by the beer stunt."

"You can't penalize me for being a winner," he said. "No escaping it."

She hesitated just a second. Then she slid her hand into his.

His palm was warm, calloused in a way that made her stomach flutter. He didn't tug or take the lead aggressively. He simply invited and let her decide.

As they stepped into rhythm, his other hand settled at the small of her back. Her breath caught. His touch was steady, confident without claiming. His body radiated heat through his damp shirt, and the span of his shoulders made her feel held. Not hemmed in. Not pinned. Just secure.

She hadn't danced with a man since William.

William had been all polish. A perfect ballroom frame both practiced and poised. She'd spent most of their slow dances worrying about her posture and whether she was performing well enough to keep his mother from commenting.

This, this was different.

Chap moved with quiet authority, like the music belonged to them alone. He didn't care who was watching, only that she was in his arms. His chest was warm, his shoulders broad and steady beneath her hands, like she could lean into him and never fall. It felt like they could be swaying in a barn, on the deck of a boat, or nowhere at all. And it would still feel right.

She let her hands slide up to the back of his neck, fingers brushing damp curls and lingering, just a moment longer than necessary.

He smelled like beer and salt and cedar and something warm and masculine. Her heartbeat louder than the fiddle.

She was aware of everything. The brush of her chest against his, the way their thighs barely touched, the tension in her lower belly that no amount of mental gymnastics could deflect. It wasn't just attraction. It was trust, and longing, and the thrill of wanting something she didn't have to earn.

Chap leaned in, his mouth close to her ear. "You smell like cinnamon and trouble."

She smiled against his shoulder. "You smell like beer, salt and incredibly bad decisions."

He chuckled, the sound low and intimate. "You like bad decisions?"

"Depends on the outcome."

They kept swaying. His thumb drew lazy circles at her waist, and her entire body became tuned to those circles. She could have stayed like that for hours.

The music slowed, then shifted to something faster. Couples peeled away, laughing, hands clapping. Chap didn't move.

"You want to walk?" he asked, voice low, almost private.

Ava nodded, not trusting her voice.

They wandered away from the crowd, past Esther's pie table and the slug races table. Children shrieked with joy, dogs barked, but the noise softened behind them. The dock stretched ahead, quiet and silvered in moonlight.

At the edge, they paused. Water lapped gently below. A breeze lifted Ava's hair.

Chap turned toward her, closer now, the heat from his body still soaking into her skin.

"Sometimes I picture you standing at the bow of my boat," he said. "Hair wild. Or laughing in Esther's kitchen. Or typing stories at the Gazette."

She smiled, eyes locked on his, "So, you think about me a lot?"

"All the damn time."

She turned toward him, confident and grounded. "You going to do something about it?"

Chap didn't say anything at first. He just looked at her, really looked, like he was trying to memorize every detail.

Ava felt her breath catch, the world narrowing to the space between them.

He leaned in, his hand lifting to brush a strand of hair from her cheek. His fingers lingered, callused and warm. Her skin tingled beneath his touch.

And then he kissed her.

It was warm and deep and slow. No hesitation, no self-doubt. Just fire. A kiss that said he'd been waiting, wanting, and wasn't going to pretend otherwise anymore.

His mouth tasted of salt and heat and something dark and sweet. She parted her lips with a sigh and he deepened the kiss. No hesitation, no apology. Just need and knowing.

When they finally broke apart, their foreheads rested together. Ava's heart pounded. Chap's thumb still brushed her cheek in lazy strokes like he didn't want to stop touching her.

Ava and Chap were still close, their foreheads touching, the warmth of the kiss lingering like sunlight after a storm.

Then a voice cut through the quiet.

"Well, I guess Spruce Cove really *is* full of surprises."

Ava turned.

Amelia stood a few feet away, her arms crossed, lips pursed. Her sundress was crisp, her makeup flawless — even in the dim light.

Chap stiffened beside her.

"Amelia," he said, voice neutral.

"Didn't realize there were festival fireworks this year," she said, gaze narrowing on Ava.

Ava, feeling oddly trashy, stepped back instinctively.

"We were just…"

Amelia shook her head. She looked at Ava then back at Chap. "You've got a type," she said, her voice light. "Someone new. Someone who makes everything feel exciting. Until it doesn't."

"That's enough," he said, firm.

But Amelia wasn't done. "Gotta hand it to this place. Pies, parades, greasy pole contests. It's like summer camp for adults. Only with beer."

She turned to leave, heels clicking on the dock. "See you around," she tossed over her shoulder.

The silence that followed buzzed louder than the music behind them.

Chap ran a hand through his damp curls. "I'm sorry."

Ava didn't say anything at first. Her heart was still hammering, though not from the kiss anymore.

"She was watching," Ava said quietly. "The whole time?"

Chap looked pained. "I don't know."

Ava stepped back. "I need a minute."

And with that, she turned and walked back toward the bonfire, trying to steady the storm that had gathered behind her ribs.

She wandered to the edge of the festival grounds, past the rows of folding chairs and into the quieter spot near the water. The hum of fiddle music and laughter felt distant now, like a party she'd been invited to and suddenly didn't belong at.

She sat on a bench near the harbor and stared out at the reflections on the water, hugging her knees to her chest.

"Mind if I join you?" a voice asked.

She turned. It was Jack, the man who taught her about sea otters and knew far too much about her mother. Tonight, he carried two cups of something steaming and held one out to her.

"I saw you leave in a hurry. Figured tea was safer than cider," he said.

She accepted it with a nod. "Thanks."

They sat in silence for a moment. The mug warmed her hands, and the scent of mint rose with the steam.

"You look like you've been through it," he said, not unkindly.

Ava smiled faintly. "Festival whiplash. One minute it's greasy poles and slug races. The next, ex-girlfriends in sundresses."

Jack let out a low chuckle. "Ah. The full Spruce Cove experience."

She glanced sideways. "You've lived here a long time?"

He nodded. "Long enough to know that the festival brings out the best and worst in people. Same with small towns in general."

"How well did you know my mom?" she asked, surprising herself.

Jack didn't flinch, but his jaw shifted. "We spent quite a bit of time together."

"She was here the summer before she got pregnant with me."

He nodded again, slower this time. "I remember."

Ava studied him, the way his eyes stayed on the water. "What was she like?"

Jack exhaled. "Fierce. Smart. You couldn't get her to change with a stick of dynamite once she made up her mind. She had this way of pretending she didn't care when something mattered more than anything."

Ava swallowed. "Sounds familiar."

He looked at her then, really looked. And something in his expression softened. "You've got her eyes. Same way of standing."

Her throat tightened.

He turned back toward the water. "She loved the ocean. Said it made her feel free."

Ava traced the rim of her cup. "She rarely talked about this place. Or anyone in it."

Jack's voice dropped, low and full of something unsaid. "Sometimes people bury the good stuff with the bad, just to survive."

Ava didn't answer. Didn't have to.

They sat in silence for a while longer, listening to the slap of water against the pilings and the distant thrum of music. She felt steadier somehow. Not better, exactly, but anchored.

When she finally stood, he did too.

"Thanks for the tea," she said.

Jack nodded. "Anytime."

She turned to go, but his voice stopped her.

"You ever have questions, the kind that don't have easy answers, you know where to find me."

Ava met his eyes, heart ticking faster.

"Okay," she said. And made her way back to the festival.

****

Ava found a quiet spot near the edge of the festival grounds, perched on an overturned crate beneath a string of lanterns swaying in the breeze. She cradled a paper cup of cider, the heat barely warming her fingers.

She was halfway through replaying the entire Chap and Amelia dock scene for the tenth time when Liz dropped into the crate beside her.

"I've been looking all over," Liz said. "You ghosted me!"

Ava took a sip. "Needed air."

Liz studied her for a moment. "You good?"

Ava gave a dry laugh. "Define 'good.' I kissed Chap, got hit with a surprise ex-girlfriend ambush, and had a conversation with a mystery man who might have known my mother better than I did."

Liz blinked. "Wow. That's a lot for one festival."

That coaxed a real smile.

Liz leaned back on her hands. "You want to unpack it? Or just sit here and watch the mayor try to flirt his way into Mrs. Walker's preserves again?"

Ava was quiet for a beat. "I didn't think I'd feel this much. Not just about Chap. About everything. This town. The people. It's like I opened a door I didn't know I'd locked."

Liz bumped her knee. "That's what happens when your heart gets tricked into showing up."

Ava exhaled. "He kissed me like it wasn't just for fun."

Liz's brow lifted. "And that's a problem why?"

"Because I liked it. A lot. And I wasn't ready for that."

They let the quiet settle again, the soft rise and fall of fiddle music threading through the night.

Liz looked at her, voice softer now. "Wanting something doesn't make you weak. It means you still believe it's out there."

Ava stared at the glowing cider in her cup. "Yeah. Maybe."

Liz nudged her. "You don't have to figure it out tonight."

Ava looked at her friend, gratitude flickering behind her tired smile. "Thank God for you."

"Anytime. Esther gave me leftover pie. Want to eat our feelings?"

Ava grinned. "Absolutely."

Chapter 11

The mud was sucking at her boots and cold water slapping her thighs. Not the usual kind like bad dates, worse exes, and that wedding hashtag she'd already deleted. No, this was messier. Wetter. Way harder to explain.

Mud clawed at her ankles like it had a vendetta. Cold. Relentless. Every step forward felt like pushing through cement laced with guilt and seaweed. Her graduation dress, once ivory and hopeful, now resembled something a shipwreck would cough up. Soaked. Sagging. Dragging her down like the past she was trying to escape.

The tide was rushing in like it had a deadline. Dark waves curled toward her, crashing against her hips with a sting. Saltwater bit into her skin, soaked through her bones. Overhead, the sky churned an angry purple gray, like a bruise that hadn't made up its mind yet. Lightning stitched the horizon, all drama, no follow-through.

Ava screamed. Loud. Desperate. Her lungs burned. The wind laughed back, tossing her voice to the waves like a secret too scandalous to keep. She tried again. Another scream. Another silence.

She flailed for balance, for something solid. A rock, a rope, a second chance. There was nothing. Just the slippery pull of the ocean and the realization that the sandbar she'd started from was gone.

Solid ground had ghosted her.

Then, from above. A shape. A silhouette. A someone.

"Ava!"

The voice broke through the wind, cracked around the edges but familiar. She squinted against the spray. One figure. Tall. Shouting her name into the storm.

Chap? William?

It could be either. Her brain, waterlogged and heart-bruised, conjured both. One steady and infuriating. The other charming and treacherous. One had her history. The other, maybe, her future. Or maybe not.

She stretched her arm out, hand trembling, fingers numb. A silent plea. The water surged higher. Her knees buckled. She went under halfway. Mouth flooded with brine and shame.

Cold pressed against her chest like a bad decision she couldn't take back. Her heart pounded. Loud, fast, furious.

Then she screamed. Not for help this time.

For herself.

And that's when she saw it. The figure leaping down from the ridge, crashing through the surf like it owed him something. Closer. Closer. A hand extended.

Outstretched. Open. Reaching.

Fingers brushed hers.

And then. Blackout.

***

Ping.

A text message.

Ava shot upright, gasping like she'd just breached the surface of the ocean. Not dreaming it but living it. Her heart thudded against her ribs like it had somewhere to be. Sweat clung to her skin, the sheets tangled around her legs like they'd staged a mutiny. Her hair was plastered to her forehead, damp and unflattering. She wiped her face with the heel of her hand, then fumbled for her phone on the nightstand. It lit up, soft and blue, the only calm thing in the room.

Chap: Are you awake or just emotionally unavailable before 7 a.m.? Asking for a friend.

Somehow, the cloud of her dream lifted and a laugh escaped before she could stop it. That was Chap, never too serious but somehow always managing to hit the exact nerve she hadn't admitted was exposed. Cute. Funny. Infuriatingly disarming.

Her thumb hovered over the keyboard as a swirl of thoughts bloomed behind her eyes. The kiss they'd shared at the Fireweed

153

Festival replayed uninvited. The hesitant start, the quiet intensity, the way her heart had thudded afterward like it was trying to tell her something. But then she remembered Amelia leaning into him on the dock and wondered. That softness between them, the quiet way he held her. It didn't look like a casual past. It looked like unfinished business.

Were they really over?

She hadn't asked, and he hadn't offered. And maybe that was the problem.

She wanted to believe Chap was different. That the look he gave her meant something. But she'd believed that once before, with William, and ended up walking in on him with her roommate.

She could not do that again. Not emotionally. Not here. Not now.

Despite herself his text warmed something in Ava. That familiar twist in her stomach, the one that said: *be careful,* followed closely by the one that said: *but what if?*

Downstairs, the house had already woken up.

From the kitchen came the sounds of Esther conducting her usual morning symphony. The cupboard doors banged open and shut. The cast-iron skillet hit the stovetop with a clang that reverberated through the walls. Somewhere, a jar of jam crashed to the floor and rolled.

"George! Did you leave the sugar in the freezer again?"

"It stays fresh that way," came the gruff reply, followed by the scrape of a kitchen chair.

"It stays hidden, is what it does."

The scent of rising bread drifted up the stairs. Yeasty, warm, a little sweet. There was something so anchoring about it, something that told her no matter what dreams haunted her, the day would still begin with Esther banging pots and George reading the same section of the paper three times.

The kettle whistled. Esther cursed it gently under her breath.

Ava smiled, the edges of her anxiety dulling slightly.

Still holding her phone, she typed:

Ava: Define 'awake.' If it involves pants and eye contact, I plead the Fifth.

She hit send and tossed the phone onto the quilt, stretching her legs before swinging them to the floor.

Her room was dim but not cold, and as she tugged on her boots, she paused. She could still hear Esther's voice rising above the sizzle of bacon.

"We're almost out of flour. Remind me to pick some up. Unless you put that in the freezer, too."

George grumbled something unintelligible.

                                    ***

Ava chuckled softly and stepped into the hallway, pausing there
for a moment to breathe in: the clatter, the comfort, the home she
hadn't known she needed.

She descended the stairs quietly, one hand grazing the worn
banister, the other clutching her phone like a tether to something she
hadn't named yet. As she entered the kitchen, the familiar chaos of
Esther's breakfast routine hit her full force. Flour dusted the counter.
A cutting board teetered on the edge of the sink, crowded with
strawberry stems and half a lemon. The oven beeped a sharp warning,
and Esther opened it with her elbow, muttering something about
uneven heat.

"Morning, sweetheart," she said without turning around.
"Bread's ten minutes from perfect. Bacon's on its way to crispy. And
if George moves any slower with the coffee, he'll fossilize."

George grunted from behind the paper. "I like to savor the
brew."

"You savor like a sloth in a hammock."

Ava smiled and leaned against the doorframe, letting the steam
and warmth envelop her. It smelled like home. Not the one she grew
up in, where bills piled up and silence did the talking. But the one
she'd always imagined might exist if life had gone another way.

Esther turned then, giving Ava a once-over. "You look like you
wrestled a seal in your sleep."

"Dreams," Ava said, grabbing a mug and pouring herself coffee. "I was drowning."

"Ah," Esther replied, as if that explained everything. "That's your subconscious telling you you're avoiding something."

Ava lifted a brow. "Since when are you a dream interpreter?"

"Since raising three kids and feeding half this town. Dreams know before we do, honey. The question is, who do you think was trying to save you?"

The words hit a little too close. Ava focused on stirring her coffee. "Hard to say. Everything was muddy."

Esther didn't push. She never did. Just turned back to the skillet with a knowing hum.

"I ran into Chap yesterday," George offered suddenly. He folded down the top half of his paper. "He was working on his halibut gear and telling Benny that he might need help fixing his engine."

"That man can build a dory out of driftwood and wire, but he can't keep a boat running for a whole season without something falling apart," Esther said with a shake of her head. Then, softer, "He asked about you, you know. Not directly. But he was asking."

Ava looked up.

"Said something about how you seemed like you were finally getting your sea legs."

She didn't reply. She couldn't. Not with her heart lurching like it was trying to leap out of her chest. So she sipped her coffee instead, hoping the heat would chase the goosebumps from her arms.

"You working today?" Esther asked, flipping the bacon.

"Yep. Liz is heading out of town. She's leaving me the helm."

"God help us," George mumbled.

Ava finished her coffee, grateful for the grounding ritual of breakfast. Even if she couldn't quite digest what it all meant.

***

The walk to the Gazette felt longer than usual. The mist still clung to the trees, draping Spruce Cove in a hush that felt almost sacred. Her boots crunched softly on the gravel, the only sound in a world still half-asleep. Seagulls called in the distance, and somewhere across the harbor a buoy bell clanged, steady and solemn.

Ava tucked her hands into her pockets, trying to shake the remnants of the dream, of Chap's text, of the press of questions still hanging in the quiet corners of her mind. That's when she saw it.

A black bear.

It stood in the middle of the dock pathway, massive and motionless. Its fur was wet at the tips, glinting slightly in the pale morning light. Steam rose from its body in lazy curls.

Ava froze.

The bear didn't move. It simply stood, watching her.

There was no growl, no sudden lunge. Just breath and stillness. Its eyes locked with hers. Dark, quiet, impossibly steady.

She felt her heart thudding in her throat, but not from fear exactly. Not now. Something else settled over her: awe. The kind that makes your skin go taut and your breath slow without you realizing it. She couldn't look away.

The bear blinked. Tilted its head slightly.

She blinked back. Her hands had gone clammy inside her pockets.

For a brief, surreal moment, it felt as if the bear was trying to tell her something. Not in some Disney-animal-sidekick kind of way. No nods, no forest wisdom. Just presence. Steady. Unapologetic. Like it could see exactly how stuck she was in life and was quietly waiting for her to figure out if she was going to run or finally stand her ground.

The same way she felt about Chap. About this town. About everything.

Maybe her grandma was right. Maybe dreams said the things you couldn't admit in daylight.

Then, with slow grace, the bear turned and ambled off the path, disappearing into the thicket beyond the trees as silently as it had arrived.

Ava stood there long after it was gone, her breath visible in the morning air.

She wasn't sure what had just happened.

But something inside her shifted. A notch, a whisper. Like the tide turning in the middle of the night.

She shook herself loose and continued toward the Gazette, her boots a little heavier now, her thoughts trailing behind like fog. When she reached the office, the familiar creak of the door and scent of old newsprint greeted her like a bracing slap of cold water.

***

The front counter was deserted, with nothing but a few sad coffee rings and a pen that hadn't worked for two years. Liz had left the printer on again, humming a quiet mechanical lullaby. But the real welcome was waiting on her desk.

A thick folder was awaiting Ava on her desk, brightly labeled in Liz's loopy handwriting: "SALMONBERRY QUEEN: Ava's Crown Jewel Assignment." A sticky note was stuck to the top: "Think tiaras, tears, and toddlers with stage moms. Try not to ruin anyone's childhood. Also: don't let Stan near the glitter. –Liz"

Ava groaned. "Unbelievable."

She flopped into her chair, pulling the folder toward her. Inside were contestant bios, sponsor ads, and a printout of last year's story. Clearly laminated by someone who took it far too seriously.

She glanced at the glittery title of the event header, then let her head fall back against her chair.

"I can't believe this is my life."

Still, she powered on her laptop and braced for the day ahead.

***

The community hall looked like a craft store explosion: glittery streamers, plastic folding chairs, and a fake backdrop of Mount Edgecumbe that looked suspiciously like it had been drawn by a bored high school student. Moms were pacing in the aisles with emergency bobby pins and backup pantyhose. One dad was arguing with a volunteer over whether his teenage daughter had been given the "good tiara" or the "backup tiara," as though world peace hinged on rhinestone distribution.

Ava took her seat in the back, pulled out her notebook, and braced herself.

The contestants trickled onto the stage, each girl more overdressed and underprepared than the last. One performed a rendition of "Let It Go" that made Ava instinctively reach for earplugs. Another twirled a baton like she'd learned her routine fifteen minutes prior. And maybe she had.

The crowd, however, was enraptured. People clapped like they were at Carnegie Hall. One woman stood to give her granddaughter a standing ovation for a haiku about jellyfish.

Ava didn't get it.

Why were grown adults crying over off-key show tunes and a papier-mâché salmon? It all felt like some collective small-town delusion, a glitter-drenched fantasy trying to convince everyone, just for a day, that life wasn't hard, the town wasn't dying, and the future wasn't quietly slipping into the sea.

She wrote it like she saw it. With a smirk.

The line that made her smirk as she typed: *"Spruce Cove's annual glitter festival showcased a passionate homage to talent, sequins, and mild emotional breakdowns. Winners were crowned. Feelings were hurt. Several glue guns were harmed in the making of this event."*

She submitted it before bed and fell asleep feeling like she'd nailed the tone.

What she didn't know. What she couldn't know yet. Was how fast the fallout would come.

***

It started with the phone buzzing. Ava ignored it.

Then came the texts.

Liz: Call me. Now.

Liz: WHY are people canceling their subscriptions?!?

Liz: I leave for one weekend and you light the town on fire with glitter and sarcasm.

Ava blinked at her screen, still in her robe, coffee in hand. The headline of her story, "Queen for a Day, Glitter for a Lifetime," blinked cheerfully at her from the Gazette homepage.

The comments were ... not cheerful.

"This is an insult to our girls!"

"Who does this outsider think she is?"

"We want Liz back!"

"My daughter cried. Cried!"

Ava sat up straighter.

Then came the calls.

Her dentist's office, which couldn't be good.

She finally answered Liz on the fourth call.

"I didn't think it would blow up like this," Ava said before Liz could speak.

"You didn't, Ava? This is Spruce Cove. They've been doing this pageant since the late '70s. Before cordless phones. Before glitter came in shaker jars. You mocked their daughters. And their deeply held belief that hot glue and duct tape can fix anything."

"It was tongue-in-cheek!"

"It was a punch in the face. To a lot of very sensitive, very vocal grandmothers. One of whom threatened to protest in front of the office. With picket signs."

Ava winced. "Over a tiara?"

"Over tradition. You didn't just poke fun. You missed the point."

Ava opened her mouth to defend herself, but the truth lodged in her throat. She had missed the point. She'd walked in assuming it was all glitter and fluff, and maybe it was, but it also meant something. To them.

Liz sighed. "We've had eighteen subscription cancellations and counting. And Phyllis from the Chamber of Commerce wants to speak to you personally."

Ava groaned. "Am I fired?"

"No. But let's just say you're not getting invited to any potlucks this year. Which, for the record, is not a great place to be."

"I'll fix it."

"You'd better. And maybe try to *not* use the words 'glue gun carnage' this time."

The line went dead.

Ava sat back, staring at the screen. Outside, a seagull screamed like it, too, was disappointed in her.

The rest of the week, the smiles had stopped.

At Annie's, her usual refill never came. Just a quick nod from the server before vanishing like everyone else lately. Ava opened her book and stared hard at the page, pretending she wasn't reading the same sentence for the third time. Pretending, she didn't care that no one had asked if she wanted more coffee. Even the barista, who used to flirt with foam art, handed her a lukewarm cappuccino like it had personally offended him.

Ava didn't need a town hall meeting to know she'd messed up. The silence spoke volumes.

She slunk into the Gazette through the side door, eyes down, heart heavy. Her desk was a minefield of passive-aggressive messages. Subscription cancellations, reprints pulled, one envelope sealed with glitter that had already started shedding onto her keyboard.

She dropped into her chair and opened her email, hoping for at least one message that wasn't steeped in rage.

There it was.

Subject: *A Letter to the Editor – From Amelia Colburn*

She clicked.

Amelia's words were polished, restrained, and sharp as sea glass. Surprisingly articulate. She wrote about growing up in Spruce Cove, about being crowned Salmonberry Queen at twelve. About how that moment made her feel seen, proud, connected to something larger than herself. She described how the crown didn't just symbolize a title, it symbolized community, roots, resilience.

She didn't mention Ava by name.

She didn't have to.

Ava read the letter twice. Then a third time. Each pass scraped something raw inside her.

She shut her laptop gently, like even it might be judging her.

Outside, the sun had vanished behind clouds, turning the windowpane gray. She stared at her own reflection in the glass, at the face of someone who'd thought she understood this place. Only to learn, once again, how little she truly knew.

Esther's words echoed faintly in her mind: *Dreams know before we do.*

Ava sighed, pulling her sweater tighter around her shoulders. The silence of the office wasn't peace. It was punishment.

And for the first time in awhile, she felt like an outsider again.

Like she'd never stopped being one.

Chapter 12

The morning after Amelia's letter to the editor ran in the *Spruce Cove Gazette*, Ava stepped into the newspaper office and immediately felt the chill. Not from the coastal air that slipped through the cracked window, but from the silence that met her.

Liz's desk was still empty. The sticky note she left Ava was still taped to the monitor:

"Emergency trip. Back soon. You've got this. — L "

Ava dropped her computer bag and sat heavily in her chair. Amelia's letter replayed in her mind. Her words had been elegant, heartfelt, and subtle in their critique of Ava's tone. It wasn't an attack, but it had landed like one.

The silence wasn't just ambient. It was thick. Hollow. Like the office itself had chosen not to speak to her.

The phone rang. The voice on the other end canceled a subscription. The next caller did the same.

By the fourth cancellation of the day, Ava felt her throat tighten. She glanced toward Liz's desk. The framed photo of Liz and her dad, a former mayor, in front of a Salmonberry Queen sign.

She hadn't just written a snarky piece. She had humiliated the paper. Liz's paper. A business that was already on the brink.

"Damn it," she whispered, pressing her fingers against her temple. "What did I do?"

She remembered Liz sitting her down that first day: *This paper survives because people trust it, more than they trust each other, some days.*

And Ava had broken that trust. With a byline, with what turned out to be really unfunny jokes.

She stood abruptly, her chair screeching against the wood floor. The notepad slid off her desk and hit the ground with a slap.

"I can't," she muttered. "I just need…"

Air. Maybe coffee. To stop thinking.

Spruce Cove was never bustling, but today it felt thinner than usual. Faces turned away as she passed. Two older women on the boardwalk stopped talking when she neared. Even Benny gave her a curt nod instead of his usual "Hey, Yale."

She'd become the girl who mocked the Salmonberry Queen. Who insulted their granddaughters and their past selves and one thing holding this town together.

By the time she reached Annie's, Ava was regretting every word of her article. She waited in line behind a woman in rain boots and a pink vest. When the woman turned and saw Ava, she offered a tight-lipped smile, then turned back around.

Ava's stomach sank. She wasn't just disliked. She was toxic. A careless outsider who didn't understand what mattered here.

She tucked her chin and pulled her jacket tighter around her frame, wishing she could fold into herself and disappear.

***

Ava took her coffee to go. No point in sticking around. The air inside Annie's was thick with judgment and cinnamon. The place hadn't changed. Martha still cracked jokes like a stand-up behind the espresso machine, and the regulars were right where they always were, perched on their mismatched stools like barflies in a Norman Rockwell painting. The steam from their cups curled into the air like contented sighs. But somehow, Ava felt like she'd been written out of the scene. Like she'd wandered into a party where everyone remembered what she did, and none of them were ready to let her forget it. Today it was still.

As she turned to leave, she nearly ran smack-dab into Chap.

"Whoa," he said, steadying her with a hand on her elbow.

She looked up. His hair was damp from the sea air, his hoodie zipped up beneath a flannel jacket she hadn't seen before. He looked tired. Or maybe she was just seeing clearly for the first time.

"Sorry," she muttered.

They stood in the narrow pass between coffee hut and gravel lot, the fog curling around their feet like it had something to say.

"You okay?" he asked.

Ava shrugged. "The town hates me. Liz left town. The phones won't stop ringing with subscription cancellations. I'm a walking cautionary tale."

Chap raised a brow. "That all?"

"I'm a pariah with a byline," she added, voice too high to be casual.

He gave a small, lopsided smile. "They'll come around."

"Will they?" Her voice cracked. "Because it feels like I spit on their salmonberries and danced on their grandmother's grave."

He winced. "Yeah. Okay. It wasn't your best moment."

Ava narrowed her eyes. "Thanks."

"I mean that as someone who's made his fair share of tone-deaf decisions." He paused. "You're not wrong about some of what you wrote. You were wrong about some of it though. The worst part is you were loud and wrong at the same time. That's a tough combo in a small town."

Ava sighed. "I was trying to be clever. You know, snarky East Coast energy."

"Wrong coast," Chap said gently. "This is a place where the highlight of the year is picking berries, catching your first spring king salmon and crowning a queen who once sang a medley of *Cats* songs."

She barked a laugh, unbidden. "You're kidding."

"Nope. I have it on VHS somewhere."

They stood in silence for a beat.

"You want to walk?" he asked.

She hesitated, then nodded.

They moved toward the docks, walking slowly. The tide was out, exposing flats that gleamed like tarnished silver. A raven swooped overhead. Kelp clung to the barnacled posts like it was hiding from something.

"You saw Amelia's letter," she said.

"I did."

"It was fair."

Chap took his time before answering. "It was honest. Kind, even. She could've gone for blood. She didn't."

Ava stopped walking. "Why does she have to be the bigger person? Why not just call me a brat and be done with it?"

"Because she knows this town," Chap said, turning to face her. "She's part of its fabric. She learned to thrive in the space between tradition and expectation. Between what people say and what they mean."

There was something warm in his voice when he spoke about Amelia. Not longing. Not romance. But reverence. Respect earned over time.

Ava felt a tiny knot tighten in her stomach.

"She's strong," Chap added. "And smarter than most people give her credit for."

Ava looked at him, half-shadowed in the morning fog, and ached. Not because she was jealous, though she was, but because she wanted someone to talk about her that way. With admiration. With fondness. With the kind of layered affection that only came from shared history.

She wanted Chap to see her like that.

But she wasn't sure she'd earned it.

"You're still learning," he said, as if sensing her spiral. "It doesn't mean you don't belong."

Another beat passed. Ava felt the words settle somewhere behind her ribs.

Then a voice cut through the quiet.

"Chap!"

They turned.

George, leaving the marine repair shop, was waving Chap to the end of the dock. His voice cracked with urgency.

Chap frowned. "That can't be good."

He took off toward the dock at a jog.

Ava followed for a few paces, then slowed. It was clear she wasn't needed. Chap was already at George's side, hunched over an outboard motor with its cover popped and a jumble of tools strewn across the dock like they'd been hurled in frustration.

Ava stopped near the railing, watching them work. The wind tugged strands of her hair loose from her bun, and she tucked them behind her ears, only to turn and find herself unexpectedly face-to-face with Amelia.

She hadn't heard her approach.

Amelia stood there, coat zipped, posture straight like she was trying to hold herself up with what little she had left. Not the kind of tired that made for a good story, just the regular kind. The kind that creeps in while you're busy pretending you're fine.

Ava opened her mouth to speak, then closed it again.

Amelia's eyes flicked over her face. "Come to watch the town implode?"

The words weren't sharp. If anything, they were weary, edged with something that sounded almost like pity. Or was it disappointment?

"No," Ava said softly. "I just needed some air."

They stood side-by-side for a long moment, neither of them speaking, the sound of Chap and George muttering over engine trouble drifting over the dock.

Ava risked a glance sideways. Amelia's face was unreadable. Regal in its reserve.

"I read your letter," Ava said.

"I assumed."

"It was well written. Gracious. You didn't have to be."

Amelia turned to face her fully. "No, I didn't. But I've learned it costs more to be unkind than it does to be honest."

Ava swallowed. "I hurt people. I didn't mean to, but I did. I made Liz's job harder. Made a joke of something people care about. Something you clearly care about."

"I do," Amelia said. "Not because of the crown. But because it gives young women a chance to feel seen. To step forward in a world that often tells them to shrink."

Ava looked down at her coffee cup, now lukewarm. "I didn't see that. I should've."

Amelia didn't reply right away. Then, she surprised Ava with a small nod. "You're seeing it now. That matters."

Ava looked up. "I want to fix it. I don't know how, but I want to start."

There was a pause. Amelia studied her, really looked at her.

"Then start with a story," she said. "A good one."

***

The next morning, Ava knocked on a bright yellow house at the edge of town, just past the bend where the blackberries overtook the fence in late July. The mailbox read "Dolores C." in curly, hand-painted script.

Dolores opened the door in a cardigan embroidered with crab apples and raised an eyebrow sharp enough to peel an apple.

"You're Esther's granddaughter," she said flatly.

"Yes," Ava replied, gripping her notepad and a pie fresh out of the oven. "I know you were a Salmonberry Queen and a past winner of the pie contest. I was hoping to ask you a few questions."

Dolores looked her over with the kind of scrutiny that made Ava feel like underbaked crust. "You brought pie?"

Ava swallowed. "I did. Apple crumble. Made it myself. And yes, I realize showing up on your porch with a pie is like bringing a kazoo to a symphony."

Dolores's eyebrow arched higher. "Bold or foolish, we'll see."

She stepped back and opened the door just wide enough. "Alright. You've got five minutes."

An hour later, Ava left with seven pages of notes, a stern warning to "get it right," and a container of rhubarb scones for Esther. Dolores reminisced about "sashes and silly songs." Over her second slice of apple crumble, she let her guard down. Told Ava how, the year she won, the whole town showed up with wildflowers. How the crown had been too big and kept slipping, but she'd smiled through it anyway. "That was the first time anyone clapped for me, just me," she said. "That sticks."

Dolores had been brisk, opinionated, and surprisingly sentimental. The crown, it turned out, had meant more than just a title. It had been a moment of recognition in a life full of quiet work and perfecting pie crusts.

It gave Ava courage.

Over the next few days, Ava set off on what felt like a scavenger hunt for redemption. If redemption came in the form of floral couches, lukewarm coffee, and stories tucked into photo albums that smelled like old potpourri. She carried a recorder, a notebook, and the kind of smile you wear when you're hoping people won't remember that you just insulted their most beloved town tradition in print.

There was Janine, whose garage was a shrine to scrapbooks and glitter glue, and who could recall the exact hue of her crown ribbon ("blush, not pink. There's a difference"). Penny still kept her sash in her lingerie drawer "for emergencies," she'd said with a wink Ava would probably think about for the rest of her life. And Shirley, who wore combat boots under her gown and hadn't told a soul until the coronation photo landed in the *Spruce Cove Gazette* and showed a flash of laces where heels should've been. "I stand by it," she'd declared. "Those heels were suicide."

They let Ava in. Sometimes grudgingly, sometimes with open arms, but always with stories. And slowly, she began to understand that the crown wasn't about glitter or fluff. It was about community. About being seen. About mattering. Just as you were.

***

Amelia was last on her list, not because she mattered least, but because she mattered *most*. Ava had put off the call the way you put off checking your bank account after a weekend of bad decisions. Amelia had already been kinder than necessary, more gracious than deserved. Facing her again felt like signing up for a second helping of humility.

Still, Ava dialed.

"I heard you were making the rounds. Figured I was next," Amelia said, her voice calm as ever, like Ava had called about a weather report and not a soul-deep apology in interview form.

"Would you be willing to talk?" Ava asked, gripping her phone with both hands like it might slip from the weight of the ask.

"I wouldn't have said yes the first time if I wasn't."

They met in Amelia's parent's living room, which looked exactly like a retired queen's living room should: filled with potted plants that were thriving in a way Ava's houseplants had never considered, lace doilies that looked like they'd been pressed that morning, and a tea set delicate enough to make Ava nervous to breathe near it.

Amelia poured tea without speaking, her movements so graceful Ava briefly wondered if they offered posture classes to former Salmonberry Queens.

"Milk?" Amelia asked.

"Yes, please. And thank you for this." Ava gestured, vaguely, to the tea, the plants, the conversation, the forgiveness she hadn't quite earned yet.

Amelia handed her the cup. "You're not the first person to misunderstand the crown."

"I might be the first to insult it in print," Ava offered, half-joking, half-dreading the answer.

"You'd be surprised," Amelia said, and for the first time, smiled.

They sat, the air between them full of possibility. Ava didn't dive in. She let the silence breathe. And then, carefully, she opened her notebook.

"Why did it matter to you?" she asked.

Amelia took a moment. "Because no one expected me to be chosen."

Ava blinked. "Why not?"

"I wasn't the prettiest. I wasn't the richest. I didn't have a big personality. But I showed up. I listened. I volunteered. And I guess somewhere along the line, people noticed. The crown didn't change me, but it told me I was noticed. That's not nothing when you're seventeen and trying to disappear."

Ava nodded, swallowing around the lump in her throat.

"And the legacy?" she asked, voice quieter now.

"That's the real part," Amelia said. "Knowing girls watched me and thought, maybe that could be me, too. Not just the crown, but the confidence. The belonging."

Ava scribbled notes, though she knew she'd remember every word.

As she stood to leave, Amelia handed her a bouquet of daisies. "For your desk. And your next apology, if needed."

Ava laughed. "Thanks."

***

By the time Ava got back to the Gazette, the bouquet from Amelia was already starting to wilt. She set it gently beside her keyboard anyway. Petals sagging, stems slightly askew, still beautiful in that tired, late-summer kind of way.

Her laptop blinked to life, and with it came the weight of everything she'd collected: the notebooks full of chicken scratch, the voice memos full of laughter and confessions, the hope in Shirley's eyes, the caution in Dolores's, the softness in Amelia's voice when she talked about disappearing.

Ava cracked her neck. Tried to breathe.

And stared at the blank screen taunting her with its smug little blinking cursor.

She'd written dozens of articles before. Headlines, features, blurbs about fundraisers and obituaries and pie contests. But this was different. This had to be *right*. Not polished. Not clever. Honest.

She started typing. Then deleted everything.

Tried again.

In Spruce Cove, the Salmonberry Queen isn't just a girl in a crown.

Delete. Too stiff. Too much like someone trying to make amends instead of telling a story.

She leaned back in her chair, rubbed her eyes, then leaned forward again. This time, she didn't try to sound like a writer. She tried to sound like someone who'd listened.

179

I didn't understand what it meant to wear a crown until I sat across from the women who wore it before. I thought it was pomp, fluff, a relic from a town too afraid to move on.

I was wrong.

She paused. Took a sip of cold coffee. Kept going.

Over the past week, I've spoken with more than a dozen Salmonberry Queens. Women who led parades, handed out ribbons, waved until their arms ached. But it wasn't the waving they remembered.

It was how they felt: valued. Connected to something bigger than themselves.

Her fingers flew now, less like typing and more like releasing something that had been waiting inside her to come out.

One woman told me the sash made her stand taller. Another said she still wears her crown to play poker on Fridays. And one, who gave me a bouquet and forgiveness in equal measure, taught me that tradition isn't the enemy of progress. It's the soil things grow from.

Ava exhaled. Her shoulders unclenched for the first time all day.

This isn't a series about crowns. It's about the women who wore them, and the community that cheered them on. And maybe, if she learned anything, it's that being part of something means taking care of it. Even when you mess up.

Especially then.

She hit save. Then backed it up in three different places.

Then, nervously with a little prayer, she hit "send to print."

***

Just after sunrise, the bell over the Gazette's front door jingled.

Ava was still in the back microwaving day-old coffee, wrapped in a hoodie and last night's anxiety, when she heard the familiar rhythm of sneakers on tile. Confident, and unmistakably Liz.

She froze.

"Liz?" she called, heart thudding against her ribs.

"Unless someone else has the keys and a habit of labeling folders in all caps," came the familiar dry reply.

Ava emerged from the kitchenette like a sleep-deprived groundhog. There she was: Liz, standing just inside the newsroom with her roller bag at her side, travel cardigan slung over her shoulders, and an expression that read somewhere between bemused and battle-ready.

"You're back early," Ava said, blinking like her editor had materialized from thin air.

"Plans change," Liz replied, eyeing the office like it might have spontaneously combusted in her absence. Her gaze stopped at the bouquet by Ava's desk, then moved to the printed article lying just beside it.

Without asking, Liz picked it up. She flipped through the pages with the cool, surgical precision of someone who'd spent decades turning rookie drafts into real stories.

Ava stood frozen, mug in hand, heartbeat rattling in her ears like loose change in a dryer.

This was it. The moment. Liz would read the first paragraph, raise one unimpressed eyebrow, and deliver a quiet, devastating verdict. Maybe she'd pull the plug on the story. Maybe on Ava.

She'd tanked things before. This wasn't just a bad lede or a missed comma.

This was someone's business. Someone's *life*.

Liz had given her the reins. Trusted her. Left the town, the paper, the whole beat in her hands. In return, Ava had written a snarky, tone-deaf feature that tanked half the subscriber base and made the town treat Liz's paper like it had insulted their grandmothers and their salmon, in that order. She'd joked about being a pariah, but the truth hit harder now, in the too-quiet room with the too-still editor scanning her words like they were an autopsy.

Ava took a sip of her scorched coffee. It tasted like burnt pride and terrible decisions.

She braced herself. Finally, Liz looked up.

"This is good."

Chapter 13

The Gaff Hook looked exactly like the kind of place where hearts got broken and patched up over a cheap beer and a bowl of pretzels that had seen better days. The ceilings were low enough that even Ava, not exactly towering, felt the urge to duck. Hundreds of dollar bills, creased, faded, some stained with what she sincerely hoped was beer, were tacked to the rafters, each scribbled with names and dates like tiny declarations of presence.

Photographs lined the wood-paneled walls: smiling fishermen in Helly Hansens, prom queens in the town parade, blurry shots from salmon derbies and Fourth of July bake-offs. Near the bar hung a framed black-and-white photo of a younger, wild-eyed Esther McCormick, her braid thick and dark, one arm raised in victory, the other gripping the tail of a massive king salmon. Winner of that year's derby, and apparently the undisputed queen of Spruce Cove.

Ava stood just inside the door, taking it all in. The air was thick with the mingling scents of fryer grease, low tide, and something sharp and citrusy that might have been cleaning solution. Or vodka. A karaoke machine warbled through a poorly tuned rendition of "Friends in Low Places," and the floor vibrated faintly with the tread of rubber boots and laughter.

"Welcome to the heartbeat of Spruce Cove," Liz said, stepping past her and brushing snow from her shoulders. She wore a hoodie that read *Deadliest Catch Meets PMS*, and her boots clunked decisively with each step.

"I feel like I need a hepatitis booster just standing here," Ava said, ducking under a driftwood beam with a smile tugging at her lips.

"That's part of the ambiance," Liz replied. "And you haven't lived until you've had your eardrums assaulted by Evelyn's Thursday-night Whitney Houston tribute."

Right on cue, Evelyn appeared in her mid-fifties, wearing a sequined top and hair teased like she had unfinished business with the 1980s. She launched into a reverent, tone-mangling version of "I Will Always Love You," eyes closed, mic clutched like it was holy.

Ava blinked. "Oh my God. She's crying."

"She always cries. It's tradition," Liz said, leading her through the crowd toward a high-top in the back.

They passed a cluster of men playing darts and a woman loudly arguing with the bartender about the difference between 'on the rocks' and 'with ice'. The walls hummed with local history. Ava caught sight of another photo of Esther, this one blurry but unmistakably her, hoisting a trophy with one hand and a beer with the other.

"She was kind of a big deal around here," Ava murmured, almost to herself.

"She still is," Liz said, nudging her gently.

They sat at a table in the corner, and a surly man with impressive sideburns came over to take their order. Liz went with something dark and probably flammable. Ava didn't hesitate.

"Gin and tonic," she said, surprising even herself a little.

The man nodded without blinking and disappeared into the crowd.

Moments later, they were clinking glasses under a ceiling of dollars and a chorus of tone-deaf locals, two women escaping heartbreak and rediscovering laughter in a room steeped in history, heartache, and second chances.

***

A voice called out from across the room, half-drowned by the thrum of bad karaoke and the clink of glass.

"Hey, Red. You any good at darts?"

Ava turned to see a trio of fishermen watching them from the dartboard area. One of them, early thirties with a beard that looked like it had trapped dinner in it and arms like tree trunks, grinned like he'd just found something shiny and mildly amusing.

"I'm sorry, are you talking to me or that redhead over there?" Ava asked, raising an eyebrow.

"All of ya," he said, gesturing to both. "But mostly you."

Liz smirked into her drink but didn't take the bait.

Ava lifted her glass, her smile sweet and just a little sharp around the edges. "Let me guess, this is the part where the local boys teach

185

the clueless city girl how to aim? I've seen the movie. It doesn't end the way you think."

"C'mon," another fisherman chimed in, "it's all in good fun. Loser buys the next round."

Ava glanced at Liz, who looked entirely unbothered, even amused. "What do you think? Should we humor them?"

Liz shrugged. "I never turn down a chance to embarrass a man with a fish tattoo."

They followed the men to the dartboard. The guys stood back, arms folded like they were watching seals balance beach balls.

Ava picked up a dart, twirled it, and immediately regretted volunteering to go first.

"How hard can it be?" she muttered, squinting at the board like it might offer tips.

She lined up her shot, took a deep breath, and launched.

The dart veered wildly left, missed the board entirely, and embedded itself in the corkboard frame next to a framed photo of someone's grandpa catching a halibut the size of a kayak.

One of the fishermen let out a low whistle. Another chuckled. "Whoa there. You trying to take out old Joe?"

"Joe shouldn't have been standing so close to greatness," Ava said, already red in the cheeks.

She handed the second dart to Liz. "Your turn, oh merciful teammate. May the gods of hand-eye coordination be with you."

Liz set it down. Then, like some kind of salty magician, she reached into her oversized purse and pulled out a battered leather case.

She unzipped it slowly and retrieved her own set of darts.

"Is that?" Ava blinked. "You brought your own?"

Liz popped a piece of gum in her mouth. "Girl Scout motto: always be prepared. Also, I once dated a guy who ran dart tournaments. Learned a few things."

The fishermen exchanged wary glances.

Liz stepped up to the line, rolled her shoulders like she was preparing for a prize fight, and threw.

Bullseye.

A gasp rippled through the room.

She threw again.

Twenty.

Then triple twenty.

By the time her third dart landed, one of the fishermen was muttering something about divine intervention.

Liz turned, handed her case to Ava, and smirked. "Your round, boys."

Ava grinned wide. "I knew I brought you here for a reason."

One of the men handed over a twenty with mock solemnity. "Remind me never to underestimate a woman with a giant purse."

As the drinks were poured and the game reset, Ava leaned closer to Liz and whispered, "That was terrifyingly hot."

"I get that a lot," Liz replied, eyes twinkling.

***

After Liz was done schooling men in darts, they settled at the bar, fresh drinks already sweating in their glasses. The din of the Gaff Hook swirled around them. Country music two decades past its prime, the dull thud of darts hitting cork, Evelyn tackling *Total Eclipse of the Heart* like she had a Vegas residency riding on it.

Liz leaned forward, resting her elbows on the sticky bar top. "So," she said, giving Ava a sideways glance, "how's your small-town exile suiting you?"

Ava snorted. "Oh, you mean the part where I flee a cheating fiancé, move in with my grandparents, and spend my nights discovering your secret dart assassin skills?"

Liz grinned. "That part exactly."

Ava swirled her straw through the melting remains of her gin and tonic, watching the lime wedge swirl like it had answers. "It's weird. I thought coming here would feel like pressing pause. But it's more like, I don't know. Pressing reset?"

Liz nodded. "This place does that. Strips you down to whatever's left when the noise is gone."

"I didn't expect to feel anything here. And then there's Chap."

Liz's brows arched with interest. "Ah. The sea captain with smoldering eyes and broody silences. Tell me more."

"I don't know," Ava said, resting her cheek in her hand. "He's complicated. And honest. And quiet in a way that doesn't feel empty, you know? Like he hears things even when you don't say them."

Liz gave a mock shiver. "Romantic and spooky. Go on."

Ava laughed, then sobered. "I think I might be falling for him. And that terrifies me."

Liz tilted her head. "Why?"

"Because what if it's just a rebound? What if I'm just desperate for something that feels good after everything with William?" She paused, swirling the ice in her glass. "And what if there's still something between him and Amelia?"

There it was. The thing she hadn't said out loud. The thing that sat heavy in her chest every time she saw the way Chap's gaze softened when Amelia's name came up, or the way he went quiet when he thought no one noticed.

Liz leaned in. "Do you think there is?"

"I don't know," Ava whispered. "She was crying in his arms the other day. And he didn't seem to mind."

"Was he supposed to throw her in the harbor?" Liz's voice was light, but her eyes were kind.

"No. I just, I thought maybe we were building something. And now I feel like the only one who didn't get added to the group chat."

Liz tapped her glass against Ava's. "You're not some extra in someone else's drama, Ava. Chap's not that kind of man. You're the part he didn't know he was waiting for."

Ava smiled despite herself. "That's dangerously close to an Instagram quote."

"Yeah, well, sometimes Instagram gets it right."

They sat with the silence a beat longer. Not awkward, just settled.

"I'm tired of running," Ava finally said. "From decisions. From feelings. From everything."

Liz raised her glass. "Then let's make a pact. No more running."

Ava clinked hers against it. "Deal."

Ava smiled, the kind that cracked something open in her chest.

***

And then, as if summoned by the universe's sense of irony, Amelia walked through the door.

She didn't slink or sashay. She just *appeared*. All jeans and windblown hair, that quiet confidence of someone who'd grown up in a place like this. Her eyes swept the room once, locked onto Ava and Liz at the bar, and without missing a beat, she crossed the floor and plopped down beside them.

"Evening," she said, like she hadn't just walked into a conversation she might have been the subject of.

Liz blinked. Ava just stared.

Amelia raised a hand to the bartender. "Ice water."

He didn't move right away. "Since when?"

"Couple weeks," Amelia said, her tone light but final. "Trying something different."

He gave a small nod and reached for a glass, but Ava caught the way his eyes lingered a second longer than they needed to. Not judgment, exactly, more like history. Liz noticed too, her brows subtly rising before she took another sip of her drink.

No one said it out loud, but the silence filled in the blanks. Maybe she'd had a problem. Maybe she'd hit a wall. Maybe she just got tired of waking up foggy. The reason didn't matter so much as the way she said it. Like a door had closed behind her and she wasn't reaching for the knob.

Amelia took her water and drank it in two long swallows. "Don't stop on my account," she said, flashing a tight-lipped smile. "I'm not here to ruin anyone's fun."

Ava opened her mouth to respond, something vaguely polite and neutral. But she didn't get the chance.

Because at that moment, the door slammed open, rattling the wind chimes above it.

***

Ava jumped. Liz straightened in her seat. Even the bartender paused mid-pour.

"Crap. Earl," someone muttered from a nearby table, low but unmistakable.

He stood in the doorway, dripping and wild-eyed, fists clenched around something crumpled in one hand. His neon Helly Hansen rain jacket was soaked and sagging off one shoulder, streaked with grease.

Ava's chest tightened.

It was him. The man from the beach. The one ranting to no one, with rage like an oil slick around him. She felt her pulse tick up, heart thudding against her ribs. But when Earl's eyes swept the bar, he didn't land on her.

He landed on Amelia.

Ava let out a quiet breath she hadn't realized she was holding.

Earl started walking, a crooked path that felt intentional, too casual to be casual. He stopped just short of Amelia's stool, close enough that Ava could smell the wet wool and motor oil clinging to him.

"Amelia," he said, like he'd just run into an old friend and not spent the last week pacing a beach yelling at the sea. "Didn't expect to see you here tonight. You look good."

Amelia didn't blink. "Evening, Earl."

"You here alone?" he asked, eyes darting to Ava, then Liz, dismissing them just as fast. "Because I was thinking maybe we could get a table. Catch up."

She sipped her water. "I'm good here."

Earl smiled, slow and lopsided. "C'mon. Don't be like that. One drink."

"I don't drink anymore."

He snorted. "Then I'll have two."

Ava felt Liz shift beside her, spine going straight.

Amelia's voice stayed even. "It's a no, Earl."

That should've been the end of it.

But something in him twitched, shoulders tight, jaw clenched. His smile dropped.

"Acting like you're too good to talk to someone who's just being nice?"

"I said no." Amelia didn't raise her voice. She didn't have to. There was steel under the calm.

The bartender was already moving, wiping his hands on a towel as he rounded the bar. "Earl," he said, l. Jow and firm. "Don't make this a thing."

Earl took a step back, half-laughing. "You serious?"

Two guys at the far end of the bar stood up. Visiting Coast Guard, judging by their jackets and tight haircuts. They didn't say anything. Just stepped forward, blocking off Earl's view of the women.

Earl looked between them, the bartender, and the crowd now watching with interest.

"This place has gone soft," he muttered. "Used to be you could buy a girl a drink without the damn Navy stepping in."

"Coast Guard," one of the men corrected coolly.

The bartender jerked his thumb toward the door. "You're 86'd, Earl. You know the rules. Go cool off somewhere else."

Earl stood still for a second too long. Then he shoved his crumpled whatever, it might've been a napkin or a receipt, into his pocket and stalked out, the door slamming hard enough behind him to rattle the glasses on the shelf.

A minute passed.

Then the bartender called out, "First round's on me if nobody talks about that drama for the rest of the night."

Laughter broke the tension, and slowly, the Gaff Hook returned to its usual rhythm. Off-key karaoke, clinking glasses, and the comfortable hum of people trying to forget things for a little while.

Amelia didn't say anything. Just turned back to her water and took another sip.

***

Without skipping a beat, the party resumed.

Then the opening chords of *A Pirate Looks at 40* rolled through the room. Slow, deliberate, like the tide coming in.

He leaned into the mic.

"Mother, mother ocean…"

He didn't have the best voice, but it was the kind that held weight. Regret. Time. Salt. People turned toward him without meaning to. Conversations paused. One of the Coasties lowered his drink mid-sip.

By the time he hit the chorus, the whole room was swaying. Barely. Gently. Like a boat drifting from its moorings.

194

Liz was locked in a good-natured argument with one of the Coasties about who really invented the longline clip. Amelia sat quiet, hands wrapped around her glass of water, her expression unreadable but calm.

And then, *clang*.

From above the bar, someone reached up and rang the brass bell, its clear, commanding chime slicing through the music.

A half-second beat, and then the room erupted in cheers.

Someone had rung the bell.

Drinks for everyone.

The bartender raised his arms in mock surrender and began pouring. The man at the mic gave a one-handed salute and launched into the next verse. Ava laughed so hard she choked on a sip of gin.

Amelia slid off her stool.

"Night," she said quietly, already moving.

Liz gave her a lazy wave. "Take care."

Ava nodded, flushed and content. "See you around."

But Amelia was already halfway to the door.

It wasn't until much later, after one drink too many, after she and Liz sang *Dancing Queen* badly and proudly, that Ava stepped outside. The chill slapped her cheeks, sobering and sharp.

She tucked her hands into her coat pockets and turned toward home , only to pause.

Across the street, beneath a flickering lamppost, she saw a familiar figure slipping into a narrow side door of an old building. Amelia.

Ava stood there, the music and laughter behind her slipping into the background like a dream fading at sunrise. For a flicker of a second, she wondered if Amelia was meeting Chap. The thought poked at her, sharp and unwelcome, but she batted it away. Blame the gin, blame the hour, blame the way everything felt slightly tilted. She was too tipsy to care, or at least too tired to figure out what caring would even mean.

Chapter 14

Ava woke to the unmistakable sound of cast iron clanging like someone was trying to contact the dead through cookware.

Clang. Bang. Scrape.

She groaned, pulling the quilt over her head. Her skull throbbed like it had its own storm system moving in, and every metallic slam from the kitchen below felt like a hammer to her temples.

The smell of bacon drifted up the stairs, thick, greasy, and cruel. It might as well have been a war crime.

She sat up slowly, and the room tilted just enough to remind her of the gin. Her hair was plastered to one side of her face, her jeans still clung to her from the night before, and her pillow bore the raccoon-eyed stamp of mascara and bad decisions.

Memories surfaced in unhelpful fragments: Liz ordering another round. The warm, syrupy buzz in her limbs. Amelia walking into The Gaff Hook like she owned the place. Alone. At midnight.

Ava winced. Her stomach twisted, not just from the hangover, but from the sharp-edged thought that had haunted her since: *Who was Amelia meeting?*

It hadn't been a casual stroll. That outfit was intentional. That smile too soft for small talk. Ava knew that kind of late-night confidence. It reeked of lipstick and secrets.

Booty call. Had to be.

She groaned again, burying her face in her hands, and then reached blindly for her phone.

No bars. Of course.

She turned it over in her hand and stared at the blank screen, willing it to light up with something. A message from Chap. A missed call. Anything.

Nothing.

She set it down with a sigh and pushed herself out of bed, her bones protesting every movement.

Outside the bedroom window, the large spruce tree caught her eye. The orange buoy swing her grandpa had hung from its thickest limb whipped back and forth, slapping against the bark with rhythmic urgency. The rope stretched tight in the wind, straining like it might snap under the pressure.

The overhead light flickered once. Then again. Then held.

Ava's stomach turned. Something was building outside, sure. But inside too. A weight in her chest she couldn't name yet.

She pulled on a sweatshirt, winced at her own reflection in the mirror, and headed downstairs toward the smell of pork fat.

***

Ava shuffled into the kitchen, blinking against the brightness like a vampire emerging from a crypt. The floor cold under her bare feet. Esther stood at the stove with the kind of focus people usually reserved for dismantling bombs. Each slice of bacon flipped with unspoken fury.

George sat at the kitchen table, hunched over the VHF radio, fiddling with the dials. The usual morning static gave way to NOAA's automated broadcast, clinical in tone, catastrophic in content:

"A storm force wind warning remains in effect for Spruce Cove and surrounding coastal waters. Sustained winds from the southeast at fifty to sixty knots. Wind gusts exceeding eighty knots have been reported in the outer channels. Inner channels remain hazardous, with gusts reaching seventy knots."

Esther turned down the heat without a word. Ava didn't move, her hand still halfway to her coffee mug.

"Seas building rapidly. Fifteen to twenty feet in outer channels, with occasional waves above twenty-five feet. Mariners in small to medium vessels are advised to seek immediate shelter. Do not attempt passage through open water."

"Next advisory at zero-nine hundred hours. Mariners are advised: this system is intensifying."

A gust rattled the windows like an impatient hand. Outside, the orange buoy swing continued to flail against the wind, rope stretching taut, twisting violently on its axis. The branch it hung from creaked under the strain.

George leaned back just enough to glance at Ava. "I wonder if Chap made it back last night."

Her stomach dropped. "He left?"

"Went to Elder Point. Had a quick run scheduled. He was dropping off gear at the lodge, I think. Told me he'd be back before the weather shifted." George turned back to the radio. "But the wind turned early. I haven't talked to him since."

Ava set her mug down with a quiet thud. That pit in her chest was no longer anxiety. It was instinct.

"He's probably anchored somewhere, riding it out," George added. But the reassurance felt thin, like a line stretched too tight.

Esther grabbed her keys and canvas tote from the hook by the door. "I'm hitting the store. Candles, propane, batteries if they've got any left."

George glanced at her. "Good luck. The whole town's already in line."

Esther kissed his cheek. Then she paused at Ava, eyes soft but knowing. "If you're going to worry yourself sick, at least put on shoes."

The door slammed behind her.

Ava stared out the window again. The orange buoy spun wildly now, the storm beginning to show its teeth.

She didn't need another cup of coffee.

She needed answers. Still no phone service.

***

Saturday dragged like a reluctant anchor. Time seemed to stretch, the hours spooled out into taut, uneasy silence punctuated only by wind rattling windows and branches slapping against the side of the house.

Ava never made it out of her sweatshirt. Her headache had vanished somewhere around the third NOAA bulletin, replaced by a sharper ache in her chest that no amount of coffee could dull.

She kept checking her phone out of habit, only to be greeted by the same mocking words at the top: No Service.

Outside, the orange buoy swing was now barely visible through sheets of blowing rain. The wind howled down the street in long, angry gusts that made even the older houses groan.

George stayed glued to the radio. He barely spoke. Just listened. Adjusted dials. Sighed. Only moving to help Esther when she returned from the store.

At one point, a neighbor came by to check on them, water already pooling in the street's low spots, and left with a flashlight and a grim shake of his head. "They say it's the worst one we've had in years," he muttered, like it was something to be proud of.

Ava sat at the kitchen table, staring through the window, watching the yard disappear a little more each hour. Her mind cycled: Chap. Amelia. The storm. Chap again.

Just as the gray outside began bleeding into early dusk, the lights flickered once, twice, and then cut out completely.

The silence that followed was brief but total. The refrigerator's hum died. The clock on the microwave went dark. Even the radio sputtered.

And then, as if summoned by instinct, Esther moved.

"Alright," she said, striking a match. "Let's light her up."

Within minutes, the cabin glowed with a soft golden halo. Candles lined the mantel. A kerosene lantern hissed to life on the kitchen counter. Flashlights were set beside every doorway. There was even a battery-powered radio, already tuned back to NOAA's droning updates. Esther started dishing up the chicken noodle soup that she had prepared.

Ava shook her head. "You're like a pioneer woman with a weather app."

Esther shrugged. "Storms come. Storms go. Doesn't mean we can't eat soup in the meantime."

But Ava couldn't eat. She couldn't sit. She couldn't stop staring at the window, at the barely-visible buoy, thrashing wildly in the dark.

She had to know if Chap was OK.

***

Ava didn't tell them she was leaving.

By the time Esther handed her a steaming bowl of soup, Ava was already pulling on her boots. The kerosene lantern flickered beside the door, casting long, nervous shadows. George opened his mouth to stop her but didn't.

He just handed her the flashlight and a spare set of batteries. The look on his face said more than words could have.

The moment she stepped outside, the wind caught her full in the chest.

It was like being hit with a wall of breath from something enormous and angry. Ava staggered back a half-step, braced herself, then pushed forward, leaning into the gusts like she was climbing a mountain.

The darkness was complete. No streetlamps, no porch lights, only the flashlight beam cutting a jittery tunnel through sheets of rain. The wind ripped at her hood, tugged her hair loose, slapped her cheeks raw. Her jeans soaked through within seconds.

The trail behind the cannery was the only path with any kind of wind break. Trees swayed dangerously, branches groaning and snapping overhead. Every few steps, she had to stop and blink against the spray, the flashlight barely able to hold steady.

Spruce Cove was a ghost town in the storm. No cars, no voices, no dogs barking. Just the scream of wind through alleyways and the occasional metallic clatter of something blowing loose.

By the time she reached the harbor, her thighs burned from fighting the gusts, and her hands had gone numb from clenching the flashlight.

Then she saw it.

The *Malahini.*

It was just barely visible through the veil of rain was Chap's boat, tied up near the end of the dock, the black hull bobbing violently in the storm surge, lines pulled taut like the boat itself was trying to escape.

A single lantern glowed faintly from within the cabin.

Ava caught her breath.

He was there.

Had been.

She gripped the railing and made her way down the slick, shuddering dock, every step a battle between footing and wind. Water splashed up through the slats. One misstep and she'd be in the harbor.

When she reached the boat, the *Malahini* rocked hard to starboard, then settled. Ava grabbed the rail, leaned over.

"Chap?" she shouted.

The wind swallowed her voice whole.

She tried again. Louder.

Nothing.

The lantern inside still burned, casting soft, shifting light across the rain-slicked deck.

Ava hesitated, soaked hair plastered to her face. A part of her, small and irrational and desperate, prayed she wouldn't find Amelia inside. That she wouldn't open the cabin door and see them embraced in some storm-shelter cliché.

She gritted her teeth.

Please, God. Not tonight.

She climbed aboard.

***

The cabin door groaned as Ava forced it open, the wind catching it before she shoved her way inside.

The galley was no more than a metal box with just enough space for a stove, a bench, and some overhead shelves packed tight with gear. The air smelled of salt, damp wool, and diesel. A rusted kettle rested cold on the burner. A single lantern cast a swinging halo of light over everything, including Chap.

He sat hunched on the bench, soaked to the bone, hair plastered to his forehead. A bottle of bourbon rested beside his boots, barely touched.

His eyes found hers immediately.

"You shouldn't be out in this," he said.

"I could say the same to you."

She closed the door behind her. The storm outside became muffled, distant. But not gone.

Chap exhaled, leaned back, and rubbed a hand over his face. "I just got back. Maybe twenty minutes ago."

"Grandpa said you left yesterday."

"I did." He let his head rest against the wall. "Figured I'd be back by supper. I was halfway across the strait coming home when the wind turned. Fast. And hard."

"Why didn't you turn back?"

He looked at her, tired and a little ashamed. "Couldn't. I was already exposed. Turning around would've meant running with the waves on my beam. I'd have rolled. So, I kept going."

He bowed his head. "One more wave and I thought the front window was going to blow out."

Ava's breath caught, and for a moment, the boat might as well have tilted beneath her. The image struck her with nauseating force: Chap, alone, gripping the wheel as the waves crashed over the bow, eyes burning from salt, hands frozen to metal. She hadn't realized how tightly she'd been holding onto the idea that he was *fine*. He was just out of reach, out of signal. But hearing it from him, the reality of it, how close he'd come to disappearing under waves tall enough to erase a man and his boat, hit her square in the chest. Grief brushed up against her, not for something lost, but for what might have been. And in that instant, everything petty evaporated into the storm.

Ava took a shaky breath.

Chap looked at her again, quieter now. "And while I was out there, soaked and battling the storm, all I could think about was you. Wondering if you were okay. Hoping I'd get back to tell you."

She stepped forward slowly, into the narrow galley. Their knees nearly brushed.

"What did you need to say?"

He paused, the tension in his shoulders finally cracking.

"That I care about you," he said. "More than I should, probably. And I didn't want to let another storm, literal or otherwise, stop me from telling you that."

Ava lowered herself onto the edge of the bench next to him. She was soaked, exhausted, unsure. But she was here.

Outside, the wind screamed around the harbor.

Inside, her storm had broken.

She kissed him.

It wasn't tentative or shy. It was soaked-through and wind-burned and hungry. She kissed him like she needed to memorize his mouth before the world could take him again, and he met her with that same wild edge. Gripping her hips, pulling her close with just enough restraint to let her know he was still asking, not taking.

He tasted like bourbon and sea spray. His hands were cold and calloused, trembling slightly against the wet fabric of her shirt. When they finally pulled apart, both of them breathless and flushed, Ava was shaking. But not from the storm anymore.

The candle on the small galley shelf flickered against the metal wall, casting uneven shadows across Chap's face. His cheeks were pink from wind and heat. His eyes wide, glassy, waiting.

She looked at him, voice low. "Not tonight. Not like this."

Chap's breath caught, then released. "Okay."

He reached for a wool blanket folded near the bunk, thick, scratchy, and familiar. He opened it in one smooth motion. Ava stepped into it, into him, and they settled onto the narrow bench, tangled and silent.

Outside, the wind pummeled the hull, relentless and furious. Bells clanged from a nearby buoy, dull and dissonant against the roar. Rain slapped the cabin roof like thrown gravel. The *Malahini* creaked with each gust, straining at her moorings.

But inside, wrapped in scratchy wool, the smell of diesel, and the not-unwelcome weight of Chap's arm around her waist, Ava felt something she hadn't expected to find tonight: comfort. Or at least the closest thing to it when you're soaked and curled up with a man who almost died but still smells better than most of your exes.

*****

The storm had passed in the night, leaving behind a harbor that looked freshly wrung out. Lines of seaweed clung to the docks, the wet planks flashing in the sun like someone had emptied their pockets of spare change. The seagulls were back, screeching, arrogant, alive.

Ava walked slowly, tugging her coat tighter against the brisk air, her boots thudding softly on the damp planks. The dock smelled of diesel, brine, and bait. The usual morning mix, but today it made her smile.

She passed a few fishermen already hard at work, coiling lines, checking hulls, shouting across the water. One of them gave her a nod. Another raised an eyebrow. She kept walking.

Her hair was still damp, her jeans creased from sleeping in them, and her face bore the faint puffiness of not enough rest and too much emotion. She probably looked every bit like a woman doing the slowest walk of shame Spruce Cove had ever seen.

But she didn't care.

She felt lighter today. Warmer. Like something inside her finally clicked into place after being off-kilter for too long.

As she reached the end of the dock and stepped back onto dry land, she turned once, just briefly, and looked out at the *Malahini*. The boat bobbed gently, sun glinting off its hull. Chap was somewhere inside, probably still asleep beneath that wool blanket, the scent of salt and bourbon still lingering in the galley.

Ava smiled.

Then, she turned toward home.

Chapter 15

The morning air was crisp and damp, laced with the scent of cedar and last night's storm.

Ava stepped carefully around a puddle by the porch steps, her boots squeaking faintly, still holding a grudge from yesterday's slog to Chap's boat. The sunrise peeked through thick clouds, painting the treetops gold, but her stomach churned with something decidedly less poetic.

She turned the corner and nearly collided with Grandpa George, who was bent over picking up wind-tossed branches near the front walkway.

"Whoa. Sorry," she blurted, pulling her hoodie up like it could shield her from embarrassment.

George straightened slowly, brushing off his hands on the thighs of his work pants.

"Chap alright?" he asked, not looking at her just yet.

Ava nodded. "He had a close call. But yeah, he'll be fine."

George gave a soft grunt. "That boy's got more grit than sense." Then, with a sideways glance, he added, "You're up early. Or late. Depends on how you clock it."

"Yeah. Turns out sleep and I are on a break."

She folded her arms, eyes on the gravel. "I'll try not to wake anyone."

"You won't," George said. "But even if you tried, those floorboards of ours have opinions."

He gave her a wry look. "You are quiet, for a McCormick."

Ava let out a breath of a laugh. "Guess subtlety skipped a generation."

George bent to pick up another branch. "Maybe. Or maybe you just save it for when it counts."

George bent to toss another branch onto the pile then looked at her dead in the eyes. "You alright?"

That question, so simple and unscripted, hit harder than any lecture could have.

"I think so," she said after a beat. "Maybe. I don't know."

He nodded, like he understood. "Storm passed. Sky's clearing."

"I don't think we're talking about the weather."

"No," he said. "We're not."

They stood there for a long moment, the silence between them steady and kind.

George pointed to the side of the house. "Your grandma's inside. Been worrying about you. She made coffee. She's less subtle than I am."

Ava groaned. "Should I be scared?"

"Nah. Just be honest. Esther doesn't expect perfection."

Ava nodded, adjusted her hoodie, and started toward the front door. "Thanks, Grandpa."

"Anytime," he said, bending back down. "And next time, check back in."

***

Ava tripped over the *Wipe Your Paws* mat on her way in, catching herself with an awkward shuffle that did nothing for her dignity. Inside, the house wrapped around her with its usual warmth, though the welcome stopped there. Esther stood at the stove in her flannel robe, flipping something in the cast-iron skillet with just enough force to make her point, her eyes cool as they flicked toward Ava.

"Morning," Ava said carefully.

Esther didn't turn. "Didn't realize we had a guest for breakfast."

Ava crossed the kitchen and poured herself a glass of water. Pretending not to notice the tension crackling like static.

"We don't," she said, trying for lightness.

Esther finally glanced over, eyes narrowing just slightly. "Hmm."

One syllable. Three layers of disapproval, curiosity, and concern.

Ava sipped her water. "I'm going to shower."

"Take your time," Esther said. "But not too much."

That, Ava knew, was code for *we'll talk later.*

She escaped down the hallway, heart pounding harder now than it had the night before, knowing full well that the storm outside had passed. The one inside was just warming up.

***

Ava emerged from the bathroom with steam still clinging to her skin, her wet hair twisted into a towel, and emotional vulnerability wrapped tightly around her pride. She could hear the soft clink of dishes and the rhythmic ticking of the kitchen clock as she padded barefoot down the hall.

Esther sat at the table with two mugs of coffee. One was clearly hers, white ceramic with *Alaska Girls Don't Cry* written in faded red. The other, mismatched and floral, was Ava's by default.

She took the offered seat without a word.

Esther didn't speak right away. She took a slow sip, eyes on Ava, not unkind, but unreadable.

"Sleep well?" she finally asked.

"Not really," Ava said, her voice small.

Esther nodded. "It's not my place to tell you how to live your life, Ava. You're grown. Smart. But grown doesn't always mean grounded."

Ava blinked. "Okay."

"I'm not mad," Esther added, setting her mug down. "But I am watching. Because I get the feeling you are getting swept up in something when the dust from your other life hasn't even settled."

Ava didn't respond right away. She stared into her coffee, tracing the rim with one finger.

"It wasn't a plan," she said eventually. "It just happened. And it feels good. Real."

Esther leaned back in her chair, folding her arms. "That's the thing about 'just happening,' sweetheart. Feels easy in the moment. Messy the morning after."

"I'm not ashamed," Ava said, but even she could hear the defensive edge.

"I didn't say you should be," Esther replied. "I'm saying don't confuse tenderness for truth. Or chemistry for commitment. Especially when you're still figuring out where you belong."

Ava exhaled, letting the words sink in.

"I don't know what I'm doing," she admitted. "One second I'm sure, and the next, I'm staring at my ceiling wondering if I'm just hiding here."

Esther's gaze softened. "You're not hiding. You're healing. But healing's not a reason to build something new before the foundation's dry."

Silence stretched between them, not uncomfortable but dense with unspoken memories. Esther's, Ava's, the echoes of her mother's.

"Are you in love with him?" Esther asked gently.

Ava's throat tightened. "I don't know. Maybe."

Esther gave her a long look, then stood, collecting the empty mugs. "Then take your time. Real love's not in a rush."

As she turned toward the sink, she added over her shoulder, "And next time you sneak in after a night out, try not to trip over the welcome mat. That thing's been loose since '98."

Ava cracked a smile, the first real one all morning.

***

The bell above the newspaper office door jangled as Ava stepped inside, the sound too cheerful for how heavy her heart felt.

No Liz. Just the hum of old equipment and the faint smell of ink and mildew. A half-eaten donut sat fossilizing on a napkin by the copier. The clock on the wall ticked like a metronome keeping time with her uncertainty.

She dropped her bag by her desk and slumped into the chair, staring at the screen.

Yesterday, she was floating, storm-kissed, desire-drunk, wrapped in Chap's flannel sheets. Half-convinced she could belong here. But this morning? She realized she was a Yale graduate scanning obituaries for typos in a one-room office where the ceiling tiles sagged.

She opened her latest article draft *'Retired Fisherman Turns Old Crab Pots into Lawn Art'* and read the first paragraph three times before admitting it was awful.

She deleted it. Rewrote the opening. Deleted that too.

Her fingers hovered over the keys, then dropped into her lap.

Was this really it? Small-town puff pieces and quirky parade write-ups?

She'd graduated with honors. Published in literary journals. Professor Campbell once told her she had a voice like a scalpel. Sharp, deliberate, impossible to ignore. And now? She was chasing pie contest quotes and trying not to get hives from a damp office chair.

Ava spun slowly in her chair, staring at the ceiling.

She could've gone to New York after she left William. Sharing a postage-stamp apartment with two strangers and submitting essays to magazines that didn't pay. Scrolling LinkedIn for unpaid internships at publishing houses. Chasing coffee for editors and trying not to lose herself in a sea of voices louder and slicker than her own.

She could've been fighting for something bigger.

Instead, she was here. Writing headlines like *"Soggy Summer Doesn't Dampen Fireweed Fun."*

She exhaled, sharp and bitter. "Grandma is right. I don't know what I'm doing."

A printout fluttered to the floor from Liz's desk. Last week's editorial layout. Ava picked it up and stared at her own byline. The words felt flimsy.

The blinking cursor mocked her. She closed the article file and opened a browser tab.

Jobs in publishing. New York. Entry level.

Her fingers hovered over the keyboard like she expected someone to stop her.

The results loaded quickly: editorial assistant, assistant to the editor-in-chief, junior acquisitions associate. Most required two years of experience she didn't have and offered salaries that barely covered rent for a closet in Manhattan.

Still, she clicked on one.

Publisher seeks editorial assistant with a sharp editorial eye, impeccable grammar, and strong multitasking skills. Experience in publishing preferred but not required.

Preferred. Not required. She clung to the loophole.

Her eyes scanned the bullet points. *Proofread galleys. Schedule author meetings. Assist with developmental edits. Answer phones with discretion.*

The words sparked something familiar. Exciting, terrifying, alive.

She opened another tab. Searched *average rent NYC studio.* Winced.

$3,200.

She opened a new search: *Remote publishing jobs.* The results were bleak.

Scrolling down, she saw a listing for a "Junior Lifestyle Content Creator" at a digital media company in Brooklyn. The job description made her want to throw up: *"We're looking for someone who can be a little bit Carrie, a little bit Oprah, and a whole lot of 'girl next door.' Must love spreadsheets, memes, and working late."*

Ava closed the tab and stared at her reflection in the blank screen.

"I could do it," she said aloud, but her voice didn't sound convinced.

Could she walk away from this town, from her grandparents, from Chap?

Would she get stuck in Spruce Cove?

Was she putting off launching her career because she afraid of failing in the world she thought she wanted?

She reached for her notebook and scrawled a single line: *Yale didn't prepare me for a town where everyone already thinks they know who you are.*

She didn't even know if she believed it.

She dropped her pen. Rubbed her temples.

Maybe she wasn't hiding. Maybe she was waiting.

Or maybe she was afraid.

***

Ava shut the newspaper office door behind her with a click and stepped into the late morning light. The breeze had picked up, carrying the scent of fish, salt, and rain still waiting its turn.

She didn't want to go home. Not yet.

She wandered toward the docks, drawn by the low hum of conversation and the creak of boats rocking gently in their slips. Familiar voices called back and forth about engine trouble, deliveries, and coffee refills.

She paused near the harbormaster's shack. The place looked like it had been patched together from old fishing crates, reclaimed wood, and optimism. Inside, the radio crackled softly with country music from another decade.

Tommy Wallis sat outside in his folding chair, a thermos at his feet and a yellow rain slicker draped over his lap like a blanket. His white beard fanned out like seafoam, and his face was a topography of wind, time, and sun.

He looked up and smiled like he'd been expecting her.

"Well, if it isn't Ava McCormick," he said. "Heard you were back. You writing stories or causing trouble?"

"Little of both," she said, folding her arms and stepping closer. "Depends who you ask."

He chuckled. "That's the spirit."

She hesitated. "You been doing this long?"

"Forty-six years," he said without blinking. "Took over from my uncle. Didn't plan on staying, but then again, life don't always ask."

"And you still like it?"

"Still love it," he said simply. "Some people chase big things. I just want to know every boat that comes and goes. I like being the person people come to when they've got a broken rudder or need a cup of strong coffee."

Ava nodded, throat tight. "And the rest? Your life?"

Tommy smiled, softer now. "Met my wife at the Fireweed Festival when I was twenty-three. She sold blueberry scones that changed my religion. Was with her ever since. Two kids. Four grandkids. Lost her last fall."

Ava's stomach clenched. "I'm sorry."

"Don't be. I got fifty good years with her. And when I'm out there on the docks, I still hear her voice every time I screw up the coffee. You do something long enough, love someone long enough and it becomes part of you."

Ava didn't know what to say. The weight of his life, the clarity, the contentment, pressed against her like a mirror.

"You ever think about leaving?" she asked.

"Sure. Thought about it. But I was always already where I belonged."

A gull shrieked overhead. The smell of fish oil drifted in.

Tommy looked at her for a long moment. "You still figuring it out?"

"Every second," she said.

He nodded like that was answer enough. "Good. Keep asking. That's the only way you'll know when the answer finally fits."

Ava headed home. Later, she settled on the porch with a cup of coffee. The porch boards creaked as Ava sunk into the old Adirondack chair, coffee mug cradled between her palms.

Beyond the railing, the harbor shimmered under late-morning sun, deceptively peaceful. An eagle cried out and dive-bombed a crab pot bobbing in the tide. The town felt too quiet. Too still.

She heard a shift of air before Chap appeared, holding a familiar brown paper bag in one hand and a cautious smile in the other.

"I figured muffins might be a reasonable entry point."

Ava didn't smile, but she didn't send him away either. "Do I look like I need muffins?"

"You look like someone who's thinking too much. Muffins help."

He handed her the bag and sat on the top step, his back to the water. He smelled like cedar, salt, and dish soap. Like he'd scrubbed his way into the morning just to feel clean.

Ava peeled the top off one of the muffins and popped a piece into her mouth. It tasted like cinnamon and nostalgia.

They sat in silence for a long beat. Chap picked at the fraying cuff of his hoodie.

"I saw the light on at the office," he said. "You working today?"

"Trying." She sipped her coffee. "More like staring and spiraling."

Chap glanced up. "Spiraling about what?"

Ava hesitated. Then, "This place. This life. Me. Everything."

He nodded, like he understood. "You thinking about leaving?"

"I don't know." She stared out at the waves. "Some days I want to get on a plane and go build a life where no one knows me. Where I'm not someone's granddaughter or the girl who wrote the Salmonberry Queen monstrosity."

"And other days?"

"Other days I think maybe I'm supposed to be here. Like there's something I'm meant to find. But then I remember, I went to Yale. I was supposed to be someone. I was supposed to make it."

Chap's brows furrowed. "You think this isn't 'making it'?"

"I think this might be a detour," she said. "Or maybe I'm afraid this is the destination."

Silence again, heavier this time. The kind that pressed on your chest like a slow tide.

"I'm not trying to be part of your detour," Chap said quietly.

Ava blinked. "You're not."

"I don't want to be the reason you stay here if your soul wants to be somewhere else."

She looked at him then, really looked. His hair was wind-tossed, his green eyes impossibly steady. A man who lived on water but craved solid ground.

"I don't know what my soul wants," she admitted. "That's the problem."

Chap stood, brushing his palms on his jeans. "Then figure it out. Take your time. Just don't lie to yourself about it."

He reached into the paper bag and pulled out a book, gently setting it on the armrest beside her.

"For when the noise gets too loud."

She picked it up. Margaret Atwood, *The Penelopiad*. Inside the front cover, a note:

"Sometimes strength looks like waiting until it feels right." – C

By the time she looked up, he was already halfway down the path.

***

At the end of the day, the house was quiet and Ava let the peace settle into her skin. Grandpa was reading in his recliner, and Esther had long since retired to bed with a mug of chamomile and her nightly ritual of muttering about the news.

Ava sat cross-legged on her bed, the fleece blanket pulled up to her waist, her journal open in her lap. The desk lamp cast a soft, amber cone across the page, making the shadows stretch long and sharp across her legs.

She clicked her pen twice. Then again.

Then she started writing.

Dear Girl I Used to Be,

Ava paused and glanced around her mom's childhood bedroom. The faded poster of Bon Jovi still hung crooked on the wall, the corners curling. Her old bookshelf sagged with used paperbacks and forgotten high school journals. She looked out the window to where the moonlight glinted off the harbor.

She continued writing, slower now, each word a thread pulling tight:

show up in fits and fragments, interrupted by bear sightings and festival pies and small-town expectations.

And still, they show up.

Just like you do.

Every day, even when it's hard. Even when you're unsure.

You're still here.

Maybe that's the bravest thing of all.

She signed her name. Not Ava the daughter, or Ava the ex-fiancée, or Ava the maybe-girlfriend. Just Ava.

She tore the page from her journal carefully, folded it once, and stepped to the mason jar on her windowsill.

The match caught quickly. The flame devoured her letter in sharp little bites.

When it was done, she pushed open the window. The breeze that came in smelled like salt, woodsmoke, and the barest hint of rain on its way.

She leaned her elbows on the sill, the cold air cutting through her like a warning.

She didn't have all the answers, not even close.

And the worst part?

She wasn't sure how much longer she could pretend that she ever would.

Chapter 16

New Haven snow blanketed the street in silence, the kind that made everything feel suspended. Like the world was holding its breath. Ava stirred the sauce again even though it didn't need it. The smell of thyme and garlic filled William's apartment. She wasn't hungry. She was performing.

The door opened with a squeak and a muttered curse as William stumbled in, juggling his messenger bag and an armload of textbooks.

"Hey," he said, blowing warm air into his hands. "Smells incredible in here."

She turned and smiled, reflexive. "Made the polenta thing."

He dropped his books with a grunt, kicking off his boots. "God, I needed this day to end. That clinical simulation was brutal. Pretty sure I misdiagnosed a virtual corpse with lupus and gave it the wrong drug protocol."

Ava laughed politely, then poured wine into two mismatched glasses. "It's not lupus. That's the rule, right?"

"You've been watching *House* again," he teased, kissing the top of her head before collapsing into a chair.

She set a steaming bowl in front of him, already knowing he wouldn't notice the way she'd plated it, the way she'd tried to impress him.

"You didn't have to cook," he said between bites. "You should be writing."

"I wrote earlier," she said. Another half-truth. She'd stared at her laptop for an hour before deleting three paragraphs of an essay about fear. Too raw, too revealing.

"Did you send anything out?"

"No," she lied again, swallowing down the rejection that had landed in her inbox that afternoon. *Not a fit for our tone. Lacked focus.*

William glanced at her, chewing slower. "You okay?"

"Of course," she said. "I'm just tired."

But she wasn't tired. She was hollow. And the worst part? She didn't know if he'd notice the difference.

After dinner, he moved to the couch and cracked open his neuroanatomy notes. "I need to memorize the cranial nerves before I dream about them. Want to quiz me?"

She nodded, even as her chest tightened. "Sure."

They went through flashcards for twenty minutes until he dozed off mid-sentence, a highlighter still clutched in his hand.

Ava stood in the doorway and watched him sleep.

She loved him. He was good, brilliant, kind.

But she had never shown him the version of herself that woke at 3 a.m. with story fragments. That hated structure. That questioned everything.

He'd fallen for the version of her that knew the cranial nerves too. The version that cooked, supported him and kept her doubts silent.

She stepped into the bathroom, turned on the light, and stared at her reflection. Still polished, still quiet, still shrinking.

"Who am I trying to be?" she whispered.

The silence that answered her was the most honest part of the night.

***

The attic nook in her grandparent's cabin had always felt a little apart from the rest of the house, like a ship's crow's nest. Tonight, it felt like the only place where Ava could breathe.

She pulled the knit blanket tighter and opened her journal to a blank page, the spine cracking quietly like it was exhaling with her.

She stared at the page for a long time. The ink in her pen hovered.

"I told myself he didn't really know me. But the truth is, I never let him."

The words came fast after that, urgent, like her soul had been waiting for this moment.

I edited myself for him. I became the "supportive girlfriend," the quiet genius who always had dinner on the table, who listened to every residency story like it was sacred scripture. I made my world small so his could be big.

And he never asked me to. That's the worst part. He never demanded anything I wasn't already offering on a silver platter of insecurity and performative maturity.

I thought loving someone meant being easy to love. Not difficult. Not chaotic. Not full of unfinished things.

She stopped writing. Her hand was trembling slightly.

I let him love the version of me that I chose to curate. Safe. The version that didn't tell him when I cried in the bathroom after reading my own story, feeling like it wasn't good enough. The version that didn't admit I hated cooking, that I only did it because it gave me a job when he had a calling.

She blinked hard. Her vision blurred but didn't fall into tears.

Maybe I wasn't afraid of him seeing me. Maybe I was afraid that if he saw the real me, the girl who doubted everything and wanted to chase poems instead of paychecks, he'd love me less. And I didn't want to test that.

So I stayed lovely. Pliable. Easy.

She swallowed against the weight of her throat.

But the thing is, I wasn't easy. I was just quiet.

She thought about the notecard from Liz taped to her work laptop: *Your voice matters.*

Ava wrote slower now, more deliberate.

He was good to me. He believed I could do anything. He loved the version of me I offered him. The one who never made waves. And I don't know if he would've loved the version who did.

The version who questions everything. Who doesn't know where she's going. Who loves too deeply, feels too much, and sometimes writes things that terrify her.

She set down the pen, her heart thudding in her ears.

She whispered, to the window, to the night, to the girl she used to be:

"I wasn't a victim. I was weak."

The words didn't echo. They landed.

They stayed.

***

She closed the journal gently, like it might bite if she slammed it shut. Outside, the wind rattled a loose shutter and inside her chest, something else stirred. A memory, inconvenient and warm.

And there it was: William. Not in the final days, when everything was unraveling, but in the beginning. Before either of them knew how much they didn't know.

Yale, late September. They were still new then, still asking each other things like "What's your favorite smell?" and "Were you weird in high school?"

She'd invited him to a student reading, her first time sharing a piece out loud. It was raw, overly metaphorical, and about her mom. She'd mumbled her way through it and left the room before the polite applause even ended.

She expected him to follow, and he did. Carrying two lattes from the vending cart and wearing that "I have no idea what to say but I'm here" look.

"I sounded ridiculous," she said, arms crossed over her chest as they walked toward the library steps. "Like a 17-year-old girl who just discovered grief and metaphors."

"You are a 17-year-old girl who just discovered grief and metaphors," he said, gently.

She stopped walking.

He handed her the latte. "I mean that in the best way. You said something real. I saw three people cry."

"They were probably just regretting their life choices."

William smiled. "Or maybe they were remembering their own mothers. Or maybe they'd never heard someone be that honest in a room full of strangers."

She stared at him, unsure how to argue with that.

He shrugged. "I don't know. All I know is you made the room go quiet. That's not nothing."

It was the first time she felt the door crack open. The moment that led to letting someone all the way in. And it wasn't because he flattered her. It was because he *saw* her. Even the messy parts. Maybe especially those.

Ava looked down at her hands.

Maybe the truth was simple: William had seen her.

She just didn't believe she deserved to keep it.

***

An hour later, Ava was on the porch with the phone pressed to her ear, the wind lifting tendrils of hair from her face. The harbor beyond was dark, scattered with the soft glint of moored boats rocking like memories just beneath the surface.

She hadn't planned to call. She didn't even remember dialing.

But when William answered, his voice was immediate. Unsteady.

"Ava?"

She closed her eyes at the sound of it. Familiar. Hesitant. "Yeah. It's me."

A moment passed, long enough to be a question.

"I thought maybe I'd never hear from you again," he said, quietly.

"I wasn't sure I'd call," she admitted.

"Are you okay?" he asked, suddenly urgent. "Is everything?"

"I'm okay," she said quickly. "I'm not in trouble. I just, I've been thinking."

He exhaled on the other end, a breath that trembled a little. "Me too."

Ava sat down on the top porch step, cradling the phone close. "I've been writing. A lot."

There was a smile in his voice, small but real. "Of course you have."

"I realized something," she said, picking at a splinter on the step. "About us."

William didn't say anything, but she felt him brace for it.

"I wasn't honest with you," she said. "Not because I didn't love you. But because I was afraid you wouldn't love the version of me that didn't fit inside a perfect future."

He let out a breath, ragged now. "Ava."

"I shrank. I made myself smaller and quieter because I thought it made me easier to love. And I thought that was what being a good partner meant. But it wasn't fair, to either of us."

There was a long silence.

Then William said, "You seemed lost. And I didn't know what to do. I thought maybe it was me. Or the pressure. Or the prospect of med school. But I saw the light go out, and I just let it. I didn't fight for us."

Ava's throat tightened.

"I've been beating myself up ever since," he continued. "Because it was the best thing about you. That glow. And I let it go out."

She blinked hard, vision swimming.

"It wasn't all your fault," she said. "I hid from you. I didn't give you a chance to see me."

He laughed softly, but there was no joy in it. "I should've looked harder."

They sat in the silence together, thousands of miles apart, but closer than they had ever been in truth.

"I want you to know," William said finally, "that I never stopped being proud of you. And not because of Yale or writing. Just because you were always trying. You were always fighting to be something honest. Even if you didn't show me everything, I knew you were there."

Tears slid down Ava's cheeks, quiet and clean. She didn't wipe them away.

"Thank you," she whispered.

"I don't know what else to say," he murmured. "Except I hope you find that spark again. It is amazing. And I hope you protect it this time."

"I will," she said. "I'm starting to."

"And Ava?"

"Yeah."

"I know I broke something I can't fix. I'll hate myself for it for a long time, maybe forever," William said, voice cracking. "But don't ever think it was about you. It wasn't. It was me. My weakness. My need for attention I didn't even deserve. You gave me plenty, and I still went looking for more. You deserved better than the half-version of me you got. You still do."

They said goodbye like people who had once loved deeply and might always, in some small, unthreatening way.

When Ava hung up, the wind had calmed.

She sat in the silence for a long time, hands folded in her lap.

***

She stayed on the porch long after the call ended, her phone resting loosely in her palm. The cold had settled in, numbing her fingertips, but she didn't move. Her mind was still buzzing. Not with regret, but with something quieter. Realization. Recognition.

Then her phone buzzed again.

William: You were always magic, Ava. Even when you didn't know it.

She exhaled. The message didn't land like closure. It landed like a question mark. Not a door slammed shut, but one left ajar. A flicker of something unfinished.

A tether.

She didn't want to leave it hanging in the silence, not this time.

Her thumbs moved slowly over the screen.

Ava: I think I forgot how to believe that. Thank you for reminding me.

She pressed send. The moment hung there, brief and bittersweet.

A second buzz followed almost immediately.

235

Chap: Waves are calm tonight. Sky's full of stars. You out there stealing constellations again?

A laugh slipped out before she could stop it. Chap always had a way of slicing through the heavy with something light.

She replied, this time without hesitation.

Ava: Only the bright ones. You know I have standards.

She set the phone down beside her, not quite ready to move. The sky above was clear, scattered with stars. The kind of night that dared you to dream too big and worry too little.

Two men.

Two pieces of her life, both holding on in their own ways.

And her?

Still unraveling. Still becoming.

But no longer hiding.

She looked out across the black water, the boats swaying gently in their slips, and whispered a quiet truth into the night:

"I'm allowed to want more than one story."

The tide was turning.

And this time, she planned to follow it wherever it led.

***

The house had gone still, the kind of deep quiet only an old home could hold. Ava padded downstairs barefoot, the phone cool in her hand, still buzzing faintly with the weight of the words she'd just sent.

She didn't expect anyone to be awake.

But there was light seeping under the kitchen door, warm and soft.

She opened it gently to find Esther standing at the stove, stirring something in a battered pot that smelled like cinnamon and sleep.

"You're up," Ava said, surprised.

Esther didn't look over. "You think I sleep through full moons and granddaughters skulking around?"

Ava smiled, despite herself. "Didn't mean to skulk."

"You meant to stew," Esther said, finally glancing her way. "There's a difference."

Ava slipped into the seat at the table. The wood was warm from the heat of the stove.

Esther scanned her eyes. "Talk."

Ava stared at the mug. "I called William."

Esther raised one brow. "Really? Why?"

Ava nodded. "I needed to, I don't know. Say some things. Hear some things."

Esther settled into the seat across from her, arms crossed but not unkind.

"I used to think he didn't really see me," Ava said, slowly. "But tonight, I realized that I didn't let him. I was scared if he saw who I really was, he wouldn't stay. So, I made myself easier."

Esther didn't speak, just watched.

"I changed," Ava continued, voice softer now. "Not that it excuses what he did, because it doesn't. He still betrayed me. But I think I wasn't exactly honest either. Not with him. Not with myself."

She looked up. "Have you ever done that? Hidden pieces of yourself to fit what someone else needed?"

Esther snorted. "Once. He was six-feet-two with forearms like a Norse god and the emotional depth of a dish sponge."

Ava laughed.

"You can love someone and still outgrow who you were when you met them," Esther said. "That doesn't make it a failure. It makes it a chapter."

Ava stirred the milk. "I texted him. I texted Chap, too."

Esther gave her a long, dry look. "Careful, Ava. Juggling men doesn't usually end with a standing ovation."

"I'm not trying to play anyone," Ava said. "I'm just still figuring out who I am."

"That's fine," Esther said. "Just don't let a man to hand you the answer."

Ava nodded.

Esther handed her a mug of warmed milk that tasted like nutmeg and safety.

They sat there awhile longer in the warm quiet, two women separated by decades and heartaches, but closer than Ava had ever realized.

***

Ava couldn't sleep, so she did the thing people always say you shouldn't do in thrillers or small-town gossip columns: she went walking alone in the middle of the night.

Down the hill toward the harbor, where the boats bobbed like sleepy dogs and the scent of salt and old rope hung in the air like a lullaby that didn't quite work.

Spruce Cove was still. Even the seagulls were off-duty.

Except for one light. Steady, faint, a little halo glowing on the deck of the *Malahini*.

Chap.

He was out there in his headlamp, crouched near the stern, elbow-deep in something with too many gears. The sleeves of his hoodie were shoved up, and he moved like someone who didn't just *know* what he was doing. He loved it.

She stayed just beyond the light's reach, watching.

The wooden planks under her boots creaked slightly as she adjusted her stance, but Chap didn't look up. He was humming under his breath; some old sea shanty Ava couldn't place. Something his grandfather probably taught him. It made her chest ache in a way that had nothing to do with nostalgia and everything to do with envy.

She slipped her hands deeper into her jacket pockets and leaned against a piling. The cold bit at her ankles.

He looked content out there. Not happy in a fireworks way, but peaceful. Anchored. Like the rest of the world could tip sideways and he'd still know how to right the boat.

And Ava, God she was tired of tipping.

She watched as he pulled a rag from his back pocket and wiped his hands clean, then reached for something in a tool box. His movements were sure, practiced. A man doing what he was meant to do, in the place that raised him.

And that's what undid her.

Because she couldn't remember the last time she'd felt that kind of certainty. Not about people. Not about places. Not about herself.

She thought of William's message. Of Chap's earlier text. Of Esther's calm but cutting wisdom.

She wasn't a girl stuck between two men.

She was a woman stuck between the person she'd been and the one she was trying to become.

And standing here, watching someone so entirely himself. It made her question if she'd ever known what that even felt like.

This wasn't a love story. Not yet.

It was a story about choices.

About standing still in the dark, trying to decide if you were the kind of woman who stayed in the shadows or stepped into the light.

Ava didn't move.

But for the first time in a long time, she wanted to.

Chapter 17

Ava snapped a photo of the salmonberry pie cooling on the windowsill, the lattice crust catching the afternoon light just right. Her grandmother's pie dish, chipped on one side and beloved for it, anchored the image in cozy imperfection. She angled the shot, added a cheeky caption ("Bet you've never seen one this photogenic"), and sent it to Chap.

She waited for the little "Delivered" bubble to blink to "Read." It didn't.

She checked again while rinsing the measuring spoons. Still nothing.

"Stalking your texts doesn't make him answer faster," Liz said from the kitchen doorway, coffee mug in one hand, judgment in the other.

Ava didn't flinch. "It's just a pie pic. Not a marriage proposal."

"Mmhmm," Liz said, leaning on the counter. "Except your eye twitched when the 'Read' never came."

Ava tossed a dishrag at her. "He's probably out on the boat. No signal."

"Or busy avoiding feelings," Liz said brightly, sipping her coffee. "Classic male strategy."

Ava turned back to her phone. Still no response. Still unread. The little bubble stared back like it knew something she didn't.

She told herself not to spiral. He'd text soon. It was fine. Probably.

Still, the silence settled on her shoulders like wet wool. Heavy, clinging, and hard to shake.

***

Ava pulled into the grocery store parking lot, already rehearsing her grocery list in her head: coffee, something chocolate, anything to keep her from refreshing her messages like a woman waiting on a verdict. The breeze drifting through her cracked window smelled like salt and rain, and the sky had that off-white Alaska glow that made it impossible to tell what time it was.

She was halfway through a mental debate between cold brew and espresso beans when she spotted him.

Chap.

Right there, near the entrance to the general store, standing in the sun like he hadn't ghosted her for two straight days. His sleeves were rolled up, revealing forearms that were sturdy, sun-browned, and annoyingly capable as he hoisted two brown paper grocery bags in one arm. And next to him?

Amelia.

Ava's brain short-circuited for a second, like someone had cut the audio. The only thing she could hear was the scratch of her own breathing and the traitorous little pop of her heart breaking open.

Amelia handed Chap another bag, said something and laughed. Chap laughed too. He was relaxed, warm, the way he sounded on their front steps, telling her stories about seagulls stealing bait. The kind of laugh that had once felt like an invitation.

Amelia reached out and smoothed something off his shoulder. Maybe it was lint, maybe a memory. To Ava it felt like a punch.

She didn't know how long she sat there, frozen behind her steering wheel, one hand hovering above the gearshift. Long enough for doubt to settle in her chest like smoke.

Chap wasn't texting her back. Hadn't read her message. She told herself he was out fishing. And now he was here. On land. Not on the water. Not unreachable or busy.

Just here. With Amelia.

She waited until they left before slipping into the store, keeping her gaze glued to the shelves. Eye contact meant conversation and conversation meant talking, which sounded impossible when she was busy trying not to come apart in the bread aisle.

By the time she eased her car out of the parking lot, it was slow and deliberate, like leaving the scene of a crime where the only casualty was her own dumb hope. Her hands trembled on the wheel, her throat tight around something jagged and unsayable.

She'd wanted to believe she was different. That what they had was new, and real, and not just Chap working through whatever Amelia had left behind. He was supposed to be waiting on her, for her to figure out what *she* wanted. Not fumbling around, confused about what *he* wanted. But maybe she'd been fooling herself. Maybe she was just the rebound who caught him mid-fall. Maybe Amelia had never stopped being The One.

She blinked hard against the pressure behind her eyes, the tears she would absolutely not let fall over a man who still hadn't answered a text.

It wasn't heartbreak. Not yet.

But it had that familiar sting. The dry run. The dress rehearsal for disappointment.

***

Back at her grandparents' house, Ava dropped the grocery bag on the counter with a thunk. A chocolate bar skidded out and slammed against the backsplash like it was trying to escape the emotional fallout.

Esther looked up from peeling carrots, one eyebrow already arched. "What'd that bag ever do to you?"

Ava forced a smile. "Sorry. Just clumsy."

Esther smirked. "Well, if you're gonna throw things, aim for the dishes with cracks. Makes for better drama."

She retreated to her bedroom before any more questions could follow her. Once the door was shut, she collapsed onto the bed, shoes still on, and yanked her phone from her pocket like it might suddenly offer absolution.

Still nothing from Chap.

Still unread.

Still silent.

She unlocked it anyway, muscle memory at this point, and was greeted not by a message.

William: Remember that time in Portland when you said you could "totally" handle a tandem bike?

Attached was a photo of a bicycle pizza cutter shaped like a tandem bike, parked on top of a deep-dish.

Ava exhaled something between a laugh and a sigh.

She typed back: I was more aerodynamic when I was full of post-grad optimism and avocado toast.

He replied immediately. You were aerodynamic. I was steering us into every trash can in the city.

She smiled, genuinely. It wasn't like the adrenaline spikes she'd felt with Chap, those nervous butterflies that fluttered too high and too often. This was lower. Softer. A warmth in the chest, not the stomach.

It was terrifying how comforting it was.

Because it wasn't just the memory; it was the ease. The way William knew how to make her laugh without trying too hard. The shorthand they had from years of inside jokes and mutual disasters. It was the kind of comfort that had once felt like home.

And wasn't that what she'd wanted this whole time?

To feel like she belonged to someone who understood her without footnotes?

She tossed the phone to the side, like it might burn her if she thought about that question too long. This wasn't about William. Or Chap. Or Amelia. Or any of it.

This was about her being so used to disappointment that she'd started to read betrayal into silence. Or worse, she was getting used to the idea that silence *was* betrayal.

She stared at the ceiling. The drywall had a tiny crack above the closet, shaped like a question mark.

Fitting.

***

By midday, Liz had declared it was time for what she called "saltwater therapy." A completely unlicensed, questionably safe mental health intervention that involved an aluminum skiff, two scones, and enough caffeine to stun a bear.

"You, me, carbs, and combustion," Liz said, tossing a life vest at Ava and gesturing toward the small skiff tied to the dock. "We're shaking the crazy loose."

"I'm not crazy," Ava mumbled, stepping into the boat with practiced caution.

"Sweetheart, you're emotionally speed-dating your past and present. Let's get you out of the fishbowl before you crack the glass."

Liz fired up the 25-horsepower outboard with a sputtering roar and steered them away from the dock. Dolly Parton's voice poured from a waterproof speaker clipped to the center seat, harmonizing with the motor's low growl as they cut across the water toward a quiet cove.

Ava sat in the bow, hair whipping in the wind, the ocean spraying salt across her cheeks. Behind them, Spruce Cove receded into postcard distance. Quaint, quiet, and entirely too observant.

They landed on a pebbled beach. Liz anchored the skiff in the shallows and jumped out barefoot.

"This cove's got good karma," Liz said, digging through a pile of driftwood. "I found my first glass float here. And a perfectly intact bottle of peach schnapps in high school."

Ava followed her lead, stepping carefully among barnacle-clad rocks. They beachcombed in companionable silence until Liz triumphantly held up a chunk of beach glass.

"Look at this. Probably started as a beer bottle. Got smashed, tossed, rolled around, and now it's sea glass. Still sharp, but pretty."

Ava smirked. "Sounds like a dating metaphor."

"Please. It's your autobiography."

Ava laughed, finally relaxing. She picked up a deflated fishing float tangled in seaweed and held it aloft.

"Ah," Liz said. "Ava's romantic life. Still floating. Still a mess."

They stood side by side, watching the tide creep in. The wind tugged at their jackets, and the ocean stretched endlessly ahead.

"You don't have to pick anyone yet," Liz said, voice softer now. "You just have to pick yourself. You remember her, right?"

Ava nodded, gripping the float tighter.

She did. She was starting to.

As they docked the skiff back at the harbor, Liz tossed Ava a towel and a look. "Feel better?"

Ava shrugged, water still drying in her hair. "I feel less insane."

"Good. Now go be productive before I have to stage another intervention."

***

Back on land, Ava felt the heaviness creep back in. Like the momentary freedom out on the water had been borrowed time. Her phone buzzed with a reminder.

Liz: Don't forget the basketball fundraiser. Ellery will flirt, but endure it for the kids.

She groaned and texted back: Do I get hazard pay for charm-induced nausea?

Liz responded with a thumbs-up emoji and a crab.

By the time Ava reached the high school gym, her jacket still carried the scent of saltwater and cedar. The emotional clarity from the cove had already started to dissolve and something about the gym's fluorescent brightness made her feel like she was walking into a test she hadn't studied for.

The gym echoed with the sharp squeak of sneakers and the rhythmic thump of a basketball. Ava stepped inside and paused near the bleachers, her tote bag slung over one shoulder, the scent of floor polish and gym sweat wrapping around her like static.

On the court, the boys' basketball team was mid-scrimmage, darting up and down in practiced chaos. Coach Ellery stalked the sideline, barking orders with a military sharpness softened by charisma. He looked like a man who still believed he was one bad injury away from a college call-back. Polo fitted, clipboard gripped like gospel.

Ava scanned the court, pretending to focus on the flow of the game, but really watching him.

He clapped once, sharply. "Move your feet! Defense isn't decorative, gentlemen!"

The players adjusted instantly, like they were wired to him.

Behind Ava, the side doors creaked open and a group of volleyball players stepped inside, laughing and clustered around a phone. They wore matching long-sleeve warm-ups over short spandex shorts, their legs bare and flushed from practice.

Coach Ellery glanced over mid-play and called out, "Watch your step, ladies. Don't want you slipping and claiming I distracted you."

The girls erupted into giggles.

"You wish, Coach," one of them teased, flipping her ponytail as she crossed behind the bench. Another flashed him a grin like she was daring him to flirt back.

He chuckled and returned to the game as if nothing had happened.

Ava's brows knit together.

Nothing technically wrong. No boundary breached. But the energy? Off. Like he'd blurred the line so gradually no one noticed it had moved.

When the scrimmage ended, Ellery jogged over, clipboard tucked under one arm. "Miss McCormick," he said smoothly. "You here for the paper? You know I photograph best from the left."

She gave him a half-smile. "Just here for a quote. Writing about the booster club fundraiser. Liz said you'd have something brilliant to say."

"Always happy to supply ink-worthy content." He handed over a glossy sheet, fingers grazing hers for half a second longer than necessary.

"Thanks," she said, folding the paper into her tote.

"You ever want to do a deeper piece on the team, let me know," he added. "We've got stories. Blood, sweat, teenage angst, the works."

"I'll think about it."

As he turned back to his clipboard, Ava made her way toward the doors, her steps slower than usual. She wasn't sure what she'd just witnessed. Harmless banter or something too familiar. Whatever it was, it sat crooked in her gut.

She paused at the threshold and glanced back. He was already shouting another play, completely in control.

Probably just a good coach.

Still, she didn't breathe easy until the gym doors swung shut behind her.

***

By the time Ava pulled into the driveway, the gym already felt a world away. Whatever weird vibe Coach Ellery gave off, it was probably just charm turned up too high. Or maybe she was just tired. Everything felt louder than usual these days.

Inside, the house was warm and dim, full of the small sounds that said everything was fine. Esther was in her recliner, a half-empty mug on the side table, eyes locked on *Wheel of Fortune*. She didn't look up, just muttered, "Should've guessed 'Tuscany.' Never buy a vowel too early."

Ava smiled and headed for her bedroom, grateful for the kind of quiet that didn't demand conversation.

The hallway creaked the way old houses do, like they're always whispering things you're not supposed to hear. Ava moved slowly, barefoot, trailing her fingers along the walls as if they might steady her.

In her room, the lamp by the bed cast a warm, golden light over everything, the knit throw her mother made in college, the chipped ceramic mug on her nightstand, the novel she'd been pretending to read for three weeks.

She sat on the edge of the bed and pulled the quilt into her lap. Her body was completely tired, but her mind wouldn't quiet.

The day still echoed. Not loud. Just persistent. A whisper she couldn't shut down.

Was she already yesterday's news?

She pictured him again, with Amelia. The ease between them. The way he carried her groceries without even looking like it was a favor. It had been muscle memory. That's what bothered her the most. Not the lie. Not even the omission.

The familiarity.

Ava leaned back, resting against the pillows, eyes scanning the low ceiling. When she was a kid, she'd trace the knots in the wood panels overhead like constellations. She used to believe the house had a heartbeat. Steady, hidden, always pulsing just beneath the floorboards.

Now it just felt like a place that remembered everything she'd rather forget.

Her phone buzzed again. This time, it was a photo from William. A cartoonishly bad drawing of a dog he'd attempted during a team meeting.

"Still an artistic genius, in case you were wondering."

She smiled. Actually smiled.

He reminded her he was predictable before the end. The kind of person who didn't make her question her memory after every conversation. The kind of person who showed up.

But that was the problem too. It was too easy. Too known.

She wondered if Chap had ever made Amelia feel this uncertain. If the version of him that Ava got, quiet and reflective and occasionally evasive, was new or if it had always been there, humming under the surface.

She stood up and crossed to the dresser, where a small photo sat tucked behind a bottle of perfume. It was her and her mom. Ava was age seven, her mom mid-laugh, arms wrapped around her like a lifeline.

Her mother had always been so sure of things. Or at least she pretended well enough that Ava believed it.

"Would you have walked away?" Ava asked the photo. "Or would you have shrugged it off like a stupid misunderstanding?"

The photo didn't answer. Of course it didn't.

She pressed her thumb to the frame, then set it face-down.

Some things were too quiet to confront out loud.

***

That night, Ava curled into her usual corner of the couch, a blanket around her legs and the scent of the ocean still faint in her hair. Esther had gone to bed after her nightly mug of chamomile tea and an unsolicited commentary on the state of Ava's love life: "Just remember, sometimes the one who makes you feel calm is the one you marry. Not the one who makes your stomach flutter."

Ironic. No one made her feel calm at the moment.

Her phone buzzed on the coffee table.

Chap: "Sorry, been out on the water. Spotty signal. Want to walk tomorrow?"

Ava's fingers hovered over the screen. Her breath caught. Not because of the message, but because of what she'd already seen.

He hadn't been on the water earlier. She knew that. She'd seen him laughing, carrying Amelia's groceries like it was muscle memory. Like she was still part of his rhythm.

Maybe it wasn't a lie. Maybe it was just the kind of truth you tell when you don't want to explain.

She stared at the text, waiting for a follow-up. Something to close the gap. But nothing came.

She looked back at the picture of the salmonberry pie she sent. Still waiting for a response.

Her hand curled tighter around the phone.

She didn't know what hurt more. The maybe-lie, or how easily it slid past his lips. Like she wasn't someone who noticed details. Like she didn't matter enough to clarify.

William's name sat just beneath Chap's in her message threads. She tapped it.

Earlier that day he'd sent a photo of a thrift-store record with a cracked sleeve and the caption: This feels like your soul in vinyl form.

She hadn't replied.

Now she typed: "Do you still burn grilled cheese?"

The response came seconds later: "Like it's my superpower. Why?"

She didn't answer. Not yet. Just let the glow of the screen and the quiet hum of being seen settle over her like a balm.

Then she turned back to Chap's message. Deleted her half-typed response.

If he could pretend, she could too.

Chapter 18

Ava didn't usually do mornings. Especially not ones that smelled like fish guts and motor oil.

But there she was, boots thudding across the slick dock, a fleece zipped tight at the neck and regret baked deep into her eye bags. The Alaskan sky hadn't decided if it wanted to be blue or gray yet, and the air had that briny chill that promised her hair would frizz no matter what she did with it.

Her grandfather was already onboard *The Surge*, muttering to himself like the engine had personally wronged him. A half-empty mug of coffee sat on the rail beside him. Black, naturally, no sugar, no cream. Because indulgences were for people who didn't grow up setting crab pots at five in the morning.

"You're up early," he said without looking up, as if she showed up at dawn every day in rubber boots ready to wrench open a crankcase.

"Couldn't sleep," she said, hopping aboard and crouching beside him. "Figured I'd come help you swear at some machinery."

He snorted. "Then you came to the right place."

They worked in a kind of silence Ava had come to appreciate. The kind where no one asked if you were okay, but somehow you still felt better. She handed him a wrench. He passed her a greasy rag. It felt good to use her hands, to do something that didn't involve scrolling or spiraling.

"You've got that look," he said eventually, giving her a sidelong glance. "Same one your mom used to get when she was thinking too hard and sleeping too little."

Ava looked away, blinking against the salt-stung air. "Yeah. She passed that down with her cheekbones and stubborn streak."

George didn't reply. Just nodded.

And then it happened.

A sound, a voice sharp and just familiar enough, cut through the calm.

Ava turned. Across the dock, Chap was walking toward the harbor store, hands in his jacket pockets, chin tucked down like he was trying to look casual. From the opposite direction came Amelia, who was looking anything but casual.

She was storming. She was flaring. She was every weather warning wrapped in a Patagonia rain jacket.

George paused, wrench halfway to the socket. "Oh hell."

Ava didn't answer. Her eyes were locked on the slow-motion train wreck happening twenty feet away.

Amelia got to Chap and stopped short. Then, without ceremony or warning, she raised her hand and slapped him across the face. Loud enough to make the seagulls startle. Loud enough to make Ava flinch.

Then came the shouting.

***

"You unbelievable jerk!"

The words flew out of Amelia like they'd been bottled up for months, maybe years, and now had no choice but to detonate in public. Loud. Raw. No filter. The kind of declaration that made fishermen pause mid-coil, tourists pretend not to listen, and the town's unofficial gossip relay perk up like prairie dogs.

Ava stood shellshocked beside *The Surge*, heart thudding in her ears. She wasn't sure what shocked her more: the slap, the volume, or the fact that Chap, steady and stoic, just stood there and took it like someone who'd been hit before and knew better than to hit back.

Amelia wasn't finished.

"You knew how much I needed you," Amelia continued, her voice rising again. "You knew I was drowning, and you stayed just close enough to make me think you'd be there for me."

Ava's eyes flicked to Chap, then back to Amelia. The implication wasn't clear, but it felt personal. Like a relationship had started and ended in the margins.

"Is this because you couldn't stand the idea of me being with someone else," Amelia added, breath sharp. "You didn't want me to be happy. You never said it out loud, but you made sure I felt it. Every damn day."

259

Chap looked like he wanted to say something, like he had something worth saying. But the moment passed.

"You let me believe," Amelia said, voice cracking now. "You let me believe I mattered. That I could tell you the truth."

She stared at him, eyes blazing, then looked at Ava, something unreadable, half-warning, half-regret. She turned on her heel. Her coat flared behind her like a banner as she stormed off.

Chap stood frozen, then bent slowly to retrieve his fallen ball cap, as if the slap had dislodged more than just his dignity.

Ava, still holding a wrench in her hand, suddenly felt like the whole dock was listing beneath her.

Around them, the harbor was a makeshift theater. Boats bobbed gently. Conversations had stalled. Everyone had pretended to go about their business, but no one had left.

*****

By the time Ava made it to the newspaper office, word of the dockside drama had already beaten her there.

She pushed open the glass door and was immediately hit with the sound of voices, urgent and overlapping, half-whispers that still managed to carry. The newsroom was usually a quiet place, more printer hum than human chaos, but today? Today it felt like a high school cafeteria with Wi-Fi.

Liz was at her desk with her feet propped up on a filing cabinet and her phone held to her ear with one shoulder. "Yeah, Marla, I heard. No, I'm not printing *that* unless you have a source who didn't hear it from their hairdresser's niece."

She looked up, spotted Ava, and gave her a raised brow that said *yep, it's that kind of day*.

Ava didn't even have her coat off yet before Nora, the summer intern with a penchant for local scandal, came speed-walking over like she was delivering a Pentagon memo.

"Did you hear?" she whispered, eyes big as saucers. "Amelia slapped him. On the dock. In front of, like, a dozen people. I wonder what that was all about."

Ava nodded slowly. "I was there."

Nora gasped, then immediately started backpedaling. "Oh my God. I didn't mean like, not that you were involved. I mean obviously, you *used* to be. Well, not *used to*, just. I'm gonna stop talking now."

"Good decision," Ava said, hanging her coat.

She made a beeline for the back room, needing somewhere without interns, or phones, or well-meaning colleagues who couldn't stop speculating.

Liz followed a moment later with two steaming mugs of coffee and a look that managed to be both sympathetic and exhausted.

"You okay?" she asked, setting one down.

Ava shrugged. "Define okay."

Liz sat across from her, leaned in slightly. "Is there something you want me to say? Because I can go full sarcastic best friend or emotionally available mentor. Dealer's choice."

Ava smiled weakly. "Just be normal."

"Normal?" Liz snorted. "I don't know what you mean."

They sipped in silence for a moment. Ava's fingers tightened around the mug.

"I was convincing myself I didn't care. He didn't matter. Until I saw her hit him," she said finally. "And then it felt like a sucker punch to the gut."

Liz didn't say I told you so. She didn't need to.

She just reached over and nudged the sleeve of Ava's sweater. "Maybe you care because you never really stopped."

***

By the time Ava walked through the front door, her body felt like it had been wrung out and hung up to dry. Her boots clunked against the tile. Her coat barely made it to the hook. She didn't bother with the second one before collapsing onto the couch in the living room.

"You've got that 'life just kicked me in the shins' look," Esther said, not looking up from her knitting. "Tea is in the kitchen, unless you need something stronger."

Ava dropped her bag with a thud. "Do we have anything stronger?"

"Depends how much you're willing to risk me dusting off the blackberry brandy."

They didn't need more than that. Esther's voice, her presence, filled the space the way only someone who knew you completely could. Ava let herself sag into the cushions.

She stared at the ceiling. "Is there a class I missed? 'How to Spot a Disaster in Disguise'? Because apparently, I keep failing it."

Esther paused, lowered her needles, and peered at her over her glasses. "Sweetheart, you're not failing anything. You're just still believing people are exactly what they say they are."

Ava gave a tired smile. "Isn't that the point of trust?"

"No," Esther said gently. "That's the point of being *young.*"

Ava exhaled, slow and unsteady. "I keep picking the ones who vanish. Or break when I need them whole."

"Maybe," Esther said, "you're choosing people who show you what you need to fix in yourself. Until you don't need them anymore."

Before Ava could reply, Esther stood with a quiet grunt and crossed to the sideboard. "Come on. You got a package earlier this week. I forgot to mention it."

She handed over a cardboard box, plain but carefully taped, the address written in elegant cursive. Ava took one look at the return label and blinked.

"Carol Hudson," she said. "That's unexpected. I haven't heard from her since before the implosion."

Esther gave a look. "Might be exactly why it's time."

Inside was a journal. Leather-bound, soft as butter, the kind of thing you didn't buy at a chain bookstore. In the bottom right corner, her initials were embossed in tiny gold letters: A.E.M.

Ava ran her hand over the cover, then opened it.

Something slipped from between the pages, a photo. It fluttered to the floor and landed face-up.

Four of them on a sun-drenched dock: William, his sister Geneva, his mother Carol, and Ava. Laughing. Tangled in each other's arms. Ava was in one of William's sweatshirts, her legs folded beneath her, her head thrown back in a laugh. William had his arm slung around her. His mother, off to the side, was smiling at them all like she'd gotten everything she ever wanted.

Ava stared down at it, breath caught somewhere between her throat and her chest.

And suddenly, she was *there* again. On that dock. Lake water lapping against the posts. Her feet bare, legs slung over the side as she dipped her toes in the cool shallows. Carol had handed her a lemonade, squeezed her shoulder, and said, "You fit here, you know. Some people take a while. Not you."

William had come up behind her, rested his chin on her shoulder, and whispered, "You're a lot. But in the way I've always needed."

She remembered blushing. And believing him.

She hadn't thought about that moment in months. Maybe because it had felt too real. Or because it had belonged to a version of herself she wasn't sure she could get back.

Esther leaned in to see the photo. "That was a good picture of you."

Ava nodded slowly. "I miss her."

"The girl in the picture?"

"No." Ava shook her head. "The one who believed the picture meant forever."

Esther didn't say anything right away. She just reached over and tucked the photo gently into the back flap of the journal, like it was a pressed flower.

"Maybe it didn't mean forever," she said. "But it meant something. That matters too."

Ava sat there a moment longer, the journal warm in her lap, her heart heavy but not in the same way it had been. Not hopeless. Not quite.

Then, almost as an afterthought, she lifted the envelope that had been tucked inside the journal's pages. The paper was thick, the handwriting as familiar as it was unexpected.

She unfolded the letter, smoothed the creases, and began to read.

Dear Ava,

I wasn't sure if I should send this.

Not because I didn't want to, but because I didn't know if it would be welcome. Or if you'd roll your eyes at hearing from your ex's mother. Or if you would throw away the journal out before even finding this note.

But the truth is, I had to write to you.

I bought the journal months ago, after William told us you'd be graduating. It's silly, I know, just a journal. But I remember how animated he got when he talked about your writing. Your ambition. The way you saw the world and wanted to put it into words. He told us, one night over dinner, that you made him feel like he had a future just by sitting next to you.

That kind of magic deserves to be remembered.

When you and William broke up, he didn't say much other than it was his fault. For a week, he didn't leave his bed. He wouldn't eat anything but applesauce. It took me two days to get him to take a shower, and even then, he looked like he'd misplaced something vital and couldn't remember how to ask for help finding it.

I know you had your reasons. I know heartbreak is complicated. But Ava, I need you to know that you are loved and very much missed.

You were already part of our family, even if we never got to made it official.

We missed you at the lake this summer. It felt strange not seeing you curled up in the hammock with a book, arguing with William about board game rules, or getting sunburned because you always forget to reapply. The Fourth of July didn't sparkle the same without you.

So, take this journal. Fill it with whatever comes next. Sadness. Joy. Confusion. Ideas. Dreams. Write yourself back to yourself. And when you do, remember that there's a family in Basin Harbor rooting for you, still.

With love. Real, unconditional, and a little overdue,

Carol

* * *

Ava folded the letter back into its envelope and held the journal to her chest. For a long, still moment, she didn't move. The weight of it, the words, the photo, the memory of belonging, settled over her in a way that didn't crush but steadied. Like an anchor. Like a reminder.

She had mattered. She *mattered.*

She stood slowly, made her way upstairs, and changed into the softest thing she owned: fleece joggers and a cardigan with a hole in the cuff she always meant to fix. When she came back down, Esther was back in her chair, knitting again, calm as a cat in the sun.

Ava smiled as she passed her, brushing a hand across Esther's shoulder in a silent thank-you. She didn't need to say anything. Esther already knew.

Her phone buzzed as she reached for the front door.

At first she ignored it, probably Liz, or someone from work asking if she'd heard the Chap and Amelia drama had exploded in the town square like a badly-scripted soap opera.

Then it buzzed again.

And again.

She checked it.

Chap.

Three messages. No subject. No warning. Just:

Need to talk.

I know you heard about Amelia. I can explain.

One minute.

Her stomach dipped like it always did when he reached out, a Pavlovian mix of longing and dread. She could hear his voice in her head already. Low, steady, just the right blend of guilt and sincerity. Apologies that left just enough unsaid to make you doubt your own clarity.

She locked the phone and tucked it under the throw pillow on the couch.

Not right now.

Not when she could still hear Carol Hudson's voice in her head, telling her she was missed. Loved. Not when there were pieces of herself she was finally starting to pick up again.

***

She pulled on a pair of sneakers, pulled her jacket, and stepped out into the evening air.

The wind had shifted. She could smell the ocean in it now. Salt and seaweed, cold and clean. Beach Road was nearly empty, save for a couple walking their dog. Ava kept her head down and let her legs lead her.

She was halfway to the lookout when she heard it.

A thunderous crash, distant but unmistakable. A deep splash that echoed across the stillness of twilight, followed by another, and then another.

She stopped walking.

Her breath caught as she scanned the water. And there, just past the point, dark, a smooth back arched through the surface. A humpback, feeding in slow, synchronized spirals. The water around it rippled and bloomed in circles of air. This was the first time Ava had seen a whale bubble feeding in person.

Another crash. The sound of power, of wildness, of something older than heartbreak.

Ava stood frozen, her pulse slowing, her lungs syncing with the rhythm of the waves. Another whale breached, lifted its fluke, and vanished in a clean, effortless dive.

She couldn't look away.

Here, now, there was no phone. No unanswered questions. No Chap. Just the ocean. The sky. The hush of waves lapping on the shore.

She sat on a worn bench, hands tucked into her sleeves.

Maybe she hadn't found forever in William. Or Chap. Maybe she wouldn't find it in anyone.

But right now, standing here in the salt and wind, hearing the crash of something ancient and alive just offshore, she felt present.

She closed her eyes. Let the sound of the whale roll over her like waves.

And for once, she didn't try to outrun the ache.

She just let it be.

Ava crawled into bed when the phone buzzed against the nightstand like it had something urgent to say. Ava didn't look. She already knew who it was.

Her fingers stilled on the pen hovering above the journal William's mother had sent, the ink bleeding a small dot into the paper. Outside her window, the Alaskan sky was an endless smear of gray, lit faintly by the last of the dusky twilight. Inside her bedroom, everything was still. Too still. Even Esther's usual humming in the kitchen had gone quiet for the night, replaced by the soft tick of the wall clock and the intermittent buzz of her phone.

There it went again. She didn't move.

She didn't need to see the name. She knew it was Chap. Her body always told on her first. The rush in her stomach, the catch in her breath. Muscle memory she hadn't asked for.

She wished she could go back. Back before Amelia had gone off at full volume on the docks, chasing away a seagull mid-screech and securing her spot as that day's hottest topic in Spruce Cove's unofficial gossip group chat. Back before Ava walked up and found Chap leaning in, rubbing Amelia's back while she cried. Not romantic, not quite. But charged. Heavy with that specific, uncomfortable weight of two people who had too much past and not enough distance.

Ava had seen it. Everyone had seen it. And while she'd tried to laugh it off later, making some offhand comment about small-town theatrics and "not my circus," the truth was uglier and less quotable.

Because the look Chap gave Amelia crawled under your skin and refused to leave quietly. Familiar. Charged. Like they'd been fighting about more than just the weather and fuel prices.

And Ava, who had spent four years learning to decode 18th-century literature, was suddenly illiterate when it came to real human emotion. Especially hers.

She closed her journal and flipped her phone face-down, smothering the screen against the blanket like it was capable of guilt. A minute later, it buzzed again. Another text.

Chap: Are you ready talk?

Simple. Direct. Just like him. And yet, the words hit her like a rock to the chest. Sudden, hard, and impossible to ignore.

She pulled the blanket up to her chin and leaned her head back against the wall, her curls fanning across the old quilt. The hum of the fridge downstairs was the only sound for miles, and even that seemed to quiet in deference to her unease.

Ava exhaled.

She wasn't angry with Chap. Not in the way she'd been with William. That sharp, scorched-earth kind of rage where betrayal wasn't just personal, it felt permanent. No, this was different. Murkier. Like trying to see through the ocean at dusk.

She was disappointed. A little humiliated. And, if she was really being honest, kind of scared. Because Chap didn't owe her anything. They'd agreed to "take a step back," her words, even. But did he have to *step all the way back* to freaking *Amelia*? Was there no in-between?

No grace period? Couldn't he have *waited a week?* Maybe just long enough for her to decide if she'd made a mistake?

She sighed and rolled onto her side, the weight of the blankets a small comfort. She opened the text again, stared at it, and then slowly typed out a reply.

Ava: Not tonight.

Then, almost reflexively, she deleted it.

She wasn't ready to draw that line, not yet. And she didn't want to give him the satisfaction of knowing she was upset. So instead, she did nothing. Let the message sit there unread. Let her silence answer for her.

She placed the phone on the nightstand and turned it off.

Just like that, the world felt farther away.

Downstairs, a floorboard creaked. Grandpa George must be up checking the woodstove again, even though the fire had died hours ago. That was the thing about this house, it was full of warmth that never quite left, even when everyone else did.

Ava pulled the covers tighter.

She didn't want to talk to Chap. She didn't want to talk to anyone. Not until the mess in her chest sorted itself out. Not until she figured out why a man she barely knew could make her feel so unsteady.

Maybe tomorrow she'd confront him. Or maybe she'd let it go. But not tonight. Tonight, she just wanted quiet.

And maybe, if she was lucky, a dream where things made sense again.

Chapter 19

Ava padded down to the kitchen on bare feet, her hair a frizzy halo of unresolved decisions and too little sleep. The smell of bacon wrapped around her like a flannel blanket, comforting like it was saying, "you're not skipping breakfast, sweetheart."

Esther was at the stove, humming along to Jimmy Buffett's *"Changes in Latitudes, Changes in Attitudes"* playing from a little radio on the windowsill. The irony wasn't lost on Ava. She'd changed latitude, all right. The attitude part? Still under construction.

George sat at the table with a mug of coffee and one of his many fishing journals, which he read like it was gospel even though half of it was written by a dude who once thought apostrophes were optional.

"You're up late," Esther said, flipping a pancake with a casual flick that suggested she'd been doing this since before Ava was born.

"I didn't sleep well," Ava muttered, grabbing the chipped *Alaska: Where the Men are Men and the Moose are Nervous* mug. She filled it with coffee that tasted like it had been reheated three times. Which, knowing Esther, it probably had.

Esther slid a plate of food in front of her: scrambled eggs, bacon, and a pancake the size of a hubcap. "You don't have to eat it all, but if I see that bacon untouched, I will haunt you until Halloween."

Ava cracked a half-smile and picked up her fork. "Understood."

George looked over the edge of his paper and gave her a small nod. The kind that meant, *You okay, kid?* She gave him the kind of nod back that meant, *No, but I'm pretending I am, so let's go with it.*

"You girls have plans today?" George asked, eyes back on the paper.

Ava shrugged. "Might go for a walk."

"Good. Clears the head," he said.

Esther snorted. "That's what men say when they don't want to talk about their feelings."

Ava sipped her coffee, letting it scald her just enough to focus. The kitchen was quiet. Her brain, unfortunately, was not.

Esther turned down the burner and leaned on the counter. "So, about yesterday."

Ava didn't look up.

"Jenny saw Chap and Amelia on the dock. Correction, Jenny heard Amelia. That girl's got a voice like a foghorn in mating season."

Ava stabbed at her pancake with more force than necessary.

"Chap apparently didn't say much," Esther continued. "Just stood there while she went full melodrama."

Ava's grip tightened around her fork. "I'm not talking about Chap."

Esther raised an eyebrow but didn't push. "Suit yourself."

A long silence fell, filled only by the radio crackling out the last chorus of Buffett's weathered optimism.

Finally, Ava stood, grabbed her coffee to-go mug, and pushed in her chair. "I need some air."

"Don't we all," Esther said, rinsing a pan. "Be back by dinner. I'm making tuna noodle casserole and I need at least one person in this house who'll pretend to like it."

George grunted without looking up.

Ava pulled on her boots by the door and grabbed her coat. The sky outside was low and gray, the kind of weather that felt personal. She didn't know where she was going — just that she needed to go somewhere.

The fresh air slapped her awake the second she stepped outside.

She needed answers.

She needed quiet.

She needed something she hadn't figured out yet.

***

Ava saw Liz before Liz spotted her, which was rare. Her best friend had the spatial awareness of a mother at Disneyland, and the gossip retention of a hairdresser. She stood outside the *Gazette* office, holding two coffees while talking on her phone with the kind of enthusiasm that usually meant someone was pregnant, getting divorced, or both.

"There she is," Liz called, holding out a cup like a peace offering. "Survival-grade caffeine with a splash of emotional support."

Ava took the cup and offered a small smile. "God, I love you."

"Obviously," Liz said, linking her arm through Ava's as they started walking down the boardwalk toward the harbor. "So. Any Chap drama?"

Ava groaned. "Ugh. Can we go one conversation without mentioning the emotionally unavailable fisherman?"

"Okay," Liz said cheerfully. "Shall-not-be-named drama."

"Better."

They passed a row of shops still shuttered from the early-morning fog. Above them, a flock of Canadian geese cut through the sky in a perfect V, so sure of their place and their path. Something Ava hadn't felt in a long time.

"Okay, I know we said we weren't going to talk about him. But.."

"You have the impulse control of a raccoon near a garbage can," Ava cut in.

Liz didn't even blink. "Exactly. So, tell me, are you avoiding him, is he avoiding you, or are you both doing that emotionally constipated two-step where no one knows who's supposed to make the first move?"

"Definitely me avoiding him. But has he shown up with flowers, a laminated apology, and a heartfelt playlist? No, he has not."

"Men never are," Liz said with a shrug. "They want credit for showing up with a pulse and moderately clean clothes."

They turned the corner near the cannery just as a tall figure in uniform stepped out from behind the shed, clipboard in hand.

Liz stopped mid-step like she'd hit an invisible wall. "Well, speak of the tall, dark, and *handcuff-equipped.*"

Ava raised an eyebrow. "Friend of yours?"

Liz exhaled, long and theatrical. "Deputy Ryan Hale. He was a class below me. Pitcher, varsity. Dated girls who wore their boyfriend's hoodies and knew how to flirt using a Gatorade bottle. Meanwhile, I had an inhaler and AP Chem."

Ava squinted toward him. The name rang faintly. Not from her own memory, but "Wait. *Ryan?* Chap's Ryan? The one who once called the Coast Guard because he ran out of coffee?"

Liz smiled. "That's the one."

Ava laughed. "Oh my God. Chap told me that story on the *Malahini.* I thought he made it up."

"Nope. Real. He's practically a local legend. Which is rude, because legends aren't usually that attractive."

Ryan spotted them and walked over, grinning like someone who'd just remembered the punchline to an inside joke.

"Liz," he said, his voice low and familiar.

"Deputy Hale," she replied, like she hadn't just rehearsed that in her head for fifteen years.

He turned to Ava. "You must be Ava. Chap's said nothing but good things. Which, knowing him, is downright romantic."

Ava smiled. "And you're the caffeine-deprived fisherman."

"Guilty. In my defense, it was a rough season. And I was twenty-two and dumb."

"He says you still owe him a thermos."

Ryan gave a sheepish shrug. "He's not wrong."

Liz looked between them, then gave Ava a look. "Excuse me, how are you suddenly bantering with the hot deputy? I had to make a fake library card to talk to him in high school."

Ryan looked amused. "That library card was very convincing."

"See?" Liz said, nudging Ava. "Quick reflexes. Great memory. Even better ass."

Ava choked on her coffee. Ryan pretended not to hear (he definitely heard).

"Well," he said, recovering smoothly. "If you two happen to spot the owner of that rusted skiff behind the bakery, let them know we're gonna haul it if they don't."

Liz tilted her head. "What if I know who the owner was? Would I be taken in for questioning? Hypothetically."

Ryan gave her a slow, amused smile. "I might have to read you your rights."

He tipped an invisible hat, nodded to Ava again, and walked off toward the harbor.

Liz watched him go. "I swear to God, if he ends up being good with kids and dogs, I'm filing a complaint with the universe."

Ava grinned, warmth blooming beneath her ribs. For the first time all morning, things felt almost right.

Almost.

***

Ava left Liz at the corner, still half-smiling at her friend's shameless commentary about Ryan's ass. The kind of flirting Liz did should've come with a soundtrack and a legal disclaimer and honestly, Ava admired the hell out of it. For a moment, it had been a relief to laugh. To feel like things could still be funny.

Then she looked up.

And there he was.

Chap was leaning against the siding of the marine supply store, sleeves shoved up, jaw tight. His hands were deep in his jacket pockets like he was trying to stop himself from doing something he'd regret. The wind had ruffled his hair, and he looked less like the laid-back fisherman she'd once thought she was getting to know and more like a man circling the edge of a storm.

Her smile disappeared without her noticing.

279

She could've kept walking. Could've turned around. But she didn't.

His gaze lifted and landed on her.

"Ava."

She stopped. Arms loosely folded. "Chap."

He pushed off the wall, walked a few steps closer. "You've been avoiding me."

She raised an eyebrow. "You know where I live, Chap. It's not like I entered the witness protection program."

He sighed. "It's not what you think."

Ava kept her expression even. "I think I saw Amelia shouting at you on the dock loud enough for the seagulls to flinch. That part wasn't subtle."

"She was upset."

"Yeah," Ava said. "I noticed. Everyone noticed."

He gave a half-smile, more like an exhale with teeth. "Figured saying something would've just made it worse."

Ava didn't return the smile. "From where I stood, it didn't look like you were doing much of anything."

"I wasn't," he said quietly. "I said something I shouldn't have. She was pissed, and I figured I'd earned the fallout."

Ava tilted her head. "Sure is a lot of tension for two people who are just friends."

Chap's jaw flexed. "Yeah. There's history. And lines that shouldn't have been crossed, by either of us."

Her eyes narrowed. "What kind of lines?"

He didn't answer fast enough.

"Oh my God," she said, the words sharp. "Is that what this is? Am I just the town idiot in the middle of some tragic love triangle I never signed up for?"

"No," he said quickly. "Ava, it's not —"

"I'm serious," she cut in. "Do you know how people are looking at me right now? Like I'm either the villain or the consolation prize. Depending on who they think you belong to."

"Ava!"

"I didn't ask to be part of this," she said. "And you didn't exactly give me a reason to believe I wasn't."

Chap didn't speak.

"I wasn't sure what we were doing," Ava continued. "Still don't. But I thought maybe we were figuring it out, slowly and awkwardly. And then I saw you two." She shook her head. "It just messed with my head."

"It's not like that with her."

"Maybe not," she said. "But from the outside? It sure as hell looks like it."

"I didn't mean to hurt you."

"I know," she said. "But that doesn't change the fact that you did."

"So, you think I'm a jerk," he muttered.

"No," she said. "I think you're a guy trying to do the right thing and getting it wrong."

Chap looked down, then up again. "You think we still have a shot at anything?"

"I think I need to figure out if I even want one."

He nodded, jaw tight. "I need a drink."

Ava raised an eyebrow. "It's not even nine a.m."

He gave a humorless laugh. "Exactly."

He walked off, and she let him. Even though part of her wanted to do something reckless, like stop him. Or forgive him. Or both.

***

Ava didn't head straight home.

She needed to walk it off. The conversation, the confusion, the sharp little ache of restraint. The ocean helped. Its steady roar had a way of quieting the noise in her head, at least a little. She headed to the beach.

The tide was low. A wide stretch of wet sand gleamed in the overcast light, the sky hanging heavy with unspoken things.

She wasn't expecting to see anyone. Certainly not Amelia.

She was perched on a log, knees tucked up, her face turned toward the sea. Wind pressed her dark hair across her cheek, and she made no move to tuck it back.

Ava paused.

She could turn around and pretend she hadn't seen her. But she didn't.

"Hey," Amelia said, not looking away.

Ava hovered a few steps off. "Hey."

There was a long silence. Then Amelia patted the log beside her. "Don't worry. I'm not in the mood to throw punches today."

Ava stepped closer. "Good. Two assaults in one week might be pushing your luck. Even if half the women in town wouldn't mind being arrested by Deputy Hale."

Amelia smirked. "Can't say I blame them."

Ava hesitated, then sat. Not close, but not far either.

They stared out at the gray-blue water. The waves lapped at the shore in slow, hushed breaths. Just enough sound to keep the silence from feeling too heavy.

Amelia broke it first, her voice was quieter than Ava had ever heard it.

"You know," she said, "I wasn't sure you'd sit down."

Ava shrugged, not looking at her. "Wasn't sure I would either."

Another beat passed.

"I've been thinking about the last several months," Amelia said. "How things played out between us."

That got Ava's attention. She didn't speak, but she turned her head slightly, listening.

"I wasn't fair," Amelia said, not quite meeting her eyes. "I let things get personal when they shouldn't have. Chap let me know. More than once."

Ava raised an eyebrow. "He did?"

"Yeah." Amelia let out a short breath, like she was annoyed at herself. "Told me I was acting like a mean girl. He wasn't wrong."

She dug her heel into the sand. "You were easy to be mad at. Not because of anything you did. Just because you showed up. For the first time, Chap wasn't available as my backup plan anymore. And I didn't know what to do with any of it."

Ava didn't jump in. Just let her talk.

Amelia gave a dry laugh. "It's easier to lash out than admit you're scared."

Ava nodded slightly. "Yeah. It is."

They sat in silence again. Overhead, a bald eagle soared past, a humpy clenched in its talons. A seagull screamed its protest, trailing behind like it had a chance.

"You and Chap," Ava said finally. "There's clearly a long history."

"There is," Amelia said. "But not the kind people like to gossip about. Or maybe exactly that kind."

She looked down the shoreline. "Things between us are more complicated than people know. That's not an excuse. Just context."

Ava didn't ask for more. She wasn't sure she wanted to know the depth of their relationship.

"I've thought about leaving," Amelia said, her voice low. "This town doesn't let you change. It decides who you are, and then it won't let you be anything else. I'm tired of pretending I'm still that version of me. The one everyone expects, whether it's fair or not."

Ava nodded slowly. "My mom used to say that's why she left. Said this place had too many mirrors and not enough windows."

Amelia and Ava sat planted on the weather log chatting for another hour before Amelia stood and dusted off her jeans.

"Be careful, Ava."

Ava looked up. "Of what?"

Amelia's gaze lingered a second too long. "People. And the stories they tell when they think no one's listening."

With that, Amelia turned and walked away, shoulders squared like someone expecting a storm.

Ava stayed put after Amelia disappeared down the beach, swallowed by sea spray and silence.

The wind tugged at her sleeves, the tide inching forward like it was trying to erase where they'd sat.

She didn't know exactly what she felt. It wasn't clarity. And it sure as hell wasn't peace.

She stared out at the horizon, wondering how many versions of herself this town would invent and how many she'd have to live down.

Chapter 20

The landline rang just after 6 a.m., slicing through the quiet of the house like a blade. Ava didn't stir at first. The blankets were heavy and warm, her body curled tight against the dawn chill that crept in around the old window frame. But she caught the shift in the air. Esther's soft rustle, then her voice, clipped and alert.

"George," she called, urgent but not panicked. That was what woke Ava.

She sat up slowly, sleep still dragging at her limbs. Her door was cracked open, and she heard the low creak of floorboards, the scrape of boots on wood.

By the time she made her way into the kitchen, George was slipping on his coat, already lacing his boots with the steady hands of a man who didn't ask for details until he had to.

"What's going on?" Ava asked, tightening the sleeves of her hoodie.

George glanced at her, his jaw working before he spoke. "The harbormaster just called. Something's washed up near the south float."

Ava blinked. "Washed up?"

"Could be debris. Could be something else," he said, not meeting her eyes. He grabbed a pair of gloves from the hook by the door.

Esther stood at the counter, arms crossed, lips pressed into a thin line. That told Ava more than words.

"I'll be back soon," George muttered. "Stay put."

But Ava had thrown her hair in a ponytail and was already pulling on her boots when Liz sent the first text.

Liz: You up? Something's happened.

Liz: Come down to the docks. It's bad.

Ava scrambled.

***

The harbor was unusually crowded for early morning. A few fishing crews had paused their loading to linger near the edge, their conversations hushed. A section near the far dock had been roped off with yellow caution tape, and the harbormaster stood beside George, who was now kneeling, his hands braced against a metal cleat, eyes fixed on something in the water.

Liz met her halfway down the dock, breath visible in the morning chill.

"They are pulling someone out," she said, voice barely above a whisper. "They haven't said who yet."

A boat hook tapped against the dock. The harbormaster gave a small nod. A tarp-covered stretcher rose from the water, slow and deliberate.

Ava's stomach twisted. She held her breath.

Then Liz said, quieter still, "I saw the shoe."

Ava didn't want to ask. Didn't have to.

Red heels. Glossy. Spike-heeled. The kind that clicked like punctuation and made Amelia impossible to ignore.

Ava's hand shot to her mouth.

"Oh my God," Liz breathed. "It's her."

The harbor held its silence like a secret. The water didn't move. Neither did Ava.

Ava quietly braced herself as her world started to spin. Amelia's limp body rising from the water was like something out of a nightmare. One she couldn't blink away.

She had never seen a dead body before.

Not like this. Not face down in the harbor that, just days ago, shimmered with early summer light. Her knees felt shaky. Her mouth tasted like metal.

It didn't seem possible. Amelia was, she was energy. A presence. Even if Ava hadn't known her well, she'd felt it.

Amelia walked into a room like it was hers the moment she crossed the threshold. People turned when she spoke. Men, women, children, deckhands. She wasn't just beautiful; she was magnetic.

Confident in a way that made people edge closer without even realizing it.

Ava had admired her from afar. Unsure if she wanted to be like her, hate her, or just borrow her confidence and flawless cheekbones for a day or two. Amelia had been one of those women who made you feel both invisible and inspired.

And now she was gone.

Ava turned her face toward the wind, trying to breathe. Behind her, murmurs swelled. Speculation, curiosity, theories. All she could think of was the last text message from Chap.

From behind her, Chief Harrow's voice cut through the fog. "We estimate she's been in the water less than twelve hours. Cold temperatures helped preserve things, but it's early yet."

Less than twelve hours.

Ava felt the floor drop inside her chest. That meant it happened last night.

After the text.

Her head started spinning.

"Can we talk?"

She hadn't answered. She'd been too upset, too confused, too afraid of what both he and she might say.

Now her silence felt like a weight.

What if he'd been trying to warn her? Or confess?

What if he was with Amelia last night?

Ava's eyes searched the harbor like the answers might be bobbing on the tide. Her stomach twisted, cold and sour.

Please don't let it be him.

Ava swallowed hard, eyes drawn to the group of men kneeling at the edge of the float. George was among them, his shoulders hunched. The harbormaster, Tommy, stood nearby, talking in low tones.

The body, guided by steady hands, was placed on the dock as volunteer EMTs shifted it into a black body bag. Ava's stomach twisted.

No one moved.

Not at first.

The sound of a seagull screeching overhead broke the silence like a bad punchline. Then the murmur began, low and speculative. People turning to one another. Names whispered. Questions launched like flares into the fog.

"Did she fall?"

"Was she drunk?"

"No, she was on the wagon."

"Who did she make mad? She burned bridges like it was a hobby."

"Someone said they heard shouting near the docks last night."

Chief Harrow stood near the edge of the float, his navy Spruce Cove PD jacket zipped halfway, the gold lettering catching a glint of early light. His posture was calm but alert, hands on his hips, eyes narrowed, like he was already building a timeline in his head.

Next to him, Deputy Ryan Hale leaned awkwardly on one foot, a yellow roll of caution tape dangling in his hand.

As Ryan started looping tape around a piling, his hands trembled slightly, and his jaw was tight. He looked rattled, like a man bearing the weight of the world on shoulders that weren't built for it. He shot a worried look at Liz and Ava.

"If they're taping it off this early, they're not thinking accident," Liz said, pulling out her notebook.

"We need to find out who saw her last," Ava said.

Liz nodded, flipping her notebook open. "Already started a list."

***

Ava's eyes swept toward the outer moorings, and there it was.

The *Malahini*.

Chap's boat, bobbing gently in its slip like nothing had changed. Lines secure. Curtains drawn. Deck empty.

Like it was just another morning. Like there *wasn't* a body being pulled from the water less than a hundred yards away.

Her stomach twisted. Did he know?

Liz followed her gaze and, as if she was reading her mind she murmured, "You think he's heard?"

"I don't know," Ava said. "But if he hasn't, he's about to."

Liz nodded and started to pull out her notebook, clicking her pen.

Ava stopped her with a look. "Not now."

Liz blinked. "What?"

"This can't be part of the story," Ava said, her voice low but steady. "Not him. Not yet. He deserves better than to find while being interviewed."

Liz studied her for a second, then slipped the notebook back into her jacket.

"Okay," she said. "We go as friends."

The walk to Chap's boat felt longer than it should have. The dock stretched ahead like something out of a dream, the bad kind, where your feet move but you don't get anywhere. Her boots hit the damp planks with a steady rhythm, but her heart was erratic and uneven. Every step closer brought more questions. Was she about to break his heart? Or discover he'd helped stop its beat?

When they reached the slip, Liz paused a few paces back, letting Ava take the lead.

She climbed onto the boat, her stomach doing anxious somersaults. She knocked once, then again, louder.

"Chap? It's Ava. You need to wake up."

A shuffle. A thud. Then the sound of a latch.

The door creaked open.

Chap squinted out, shirtless and sleep-rumpled, his hair doing something that defied physics. He looked like a man who'd lost a bar fight with a bottle of bourbon and barely lived to tell the tale.

When he saw her, that familiar crooked smile tugged at his lips.

"Well," he rasped, "if I'd known that waking up meant finding you on my deck, I'd have left the door unlocked and made coffee."

Ava's breath hitched.

For half a second, it almost worked. His charm, the casual flirtation. She could feel herself teetering on the edge of whatever it was they hadn't quite defined.

Then he saw her face.

The smile disappeared.

He glanced at Liz. Then back to Ava. "What's going on?"

She swallowed hard. "They found a body this morning."

Chap blinked, straightening slightly. "Who?"

"They haven't said officially," she said gently, "but we think. No. We *know* it's Amelia."

Chap stared at her, shellshocked.

Then, barely audible: "How?"

It was the kind of question you asked when your brain refused to catch up. When it needed someone, anyone, to offer a better version of reality.

He rubbed his face and leaned hard on the hatch frame, eyes darting between the water, the dock, his bare feet. As if searching for answers in the texture of the grain.

He looked wrecked.

And Ava?

She didn't know what scared her more: that he had no idea what had happened.

Or that he did.

It wasn't even a question, not really. More like a reflex. Like his mouth said something because his brain couldn't.

Ava took a step closer. "We don't know yet. I'm sure they will send her north for an autopsy."

He shook his head, jaw tight. "She was just here. She was fine."

Nobody said anything.

"You think I —" He stopped himself, shutting his eyes for a second. When he opened them, they looked older. Wrecked.

"I don't know what happened," Ava said, voice gentle but steady. "But I know you need to take care of yourself right now. Shower. Eat something. Don't drink."

Liz cleared her throat behind her, her tone careful. "Let's go. The longer we wait, the more the town fills in its own blanks."

Ava nodded slowly, then turned back to Chap. "You want help with anything? We can call someone. Or I can stay. If you need."

He shook his head. "No. I just, I need a minute."

A moment passed. Ava stepped forward and hugged him. Awkward at first, like she wasn't sure how to land it. But then his arms came around her, and it stopped being awkward and started to feel real.

Liz hesitated, then joined them. A three-person, clumsy, quiet circle of grief.

When they pulled away, Chap didn't say a word. He just sat down on the edge of the deck, barefoot, shirtless, elbows on his knees. His head dropped into his hands.

They left him there, rocking slightly with the tide, alone with the sea and whatever ghosts had come in with it.

***

Ava and Liz walked in silence at first.

The dock creaked under their steps, seagulls calling overhead, the salty air sharper now, like it had sobered up too. The harbor was still a blur of motion. Chief Harrow talking with the harbormaster, Deputy Conner stringing more yellow tape around the floats.

The crowd was swelling. Locals clustered at the edge of the lot, arms folded, voices low. Not crying. Not even shocked. Just hungry for details, for someone to blame.

Ava kept her eyes ahead.

"He didn't ask any questions," Liz said quietly.

"No," Ava replied.

A couple of kids on bikes skidded to a stop near the docks, craning their necks for a look.

"People are already talking," Liz said.

"I know."

"We need to get something on the record."

Ava didn't argue. This was what they were good at, after all, sorting truth from hearsay. Holding space between grief and gossip.

But her thoughts were still on Chap. Devastated. Blinking. Lost.

They reached the edge of the harbor lot just as Joyce Turner, busy body of Spruce Cove, stepped out of her Subaru. She was halfway through her second iced coffee of the morning when she spotted Liz and Ava.

"Ava," she called, voice pitched with performative concern, "have you heard? About Amelia?"

Ava nodded. "Yeah. We were down there when they pulled her out."

Joyce's eyes widened, the kind of wide that begged for details. "So it's true? She was found in the harbor? Dead?"

"Yes," Liz said before Ava could answer. "And that's all anyone knows so far."

"Well," Joyce sniffed, lowering her sunglasses, "I heard from Dean who heard from someone at the Gaff Hook that she and Chap. Well, there was some sort of scene last night."

Ava stiffened. "What kind of scene?"

"You know how Amelia could be," Joyce said, with a flutter of her hand. "Always the center of something. Dean said Chap left early. Stumbling, I think was the word."

"Dean was there?"

"Of course. Half the town was. The boy's baseball team won regionals. It was packed."

Liz stepped in smoothly. "Thanks, Joyce. We'll make sure the paper prints facts, not rumors."

Joyce smiled, unfazed. "Just trying to help."

She walked off toward the docks, likely hunting down someone else to interrogate.

Ava turned to Liz. "It's already happening."

Liz nodded. "Let's get ahead of it."

***

The smell of low tide wafted through the air as Ava and Liz returned to the far end of the dock armed with tape recorders, notepads and a camera. Behind them, the town buzzed like a beehive someone had knocked over gently. It would only get louder.

Just ahead, Esther was coming down the ramp of the harbor. She had changed into her fleece vest and walked like her feet couldn't carry her fast enough. Below, George had that look he wore when someone had overcooked the halibut special; tight-lipped and ready to fix something.

"They're going to see Chap," Ava said.

Liz followed her gaze. "Of course they are. He's one of their people."

Ava watched until they disappeared onto Chap's boat, then turned toward the police tape.

Chief Harrow was standing at the far end of the dock, arms crossed over. His eyes scanned the water like it might speak to him if he just stared long enough. Deputy Hale stood nearby, hands in his pockets, his jaw working like he was chewing over something too complicated to swallow.

"Chief," Liz called out, calm but clear.

Harrow turned as they approached again, his expression unreadable. "Back already," he said. "Didn't get enough the first time?"

"We're not writing anything yet," Liz said. "We're just asking some questions."

"Town already is," he muttered, jerking his head toward the crowd. "You can practically see the torches forming."

Ava stepped closer. "Are you releasing the name?"

Harrow nodded once. "Amelia Colburn. No sign of foul play so far, but we're checking. Autopsy'll tell more."

"You're calling it accidental?" Liz asked.

"For now," he said. "Maybe a fall. She'd been at the bar so she could have been drinking. There was a big celebration."

Liz glanced at Ava.

"Anyone see her last?" Ava asked.

Harrow's jaw ticked. "A few. Working through that. I know about as much as you do at this point."

"But you think this'll be wrapped up quickly?" Liz said, tone even but pointed.

He didn't flinch. "I do."

Ryan shifted beside him. Not a word, just a glance across the dock, toward Liz. Not long. Not dramatic. But enough.

Ava saw it. So did Liz.

That one flicker of worry said everything the chief didn't.

"We'll let you get back to it," Liz said, her voice lighter now, the reporter mask back in place. "Thanks for the update."

Harrow nodded, already turning back toward the water.

As they turned to leave, Ava caught it. Just a flicker.

Ryan was watching them.

His arms were crossed, his stance casual, but his eyes? Not so much. There was a crease between his brows like he was trying to work out a puzzle he didn't like the shape of. He didn't say a word, but the look he gave them was sharp. Appraising. Nervous. Like he knew something wasn't adding up and didn't trust anyone to say it out loud.

As they walked away, Ava leaned in. "You see that?"

"The glance?" Liz said. "Yep. Ryan's not convinced this is an accident."

They moved toward the edge of the lot, where the crowd had begun to thin. The ambulance was gone now. Just a few lingering faces, still hungry.

"What if the chief's wrapping this up too fast?" Ava asked.

"Then we make sure it doesn't stay wrapped."

Chapter 21

The email came just after noon.

Ava was in the newsroom, standing at the whiteboard covered in color-coded timelines and scribbled names, when Liz came in, her expression unreadable.

"They just released the autopsy report," Liz said, holding out her phone.

Ava wiped her hands on her jeans before taking it. Her eyes skimmed the screen. With every line, her stomach twisted tighter.

Amelia Colburn.

Blunt force trauma to the back of the head.

Time of death: between 10:30 p.m. and midnight.

Presence of ocean water in the lungs—she was still alive when she hit the water.

No alcohol. No drugs.

Bruising on her upper back and arms. Restraint or defensive marks.

And then, buried at the bottom like it barely mattered:

Approximately nine weeks pregnant.

Ava read the line twice. Then a third time. Her throat closed around it.

"Jeez," she breathed.

She felt the words land somewhere low and deep, like a stone dropped into her gut. Murder was bad enough. But this?

"She was pregnant," she whispered. "She was pregnant and someone…"

Liz reached out, steadying Ava with a hand on her arm. She didn't say anything. She didn't have to.

Ava swallowed hard. "No alcohol. Not even a glass of wine. And bruises on her back and arms."

"She didn't fall," Liz said, quietly finishing the thought.

"No." Ava's voice was sharper now, more certain. "She was pushed."

The office buzzed around them. Printers whirring, chairs creaking, someone arguing about page layout in the corner. It all faded beneath the throb of something rising in Ava's chest. Not just shock. But anger, grief, fear. That terrible combination that told her this wasn't just a headline.

It was about to be everything.

"We have to talk to Harrow," she said. "Now."

They didn't speak for the first few minutes of the drive.

Ava kept her hands tight on the wheel eyes fixed on the two-lane road that wound through Spruce Cove like a scar. The sky was overcast again, the clouds pressed low, heavy and bruised. The kind of weather that made everything feel closer. Like the town itself was eavesdropping.

"She didn't tell anyone," Liz said finally, her voice low. "About the baby."

Ava nodded, slow. "If she had, it would've been all over town in twenty-four hours."

"Do you think it was Chap's?"

The question hit like black ice, invisible until she started to spin. Ava's fingers tightened on the steering wheel. Her breath was sharp and unsteady.

It wasn't the question itself. It was the way it peeled back something she hadn't let herself look at too closely. Not yet.

"I don't know," she said. She kept her eyes on the road, even as her vision blurred around the edges. "It's possible. They were on-again, off-again for years."

She paused. The silence was louder than anything Liz could have said.

"But she was pulling away. Working on herself. She was going to apply for jobs outside of town."

"She didn't seem like someone planning a family," Liz murmured.

Ava shook her head, more to clear it than to agree. "No," she said quietly. "She seemed like someone trying to get out."

The words sat heavy between them. Ava didn't add what she was thinking. That if it *was* Chap's baby, then everything about Amelia's final days got messier, and scarier. That there was a version of the story she hadn't let herself imagine. Until now.

And once the idea was out there, she couldn't unthink it.

The silence stretched again.

"You think he knew?" Liz asked.

Ava exhaled through her nose. "If he did, we would've noticed something by now. Chap's not exactly subtle when he's spiraling."

Liz leaned her head against the window. "And if he didn't know?"

Ava's throat tightened. She gripped the steering wheel like it could steady the mess unraveling in her chest. "What if it *was* his?" she whispered. "And this, this is how he finds out? Not from her. Not from a quiet conversation or a moment where he could at least try to do the right thing. But like this. A rumor. A maybe. A baby no one even knew about, and now…"

She blinked hard, like that might hold back the tears she refused to cry. "Now it's too late for everything."

Neither of them said anything else as they pulled into the lot beside the station. The harbor wind tugged at the police tape still fluttering at the dock, like it refused to settle until the truth did.

Chief Harrow looked like he hadn't slept. He was behind his desk when Ava and Liz walked in, rubbing his temple with two fingers like he could smooth the truth out of his skull if he just pressed hard enough.

"You saw the report," he said without preamble.

Ava nodded. "It wasn't an accident."

"No," Harrow said flatly. "Someone killed her, then tossed her in the harbor like they were taking out the trash. Bruises on her arms. Defensive, maybe. Maybe not."

Liz leaned forward. "And the pregnancy?"

"Confirmed. We'll run DNA if we have to."

Ava's breath caught. *If we have to.*

"You don't already have a list of potential fathers?" she asked.

Harrow narrowed his eyes. "I've got theories. But I'm not saying a damn thing until I've got more than bar gossip and gut feelings."

"You think it was Chap," Liz said.

"I think a lot of people *think* it was Chap," Harrow replied. "He was drunk. He was angry. He's not talking."

"He's probably scared," Ava said, the words escaping before she could stop them.

"Maybe," Harrow said, his gaze fixing on her now. "Or maybe he's guilty."

He let the silence stretch before adding, "And maybe I shouldn't be discussing an active investigation with someone who's been romantically entangled with my prime suspect."

Liz's eyebrows shot up. "*Prime* suspect? That's interesting. So, it's official now?"

Harrow refused to answer.

Then she scoffed. "Come on, Chief. Half the town's slept with each other. You can't avoid a conflict of interest in Spruce Cove."

Ava lifted a hand. "For the record, I haven't slept with *anyone* in this town."

That earned a flicker of something in Harrow's eyes, part amusement and part warning, but he didn't push it.

Liz leaned in again. "Was Amelia acting strange lately? Quiet? Paranoid?"

"She was planning a move," Harrow said. "Talked to someone in Anchorage about a museum job. That's what I heard. She was trying to leave."

"Then why Chap?" Ava asked.

Harrow shrugged. "You tell me. You knew her better than I did."

It felt like an accusation. Ava didn't answer.

"We'll have a public statement by morning," Harrow said, reaching for a folder. "In the meantime, keep the pregnancy out of the story. For now, for the family."

His eyes moved between them. "We don't need to be making this mess worse."

As they stepped into the hallway, Liz muttered under her breath, "There's no way he keeps that quiet."

***

They were halfway to the car when the door behind them opened again.

"Wait," Ryan called, jogging down the steps. He glanced over his shoulder, making sure no one was watching. "Can we talk? Just for a second."

Liz and Ava stopped.

"I couldn't say anything earlier," he said, his voice lower now, more urgent. "But I want you to know, the chief thinks Chap did it. He's not saying it publicly yet, but he's building that case. Quietly. Methodically. Like he's already convinced."

Ava felt her stomach sink. "But you don't believe it."

Ryan looked between them, his eyes searching theirs like he was desperate for someone, anyone, to believe his version of the truth.

"Chap's my best friend. Has been since we were twelve. He's got a temper, sure, and sometimes his mouth runs faster than his brain. But he's not the kind of guy who could do something like this. Not to Amelia. Not to anyone."

Liz studied him. "Then who do you think did it?"

"I don't know," he said. "But I do know this, Earl Atwood came in the same time Amelia did. Had words with Chap. He apparently looked like a man sweating through something. And when he left, he avoided eye contact with every person in the room."

"Why hasn't the chief looked at him harder?" Liz asked.

"Because Chap's the obvious suspect. The ex with a temper, a messy breakup, rumors already swirling. People hear 'unwanted pregnancy' and start filling in the blanks. He fits what they want to believe. Earl doesn't even register in the version Harrow's building."

He glanced around before adding, "But the thing is, Earl wouldn't leave her alone. Came into The Gaff Hook that night and zeroed in on her. She shut him down."

Ava and Liz exchanged a glance, because they'd seen it too. The look. The tension. The way Amelia had turned her body away from him, stiff and dismissive. And the way Earl had lingered anyway.

"And the chief?" Liz asked.

Ryan shook his head. "Brushed it off. Said it was just Earl being Earl. But I have seen the way he looked at her. It wasn't harmless."

He turned, already retreating toward the station.

"Thank you," Liz said after him.

He didn't turn around.

***

They found Earl Atwood outside of Annie's, a half-eaten donut in one hand and a coil of rope in the other. The gulls screamed overhead, but he didn't look up when they approached.

"Earl," Liz called out, her voice brisk.

He turned, slow and suspicious, like he'd already decided they were trouble. "Well, well. The press ladies," he said. "What's the headline now?"

"We just have a few questions," Ava said. "About the night Amelia died."

His jaw twitched, a flicker of something mean darting through his eyes. "I already talked to Harrow."

"We're not Harrow," Liz said. "Did you see Amelia after she left The Gaff Hook?"

He shrugged. "Didn't keep tabs on her."

"You were talking to her earlier in the night," Ava pressed. "People said it looked tense."

Earl narrowed his eyes. "We were just catching up."

"We heard she wasn't smiling," Liz said. "Didn't look too comfortable."

Earl snorted. "That girl never knew how to take a compliment."

He turned back to his rope, then added, almost like it hurt to admit, "Like I'd be interested in a pregnant woman anyway. What the hell was I supposed to do? Raise a kid?"

Liz's head snapped up. "Funny," she said softly. "We didn't say she was pregnant."

Ava folded her arms. "Or that anyone knew."

Earl froze. The silence that followed was heavy enough to sink a skiff.

"I heard things," he said finally, his voice too quick, too forced. "Small town, you know how it is."

"Except nobody else heard it," Liz said. "Not until today. So, unless you've got a crystal ball in your tool shed, you knew something no one else did."

Earl's jaw clenched. "I didn't touch her," he growled.

"She told you to leave her alone," Ava said.

His eyes flared. "You don't know what you're talking about."

Liz's tone cut like wind off the water. "This sounds a lot like the other night, when you got 86'd for not leaving her alone."

He didn't move. Then he forced a laugh that was too loud, too short, all wrong.

"Whatever," he muttered. "You're barking up the wrong damn tree."

They walked away without saying goodbye.

Shivers were still crawling down Ava's spine, the kind that felt like they'd settled under her skin and might never leave. She didn't mean to look back, but she did. Just a quick glance over her shoulder, just to be sure Earl hadn't decided to follow them. He hadn't. Thank God.

Still, she picked up her pace, like putting more sidewalk between them might calm the adrenaline fizzing in her veins.

"He's hiding something," she said, trying to sound cool, like her voice hadn't just wobbled a little.

Liz didn't even blink. "They always are."

Ava nodded, jaw tight. She kept walking, hoping Liz couldn't tell that her heart was still pounding like it was trying to outrun her body.

***

Chief Harrow didn't look up from his desk when they walked in.

"If you're here to tell me Chap's a misunderstood saint, save it," he muttered, flipping a page in the folder before him.

"We're not," Ava said evenly. "We're here to talk about Earl Atwood."

Now he looked up.

Liz stepped forward. "We just spoke to him. He got defensive. Quick to anger. And he knew about the pregnancy. We didn't tell him."

"That doesn't prove anything," Harrow said. "Half the town probably knows by now. I told you to keep it quiet."

"Then either someone's talking," Liz said, "or Earl knew before anyone else had a reason to."

"And he had motive," Ava added. "He was bothering her. She told him to back off more than once. Didn't even want to be in the same room with him."

Harrow sighed. "Earl's harmless."

"He was kicked out of The Gaff Hook last week for harassing her," Ava said. "That's not harmless. That's stalking."

The chief leaned back in his chair, arms crossed. "Chap was drunk. Angry. Jealous. And he left the bar before she did."

Liz didn't miss a beat. "That sounds like half of The Gaff Hook on any given Friday night."

Then, more measured, "It doesn't make him the *only* suspect."

"No," Harrow said, "but it makes him a strong one. And he's not talking. He looks guilty."

"Or," Ava said softly, "he's terrified."

For a moment, none of them spoke.

Then Harrow sat forward and stared at Ava. "Look, if Earl did anything, I'll find it. But I'm not going to stop looking at Chap just because you two have history."

Ava flinched, barely. But she didn't look away.

Frustration coiled inside her, sharp and insistent. They were running out of time. Outpaced by rumor, drowning in everyone else's version of the truth.

Liz's voice was cool but firm. "I'm sure you'll investigate every lead, Chief. Fully. So, when the time comes, you know you got it right."

Harrow didn't answer.

That night, Ava climbed aboard the *Malahini*, her boots thudding softly against the worn wood of the deck. The cabin was dark, quiet. No lights, no voices. Just the hush of the harbor behind her.

The soft creak of the planks must've been enough. Moments later, the cabin door cracked open.

Chap squinted out, bleary-eyed and bare-chested, hair tousled like he'd just wrestled sleep and lost.

He blinked at her, then at the thermos in her hand. "Tell me that's not whisky."

"Chamomile. With honey."

He exhaled and stepped aside. "That might be the kindest thing anyone's ever done for me."

The cabin was warm from the little space heater tucked in the corner. She sat across from him while he poured the tea into two mismatched mugs. One with a chip at the rim, the other with a faded fish painted on the side.

He slid hers across the table.

"Still hungover?" she asked.

"Let's just say my skull's not accepting new tenants," he muttered. "But I'm upright, so I'll take it."

They sat in the kind of silence that felt earned. Comfortable, even now.

"I knew," he said quietly.

Ava looked up.

"About the baby," he added. "She told me a few days before. Everything. When she slapped me on the dock."

Ava's voice was soft. "Why didn't you say anything?"

Chap didn't look at her. "It wasn't my secret to share."

Ava blinked.

He stared into his mug. "I told her she wasn't ready to be a mom. Not with everything going on. Not with the way she was feeling about the town, her job, her future. I thought I was being honest."

"And she got mad."

"Yeah," he said. "She got really mad."

"Was it yours?"

The question slipped out before she could stop it.

Ava held her breath, instantly wishing she could take it back.

Chap looked at her, really looked at her, and raised an eyebrow. "Really?"

She felt the heat rise to her cheeks. She didn't answer, just stared down at her tea.

She didn't press. But the silence that followed felt different.

And she let it drop. For now.

Outside, the harbor kept its secrets. Inside the *Malahini*, the truth was starting to slip free. One painful drip at a time.

***

Later, back at the house, Ava stood at the kitchen sink, staring out at the moonlit yard. The steam from the kettle curled up around her face, soft and warm.

The conversation kept looping in her head. Not the words so much as the spaces between them. The way Chap had said it wasn't his secret. The way he hadn't said more.

Esther came in wearing her robe, her face drawn with sleep and worry. "Did you see him?"

Ava nodded. "He's holding it together. Barely."

George shuffled in behind her, rubbing at his temple. "He's not a killer, Ava. Whatever the town says."

"I know," she said. "But knowing and proving are two different things."

Esther poured her own cup of tea and joined Ava at the sink. "He needs people in his corner right now. Real ones."

"He's got them," Ava said. "He just doesn't know it yet."

The house was quiet again, save for the slow tick of the kitchen clock. And somewhere under it all, the low hum of a storm still gathering. Just out of reach.

***

That night, Ava lay in bed staring at the ceiling, the faint glow of the streetlight outside bleeding through the curtains in soft gray lines.

She heard Amelia's voice sitting on the log the last time they talked.

"I feel stuck," Amelia had said, voice low and tired. "Like Spruce Cove has its hand around my throat. Every time I think I'm about to get free, someone pulls me back in."

Ava had laughed then, not unkindly. "Isn't that just being from here?"

But Amelia had looked out at the water, her eyes distant. "No. It's more than that. I'm not meant to stay. If I don't leave now, I will never get out."

Now, lying in the dark, Ava saw it for what it was. Not just a moment of vulnerability, but a warning. A quiet kind of goodbye.

She blinked at the ceiling.

Amelia hadn't said she was pregnant. She didn't need to.

She was telling her she was trapped, angry and scared.

And now she was gone.

Ava turned her face into the pillow, her voice barely a whisper into the dark.

"I should've listened."

Chapter 22

Ava was dreaming of the ocean again. That lull of dark water, the familiar sway of a boat she hadn't stepped on in years. Then a sound broke through it. Three sharp knocks, cutting through sleep like glass.

She blinked into the dark, heart thudding. Another knock. Firm. Urgent.

She threw off the covers, pulled on the sweatshirt draped over her chair, and padded to the front door, her footsteps soft against the cold floorboards.

Through the window, she saw Liz on the porch. Coat zipped to the chin. Arms crossed tight over her chest like she was holding herself together.

Ava opened the door. "What the?"

"We need to talk," Liz said. Her voice was quiet, but it had that edge. The kind that said this wasn't just news. It was damage.

Ava stepped aside. Liz entered.

They didn't speak again until they reached the kitchen. Ava flicked on the small light over the stove, and everything felt surreal. Familiar objects in unfamiliar quiet.

Liz sat. Ava stood.

"Tell me," Ava said, her voice urgent.

Liz didn't hesitate. "There's been a tip. Someone says they saw Chap and Amelia. Outside. The night she died. Arguing. Loud. Heated."

Ava tried to play it off: "Like they always fight?"

She gripped the edge of the counter. "Who gave the tip?"

"Anonymous. Came in late. Harrow says it's detailed enough that he can't ignore it."

"Does he think?" Ava couldn't finish.

Liz answered anyway. "The Chief is publicly calling Chap the prime suspect. This will be part of the story."

Ava turned toward the dark window over the sink. "Grandma and Grandpa. They're going to hear about this."

"They will," Liz said.

A floorboard creaked.

They turned to see George in the doorway, robe cinched tight, eyes bleary but alert. Esther was right behind him, wrapped in her shawl like armor.

"We didn't mean to eavesdrop," George said gently. "But we heard enough."

"Is it true?" Esther asked, voice soft. "They think Chap?"

Liz nodded. "They do."

George's gaze found Ava. "And what do *you* think?"

Ava didn't answer. Her throat was too tight.

Esther stepped closer, her hand finding Ava's arm. "This doesn't sound good."

The kettle whistled from the stove. No one moved.

***

Ava didn't sleep.

After George and Esther had gone back to bed quiet, shaken, and pretending not to be, Ava stayed in the kitchen long after Liz left. The kettle had gone cold. Her tea sat untouched, the bag still sitting like an anchor in the mug.

She sat at the table with her arms wrapped around herself, staring at nothing. Just listening to the hum of the refrigerator and the occasional groan of old pipes in the walls.

Outside, the dark started to lift. First a dusty gray, then that bruised blue that always came before sunrise. Eventually, the first fingers of light crept across the linoleum, like even the sun was tiptoeing through this.

She was trying to wrap her head around the fact that Chap was a suspect.

That word hadn't stopped echoing in her head. *Suspect.* Like he was some man they barely knew. Like he hadn't stood in her kitchen.

Slept in her bed. Laughed at her terrible jokes and touched her like he meant it.

She pressed her palms flat against the table.

She wanted to believe he was innocent. God, she wanted that. But the part of her that had spent childhood summers in this town, the part that knew how people could change and how sometimes they didn't, kept whispering: You don't know everything. You never did. She thought of Amelia. Her bright, restless energy. The way she'd started pulling away that last year. A girl trying to leave. A girl who never got the chance.

Ava swallowed hard. What if Chap *had* hurt her?

She stood abruptly. The chair scraped against the floor. Her legs were shaky, her body aching with fatigue, but her mind was wired, alive in the worst possible way.

She went upstairs to shower. The hot water scalded her skin, but she didn't flinch. It grounded her. Made her feel real again.

By the time she stepped out, the sky was fully awake. Bright and cold and indifferent.

She dressed quickly, pulling on jeans and a sweater without thinking. Her hands moved automatically, but her chest was tight.

She didn't know what she'd say when she saw him. Didn't know what she believed anymore.

But one thing was certain.

If she didn't look him in the eye, she'd never stop wondering.

Ava checked the *Malahini*. He wasn't there. She found Chap behind his workshop, the sleeves of his flannel rolled to the elbows, his hands busy doing nothing, just rearranging the same pile of firewood.

He looked up when he heard her footsteps crunch over the gravel. His eyes were bloodshot. He hadn't shaved. For a second, she hesitated. Then she forced herself forward.

"We need to talk."

He exhaled through his nose, didn't speak.

"Someone saw you with Amelia," Ava said. "Arguing. The night she died."

He looked away.

"Harrow says you're the prime suspect."

His jaw tensed. "Of course he does."

"I need to ask you something," she said, stepping closer. "And I need you to look me in the eye when you answer."

That got his attention. Slowly, he turned toward her.

"Did you do it?" she asked. Her voice was steady, even though her heart was racing so loud she could barely hear herself.

"What?" His eyes widened. "You think I? Jesus, Ava." He shoved a hand through his hair and turned away, pacing a tight line in the gravel. "You *really* think I could've?"

"I don't *want* to think it," she said. "But you won't talk to the police. You won't tell them what happened. Why wouldn't you clear your name? So tell me, right now. Why won't you?"

He stopped pacing. His back was to her. For a moment, she thought he might just keep walking.

Then he turned. And the look on his face wasn't anger anymore.

It was shame.

"Because I don't remember," he said.

The words dropped between them, heavy and unforgiving.

"I remember being at The Gaff Hook. I remember drinking too much. And I remember Amelia showing up." He paused. "We talked. Maybe argued. I don't know. It's a blur. I left. And after that, nothing."

He lifted his hands, helpless.

"I blacked out, Ava. I woke up in my bunk with no clue how I got there. No idea what we talked about. I don't even know what time I left the bar."

Ava's throat tightened. Her arms crossed tightly over her chest.

"You could've followed her."

"I could've," he said quietly. "I don't think I did. I *hope* I didn't. But I don't know."

The silence that followed was thick and sickening.

Ava stared at him, searching for something: remorse, panic, truth. All she found was devastation.

And maybe, worst of all, doubt.

Ava didn't say anything.

She just stood there for a moment, the wind tugging at her sleeves, her thoughts too loud and jumbled to sort through. Then she turned and walked away.

Gravel crunched under her boots. She didn't look back at first. Couldn't. Not until she reached the corner of the building and curiosity, or something crueler, forced her to glance over her shoulder.

Chap was still standing there.

Arms limp at his sides. Shoulders slumped. The man who'd always seemed too stubborn to break looked, suddenly, breakable.

And that might've hurt more than anything.

Ava turned away again and kept walking.

She didn't know what she believed. She didn't know if she was angry or heartbroken or just empty.

But she knew where she had to go.

***

Liz was still at the office, the lamplight spilling out across the sidewalk like a halo. Inside, her desk looked like chaos. Three coffee mugs, an open notebook, a trail of highlighters. But she looked up the second Ava stepped in.

Ava didn't say anything at first. She shut the door and leaned against it, like she wasn't sure her legs would keep her up.

324

"He doesn't remember," she said finally. "He blacked out."

Liz froze, her pen still hovering above the page. "What?"

"After The Gaff Hook," Ava said, voice thin. "He remembers drinking. Talking to Amelia. Then nothing. Just, nothing."

Liz stood, slowly, like the air had gotten heavier.

Ava's hands started to shake. She crossed the room and sat on the floor, her back to the wall, knees pulled up like a shield.

"I don't know what's worse," she said, "that he might be lying or that he's telling the truth."

Liz crouched beside her. "I'm sorry, Ava."

"I stood up for him." Her voice cracked. "I believed in him. I said he wouldn't, he couldn't, do something like this."

She tried to hold it back, but the tears came anyway. Not pretty ones. These were the kind that made your whole face ache, made your body curl inward like grief had physical weight.

Liz said nothing for a moment. Just rested a hand on Ava's back, grounding her.

"I let him back in," Ava whispered, more to herself than to Liz. "And now I don't know who he is."

Liz's voice was low. "You knew the version of him he showed you. That doesn't make you foolish. That makes you human. Hell, we all saw that same version."

Ava sniffed, rubbed her sleeve across her nose. "What if I fell for someone capable of something like this?"

"You fell for someone complicated," Liz said. "But you don't know the truth yet. Neither do I."

Ava looked at her, eyes rimmed red. "Then how do I hold both truths at once? The part of me that still wants to believe and the part that's terrified? What if he's innocent? What if he's guilty?"

Liz exhaled, slow and steady. "One hour at a time. One piece at a time. That's how we survive these things."

For a moment, the room was quiet but for the hum of the old radiator and the storm outside beginning to pick up.

Then Liz added, "But you should start preparing. Not just yourself. Your grandparents, too. Because if this turns, if it gets darker, you need to be ready."

Ava nodded. Her hands were still trembling, but something in her had steadied.

"I can't just wait around," she said, her voice low but certain. "If there's any chance he didn't do this, I have to find out who did."

"Then we'll keep digging," Liz said. "Together."

Ava wiped her face, took a breath that felt like the first clean inhale in hours.

She didn't feel strong. But she didn't feel entirely broken either.

Not yet.

***

The house was warm. Usually too warm for Ava, who often cracked a window just to feel something crisp on her skin. But tonight, she didn't mind it. Tonight, she let the heat wrap around her like a memory she didn't know she'd been missing. It was something familiar, something steady. Something that didn't ask questions.

She stepped through the door quietly, careful not to let it slam. The living room was golden with fire light, the kind that made everything look like a memory. George sat in his recliner, glasses perched on the end of his nose, a thick book open in his lap. Esther was curled on the couch, knitting needles clicking in a soft, steady rhythm. The scent of peppermint and cedar hung in the air.

Ava hesitated in the doorway.

"Hi," she said, like a kid arriving home past curfew.

George looked up first. "Hey, kiddo."

Esther glanced up, her expression warm but searching. "Everything okay?"

Ava shook her head lightly, then nodded. Then, as if to change the subject, gestured to the book in George's lap. "What're you reading?"

George held up the cover. *A History of the Pacific Trollers, Volume II.* "Just revisiting the glory days."

Ava forced a small smile. "Sounds riveting."

Esther's needles kept moving. "I'm making a shawl for Mary next door. She saw mine at the Christmas potluck and practically chased me to the car with a bag of yarn and a promise of blackberry pie."

"That sounds like Mary," Ava said. She didn't sit. Her arms crossed tightly over her chest, as if holding herself together had become muscle memory. She took a step forward, and then another.

The room felt smaller tonight. Closer. Like the walls had leaned in just enough to notice.

Esther's needles paused. George lowered his book.

"Ava?" Esther asked gently. "Honey, what is it?"

Ava blinked. Her mouth opened, closed. She felt the words forming, heavy in her throat, but they wouldn't come out. Not yet. She stared at the fire instead, her heartbeat in her ears.

Then, softly, almost too softly, she said, "I talked to him."

The silence that followed was immediate and dense.

George straightened. "Chap?"

She nodded. Her voice was barely audible. "He doesn't remember. The night Amelia died. He said he blacked out."

Esther's knitting fell still in her lap. George's eyes narrowed, not in suspicion, but in concentration. Processing.

The fire crackled quietly, like it was trying to fill the space between them.

"He said he was drinking," Ava continued. "That they talked. Maybe argued. But after that, it's blank."

She paused, her voice breaking a little on the word. "He woke up on his boat. Alone. No memory of how he got there."

For a moment, no one spoke. The soft tick of the mantle clock, the occasional pop of firewood, it all felt magnified, like the world had shrunk to just this room.

Esther sat back slowly, as if her body had suddenly grown heavier with the weight of what she'd just heard. Her knitting slipped from her lap without her noticing, needles clinking softly against one another as the yarn tumbled to the floor.

Her face shifted. Not just worry, but something deeper. A kind of grief that didn't have a name yet. Her eyes, normally so sharp and knowing, looked pained. Hollow. Like someone had cracked the foundation beneath her feet.

"So," she said, her voice faltering, "he might've done it."

She didn't say it with accusation. She said it like a question that hurt to ask. Like it cost her something just to form the words.

Ava didn't answer right away. She couldn't.

"He says he doesn't think he did," she whispered. "But he can't be sure."

George exhaled through his nose, a slow, deliberate breath like he was trying to steady something inside him. He leaned forward in his chair, elbows on his knees, the book forgotten now at his feet.

"I don't want to believe that," he said. His voice was quiet, but it had weight. "I've known that boy since he was knee-high. Taught him how to tie a proper knot. He used to bring me deer meat, proud as a prince."

He looked up at Ava then, his expression caught somewhere between disbelief and disappointment. "But I also know what a blackout means. What alcohol can do. Especially when you mix it with pain and anger."

He shook his head, as if trying to clear the thought before it settled too deep.

"Chap's got a good heart," George said, softer now. "But sometimes even good hearts don't stop people from breaking."

Ava took a step back, suddenly aware of how tight her chest felt, how heavy her limbs had become.

"I'm going to head to bed," she said, trying to sound casual, but the words came out brittle. "It's been a long day."

Neither of them argued. Esther stood slowly, smoothing her skirt, and crossed the room. She didn't say anything, just wrapped Ava in a hug that lasted longer than usual. One of those lingering embraces that tried to pass strength through skin. Ava let herself lean into it, just for a second.

"Get some rest, sweetheart," Esther whispered into her hair.

Ava nodded, stepped back. She turned toward the stairs, keeping her shoulders straight, her pace steady. But as she reached the corner, half-swallowed by the shadows, she heard them.

Esther's voice, low but urgent. "What if we were wrong, George?"

"I thought we were bringing her home. Somewhere safe. But what if this wasn't the safest place after all?"

A chair creaked. George's voice, low and unreadable: "We didn't know."

Esther again, quieter now. "We may have introduced her to a murderer."

Ava didn't stop. She kept walking, each step heavier than the last, the words chasing her down the hall like ghosts. She reached her bedroom, closed the door behind her, and leaned against it. Her eyes stinging, chest aching.

She hadn't come to Spruce Cove for this. But here she was.

Alone. Again.

And for the first time in weeks, she wasn't sure if anyone in the house still believed in him.

Or in her.

She sat down on the edge of the bed, the mattress creaking beneath her like it, too, was tired of holding the weight of this story.

Her phone buzzed against the nightstand, sudden and loud in the quiet.

She didn't want to look. Not tonight. But habit won out over exhaustion.

William: Hey stranger. Haven't heard from you in a bit. Just checking in. You still surviving the land of salmon and bear spray?

A second buzz.

William: Also, I passed a bakery that sold lemon bars. Made me think of you. And of your very strong opinions about "mushy crusts."

Ava stared at the screen, something unfamiliar pressing at the corners of her eyes. Not quite tears. Not quite a smile.

It was the first message in what felt like weeks that didn't demand something from her. It just offered warmth.

Ava stared at the screen, her thumb hovering over the keyboard, unsure whether to reply or let the message sit like a postcard from a different life. One where things made sense. One where people didn't vanish into silence or suspicion.

She set the phone down without answering.

Somewhere across the hall, floorboards creaked. The fire had burned low. The night folded in around her like a closing door.

She pulled the covers up, let the dark consume her, and told herself she'd figure it out tomorrow. Not because she believed that.

But because she didn't know what else to do.

Chapter 23

The scent hit Ava first. Cinnamon and butter, warm and insistent, like it was trying to remind her there were still good things in the world. She stepped into the kitchen barefoot, drawn by the smell and the sound of quiet industry.

Esther stood at the stove, lifting the last foil-covered pie from the oven with practiced care. The counter was already crowded. Pies of every variety, lined up like offerings: golden crusts, glistening with sugar, resting on cooling racks and cookie sheets. Rhubarb, apple, blueberry. Lemon chess, her specialty. One peach, set aside for Darlene.

"Number nine," Esther murmured, mostly to herself. "God help us if I didn't bring enough."

The kitchen looked like it had weathered a small, flour-based storm. There were smudges on the cupboards, butter wrappers curled near the sink, and Ava could've sworn the smell of nutmeg had woven itself into the curtains.

George came in from the garage, balancing two pie carriers in his arms. "Car's loaded," he said. "But I had to rearrange the backseat three times. These pies take up more room than we did on that camping trip to Yellowstone."

Esther didn't laugh, but her mouth tugged upward for a second. "Put the lemon ones on the side closest to the community hall door," she instructed, wiping her hands on her apron. "They need to be cut last. Keeps the crust from getting soggy."

Ava leaned against the doorway, arms crossed loosely over her chest. She hadn't spoken much that morning. None of them had, really. The silence between them felt respectful, like they were walking around something fragile.

"They're going to appreciate all this," Ava said finally, nodding toward the pies.

Esther gave a small shrug. "It's what we do. People lose someone, we feed them."

It wasn't just tradition. It was ritual. Grief wrapped in sugar and pastry crust.

George disappeared again, and Esther finally stepped back from the counter, rubbing her lower back with one hand. "Go change," she said softly. "We need to leave in twenty minutes."

Ava hesitated. "Do you want help ironing your blouse?"

Esther looked surprised, then nodded. "If you don't mind. It's on the bed."

By the time Ava brought it to the laundry room, George was already there, wrestling a crease from his tie with all the grace of a man who wore one maybe twice a year.

"You look nice," Ava said.

He grunted. "I'm pretending that I'm a man who owns more than one tie."

Ava set the iron down on the board and smoothed Esther's blouse beneath her hands. The fabric was thin, delicate. Light lavender with tiny stitched flowers near the collar. The kind of shirt that felt like something someone wore to be seen.

She pressed slowly, methodically. The iron hissed. Outside, a crow cawed once, loud and sharp, like it was announcing something no one wanted to hear.

In the living room, Esther called out, "Ten minutes."

Ava didn't rush.

***

Before heading into the sanctuary, Ava, George, and Esther made the turn down the side stairwell to the basement, carrying their cargo like sacred offerings.

"Hold those level," Esther said over her shoulder, navigating the steps with a pie in each hand. "If anyone drops my lemon chess, this funeral's becoming a double-header."

The usually musty church basement smelled like warm casseroles, buttered rolls, tangy mustard dressing, and something unmistakably marshmallow based. Every folding table was already brimming with foil-tented dishes, Jell-O salads quivering in glass bowls, and crockpots humming on low, their cords trailing like roots.

335

Esther led the way. George followed with the last of the crates. Ava brought up the rear, arms full of lemon chess.

The room buzzed with motion. Women in quilted jackets and sensible shoes darted from one table to another, adjusting placements, scribbling labels, and barking friendly commands over the noise. At the center of it all, Joyce stood with a clipboard, her hair perfectly set, her mouth moving a mile a minute.

"No, no. Put the potato au gratin next to the meatballs. We can't have two heavy meat dishes at the same end. We'll lose balance. This has to be perfect!" she called, her voice sharp enough to slice bread.

She caught sight of Esther and broke into a wide, tight smile. "Esther! Thank God. We need your pies."

Esther gave a faint smile. "Lemon's on the end, peach is front and center."

"You're a saint," Joyce said, already motioning to two younger women to clear space on the dessert table.

Ava set the pies down, suddenly aware of just how many eyes were on her. Curious glances, quick whispers. Everyone was polite. No one asked questions. But their faces said enough: *Were you the reason he killed her?*

Esther's hand found her back. Not pushing. Just steadying.

Joyce leaned closer. "You holding up, honey?"

Ava nodded, not trusting her voice.

"Well," Joyce said with a sigh, "go on upstairs when you're ready. We'll have the tables looking perfect by the time you come down."

And just like that, the moment ended. Joyce clapped her hands and spun back to her task force, redirecting a tray of deviled eggs like she was commanding troops.

Ava followed her grandparents back upstairs stairs, her hands now free but her chest heavier somehow. She took a deep breath.

Time to face the rest.

***

A man at the upright piano played the opening notes of *Amazing Grace*, the sound both familiar and newly unbearable. Slow, measured, and aching. The kind of melody that knew exactly where in the chest to land.

Ava stepped through the double doors behind her grandparents, and for a moment, all she could see was light.

The stained glass over the altar cast a prism of gold and violet across the floor. A single lamb, its face lifted toward a painted sky, dominated the center panel. On a brighter day, it might have looked hopeful. Today, it just looked alone.

The pews were packed with coats and collars, with shoulders pulled tight by grief. The entire town had shown up. Some were crying openly. Others stared forward like they were still trying to convince themselves this was real. The air felt weighted, thick with perfume and sorrow.

337

In the middle row, Ava spotted Chief Harrow and Deputy Hale, their uniforms crisp, their faces unreadable. The pew creaked slightly when Harrow shifted, but he didn't look around.

Ava searched for him. Her eyes scanned every shadowed corner, every pew edge, expecting Chap to be somewhere. But he wasn't.

Not yet.

A hush swept the room as the doors at the back opened again.

The pallbearers entered, six in total. Each wore a small daisy boutonnière pinned to his lapel. Bright and simple, like something Amelia would have chosen herself. They moved with the steady, careful choreography of ceremony. At the front of the group was Mason, his jaw tight, his eyes fixed straight ahead. The boutonnière on his lapel had a faint smear of something, pollen or maybe the thumbprint of someone who'd tried to pin it on him.

Behind them, the casket gleamed. A rich, honey-colored cedar, its grain soft and warm in the morning light. The men in town had built it themselves. A quiet tribute. A final act of love and labor for one of their own. No flowers on top. Just a single folded cloth. Blue, like her favorite dress.

Ava's breath caught. The room spun just slightly.

Esther reached for her elbow.

She followed them down the aisle, numb. George guided her to a pew on the left side, about four rows from the front. Esther sat beside her, her hand still resting lightly on Ava's arm like she didn't quite trust the moment not to collapse. Liz slid next to Ava.

As the casket was set gently on the supports, the piano began to fade.

The pastor stepped forward, his notes tucked into a leather-bound folder. His eyes were red-rimmed behind his glasses, and when he spoke, his voice cracked, just once, but he didn't apologize for it.

He spoke of light. Of a life too brief and too bright. Of questions we never get answers to. Of faith in the face of uncertainty. Of community and the way it carries us, even when we're too tired to walk.

Ava barely heard the words. Her eyes drifted again toward the back of the church.

She saw him.

Chap had slipped in during the hymn. He sat alone in the last pew, his shoulders back, his eyes lowered. No boutonnière. No coat. Just him, in a plain black shirt, looking every bit uncertain and shattered.

No one sat beside him.

No one even looked.

Except Ava.

***

The sanctuary fell still as Amelia's sister stepped up to the lectern.

She was a quieter version of Amelia. Same dark eyes, same sharp cheekbones, but without the mischief always sparking behind them.

339

Today, those eyes were swollen with grief, and her hands shook slightly as she unfolded the piece of paper in her hands.

"My name is Caroline," she began, her voice soft but steady. "I'm Amelia's older sister. And I want to tell you what it was like to grow up in her orbit."

A few people smiled, the kind of expressions pulled from shared memory more than comfort.

"Amelia didn't enter a room," Caroline said. "She *arrived*. Like a storm cloud with glitter in it. She was always a little too much, but in the best possible way. If she loved you, you knew it. And if she was mad at you, well, you knew that too."

Soft laughter rippled through the room.

"She once told me she hated beige because it looked like giving up. She wanted color. Bright, bold color. She wore purple eyeliner in seventh grade and didn't care that people stared. She gave people nicknames they never escaped. And she always, *always*, snuck extra whipped cream when no one was looking."

Ava smiled, briefly, and bit the inside of her cheek to stop the tears.

"But she wasn't just wild," Caroline went on. "She was soft. She was the first one to notice when you were having a bad day. The first to text a funny meme or a link to a ridiculous TikTok. She didn't say *I love you* in words. She said it by making you playlists. Or stealing the last cookie off your plate because she didn't want you to feel guilty for eating it."

The laughter faded, replaced by the thick quiet that comes before a sob.

"She was getting ready to leave this town. You all know that. She had plans. Big, impossible ones. She wanted to be a climate activist, a podcast host and talked about opening a food truck called 'Bad Egg' just for brunch. She didn't need to be famous. She wanted to *matter*. She wanted to fix something. Or everything."

Caroline's voice broke then. She paused, pressing a hand to her chest.

"She was complicated. Beautiful. Messy. Brave. And she should be here."

Silence.

Liz looked down at her hands, her expression unreadable.

Caroline sniffed, collected herself and looked directly at Liz. "Before I sat down to write this, I called someone who knew Amelia well. I needed help finding the words. I'm grateful for that help. Because this, this is the hardest thing I've ever had to write."

She folded the paper again, her hands steadier now.

"But here's what I'll leave you with: Amelia was the kind of person who made you feel more *alive* just by standing next to her. The kind of person you never, ever forget. And I hope, when you think of her, you don't just remember the way she left. I hope you remember the way she lived."

She stepped back from the lectern. For a long moment, no one moved. The sanctuary held its breath.

Then the pianist began again, soft and slow.

Be Still, My Soul.

The notes unfurled like prayer. Low, steady, aching. A hymn for the broken. A lullaby for the ones left behind.

Ava stared straight ahead, her vision blurred.

Beside her, Liz's shoulders shook in silence, her face wet. Ava reached blindly for her hand, and Liz squeezed back, fingers trembling.

Esther, always prepared, reached into her purse and pulled out a travel pack of tissues. She passed one to Ava, then one to Liz, her own hands armed with tissues as her eyes filled.

Finally, she offered one to George.

He didn't speak. Didn't blink.

Just nodded once, taking the tissue in silence.

A single tear traced down his cheek, carving a line through skin that had seen decades of joy and grief.

***

As the final chord of *Be Still, My Soul* lingered in the rafters, the pallbearers rose again, slowly. Six men, six steps, and the cedar casket lifted from its supports with reverent care.

Mason didn't look up. His jaw was locked tight, his boutonnière now wilted slightly against the tension in his chest.

The pastor stepped to the front, hands folded over his Bible.

"Thank you, all of you, for being here today," he said. His voice was warm, measured. One of those tones people trusted without realizing why. "Per Amelia's family's wishes, the graveside burial will be private. You are all invited to join us downstairs for the meal her community has so lovingly prepared."

Pastor Grady, who'd baptized half the town and buried the other half, stepped back as the pallbearers moved again. The casket led them down the aisle, the soft scuff of dress shoes against wood the only sound.

Mason's eyes scanned the crowd and landed on Chap.

For just a second, everything in the church seemed to pause.

Mason's glare was cutting. Not loud. Not theatrical. Just pure and clean and burning. The kind of look that didn't need words to wound.

Chap didn't flinch.

Behind Mason, Amelia's parents followed, their faces hollowed out by grief. Her mother gripped her husband's arm like she needed it to stand. Caroline trailed behind them, her shoulders rounded, her face pale and raw.

They all passed Chap without acknowledgment.

Ava watched it all unfold from her seat, her breath shallow.

Then, in the blur of movement and murmured condolences, she saw Chap slip out the side door.

She instinctively followed.

Outside, the air was sharp with pine and faint woodsmoke. Chap stood a few yards from the church steps, his hands stuffed into his pockets, his face turned toward the tree line.

He didn't turn as she approached.

"I wasn't going to come," he said.

"I know."

He exhaled through his nose. "Thought I'd just watch from the back. Say goodbye in my own way."

"She would've wanted you here," Ava said quietly.

"We don't know if that's true," he replied. "But thank you for saying it."

Ava stood beside him for a long moment. The sound of muffled voices spilled out from the church basement windows. The clatter of serving spoons and the soft wail of a child too young to understand why everyone was dressed in black.

Chap looked like he might speak again but didn't. His shoulders rose, then fell, like breathing had suddenly become a burden.

She stepped closer. Without thinking, she wrapped her arms around him.

He froze for half a second. Then clutched her back with a force that startled her.

Not aggressive. Not even desperate.

Just afraid.

Like letting go might undo him completely.

"I'm sorry," he whispered, voice breaking. "I don't even know what I'm sorry for. Just, all of it."

Ava didn't say anything.

She just held on tighter.

***

Ava slipped back into the building through the side entrance, the hum of voices rising with every step toward the basement. The warmth hit her first: roast beef and gravy, dish soap, over-perfumed coats. Then the sound. A hundred conversations braided into one steady current of human noise: laughter, murmurs, sniffles, clinking forks.

She paused at the top of the stairs, unnoticed for a moment.

The usually stark basement had been transformed. The food Esther and others had brought now covered every table. Plates were loaded. Chairs had been dragged and scooted and filled again. Kids were spinning in circles near the coat rack. Women dabbed at their mascara with napkins. Someone laughed too loudly, then covered their mouth like it wasn't allowed.

Liz stood near the drinks table in a deep, animated debate with the Little League coach. Something about the Chicago Cubs and whether the curse was real or just an excuse for bad pitching. She was smiling in that way she did when she knew she was right, her whole body leaning into the conversation.

George had found a corner full of old men, one foot up on a chair, miming the arc of a cast with his arm. The group around him nodded solemnly, the way only fishermen and eulogized husbands do.

And for a second, Ava almost felt like she could breathe.

But then she heard it, just behind her near the stairwell: a voice.

"I can't believe he showed up."

"Had the nerve to sit in the back like he belonged here. Her poor parents, having to see him there."

"God help that girl."

The words were soft and too practiced to be new. The kind of gossip that bloomed in grief like mold in a sealed room.

Ava stood frozen. Her plate was empty. Her throat was tight.

She didn't turn. Didn't look.

She just stepped back quietly up the stairs and into the silence of the hall, the sound of casserole and condemnation trailing behind her like smoke.

***

The house was quiet when Ava got home.

She walked past the kitchen, still a wreck from Esther's baking bonanza, pie tins stacked, flour dusting the counter like snow, a cooling rack abandoned beside the sink.

Ava moved through it all seamlessly, slipping out of her dress, into pajamas, brushing her teeth on autopilot. Her body felt heavy, like grief had weight. Like it had settled into her bones.

She climbed into bed and pulled the blanket up to her chin.

She didn't expect to sleep.

But she did.

In her dream, Amelia stood at the edge of the dock, her hair wild from the wind, her dress was lemon-yellow.

She was barefoot. Calm.

"You still don't believe it," she said, not accusatory. Just matter of fact.

Ava shook her head. "I don't know what to believe."

Amelia smiled, that half-smirk she always used before saying something uncomfortably true. "He didn't do it," she said. "You know that."

The dock swayed beneath them.

"I don't know anything anymore," Ava whispered.

Amelia didn't answer. She just stepped back into the fog, her body already blurring at the edges.

***

Ava woke to the sound of her phone vibrating on the nightstand. One long buzz, then another. The room was pitch black.

She blinked, disoriented, the remnants of a dream still clinging like sea mist.

Liz.

She answered, her voice rough. "Hello?"

Liz didn't hesitate.

"They arrested Chap."

EPILOGUE

The sea didn't speak in words, but Chap had learned to understand its silences.

It was too quiet now. No seagulls, no creak of dock lines, not even the slap of water against the hulls. Just fog curling in from the harbor like breath held too long. Thick, cold, and suffocating.

Chap stood at the edge of the dock, staring at the slow sway of his boat. It bobbed like it always had, tethered to the post by a weathered rope, but today it looked foreign. Like he was seeing it through someone else's eyes. Like it belonged to a story he didn't want to be in.

He tried to stitch the night back together.

It started at the bar.

Amelia had shown up late, shoulders stiff, face pale but determined. She was already on edge. Then Earl started in. Hands too familiar, voice too loud, laughing like it was all a joke. She tried to shake him off. Chap stepped in.

He hadn't planned on a scene. But the moment Earl smirked and said, "Didn't know she was your girl again," something snapped.

The bar got quiet real fast.

They took it outside. Chap shoved him. Hard. Earl hit back. A busted lip, a split knuckle. Nothing new in a town like this. But what Chap said next, that was the mistake.

"She doesn't need your crap Earl. She's got enough going on already."

Earl sneered. "Like what?"

Chap hesitated, blood pounding. "She's in a special state that's all. Back off."

The words left his mouth like a slap.

Amelia froze. Her eyes got wide. Not in fear, but betrayal. She turned on him, voice shaking. "You told him?"

"I didn't."

But she was already backing away. Her face had gone blank, her defenses snapping into place like armor. She didn't yell. Didn't cry. Just looked as if he had shanked her in the back. She turned and walked away. He knew for certain he would hear about this later.

That was the last clear moment.

Everything after was fog. Literally and otherwise.

He didn't know where she went. He didn't follow. Hours bled into each other, his mind fraying at the edges. The next morning, she was found near his boat.

They said there was a burner phone. A message sent around the time she died: I'm here. Are you?

They said it was to him.

The knock came just after sunrise.

One knock. No shouting. No sirens.

Just Chief Harrow's face on the other side of the door, set and sure.

"Need you to come with me, son."

Ryan was behind him.

No cuffs yet. That came later.

As they paraded him past the trollers and crab pots, through fog that smelled like salt and rust, Chap realized the truth was already buried.

Amelia was dead.

And they'd already decided who to blame.

Stay Hooked

Spruce Cove Series Book 2

Spruce Cove isn't done keeping secrets.

Chap Fisher is behind bars, accused of murdering his ex-girlfriend, Amelia Colburn. The town has already decided he's guilty. But Ava McCormick isn't so sure. Together with Liz, her sharp-tongued best friend, Ava sets out to uncover the truth about Amelia's death. A truth the town seems determined to keep buried.

As Ava digs deeper, the past refuses to stay quiet. Amelia's secrets run darker than anyone imagined, William is pushing his way back into her life, and Ava's own heart is caught between loyalty, desire, and doubt. Every answer only raises more questions, and every clue pulls her further into a web of betrayal, obsession, and danger.

With Chap's future and her own on the line, Ava will have to decide how much she's willing to risk for the truth.

Be the first to know when **Stay Hooked** releases. Sign up at joyoffiction.com.

ACKNOWLEDGEMENTS

Writing a book is like heading off on a fishing trip before sunrise with no charts, no guarantees, and a cooler half full of bait and beer. You might get lucky, skunked, or hit a rock and need help making it home in one piece.

To Greg, my co-captain, thank you for cheering at the right moments, copy-editing at the wrong ones, and handling carpool like a boss while I wrote emotionally fraught scenes about cheating fiancés and stubborn Alaskan fishermen.

To my mom, Karen, and my sister, Geneva, thanks for the encouragement, tough love, and the "try again" texts. Mom, your edits turned rough pages into chapters. As usual, you two were always right (so annoying).

To our kids Ava, Tim, and Theo thank you for your patience, hugs, and daily dose of comic relief. You remind me daily why stories matter.

To the people of Southeast Alaska, thank you for the voices, grit, and salty charm that helped shape me and this book. You might not see yourselves in these pages, but trust me, you're there.

And to every woman who's ever packed a suitcase with more questions than answers, this one's for you. May you find your Spruce Cove, your people, and your own brave, beautiful beginning.

ABOUT THE AUTHOR

Joy Thomas grew up in a Southeast Alaskan fishing town where boots were non-negotiable and stories were as common as rain (some of them even true). A former journalist, she writes modern fiction with heart, grit, and a splash of mystery. Her debut novel, Stay Salty, kicks off the Spruce Cove Series: a romantic mystery set in a coastal town where secrets rise like the tide and the past has a habit of washing back ashore. She lives in the Charlotte, North Carolina metro area with her family of five and a beagle named Magnolia.

VISIT JOY THOMAS ONLINE:

www.joyoffiction.com